BEYOND
REASON

KARICE BOLTON

DEDICATION

I want to say a heartfelt thank you to the readers of the Beyond Love Series. You have made the series soar and my heart sing with your kind notes, messages, and posts about the stories and characters. I look forward to sharing many more stories about Jason, Gabby, Brandy, Aaron, and Lily with you all. Also, a big thank you to Natalie C. who came up with the name Austin during a 'Naming Contest' I held. It fit perfectly! As always, a big thanks to my amazing husband and wonderful mom for putting up with me while I type away.

BOOKS BY
KARICE BOLTON

THE WITCH AVENUE SERIES
LONELY SOULS
ALTERED SOULS
RELEASED SOULS
SHATTERED SOULS

THE WATCHERS TRILOGY
AWAKENING
LEGIONS
CATACLYSM
TAKEN NOVELLA (A Watchers Prequel)

THE CAMP

BEYOND LOVE SERIES
BEYOND CONTROL
BEYOND DOUBT
BEYOND REASON
BEYOND INTENT ~ Coming Soon

LUKE FLETCHER SERIES
HIDDEN SINS

AFTERWORLD SERIES
RecruitZ
AlibiZ ~ Coming Soon

One

I glanced around the steakhouse, which was packed with couples and families celebrating birthdays and anniversaries. And I was on a date. Rob had asked me out several times, and I'd finally agreed. He was a co-worker at the PR firm in Portland where I worked. His father, also, happened to be the president of the firm so that was a bit of a sticky situation.

In the past, I seemed to have gotten myself in trouble with people who had some sort of authority over the direction of my life. The professor was a mistake, but I wouldn't take it back. I wouldn't take back any of my mistakes. And that was the exact reason I'd told Rob "no" so many times. I'd been trying to avoid making those slip-ups quite so frequently.

I was attracted to Rob and was trying to be good, but my willpower finally gave up. I'd felt the slightest sweep of his fingers across mine after a meeting last Monday and here I was.

Besides, he *wasn't* my boss.

However, I also hadn't expected to feel completely dead when I looked at him tonight.

And I did.

So that was great!

Where did the spark go? Why did this always happen? Was I just always looking for something that only existed in fairytales and movies? I blamed my mom and her incessant need to watch *Pretty Woman* when I was a kid.

"Is it just me or are these drinks really strong?" I asked.

I felt Rob's eyes on me and knew I should turn my attention back to him. But something wasn't working for me. I mean, he was completely my type, and I'd day-dreamed about him almost nonstop from the moment I started my job several months ago. Yet, here I was sitting across from one of the sexiest men in Portland, and some-how, I was managing to stare at a light fixture attached on the wall next to me rather than at him. Eartha Kitt and Bing Crosby Christmas music wrapped around me and fit the seasonal vibe of the steakhouse to perfection, but I was feeling anything but in the holiday spirit. The spirit I was in made me want to bolt right back home into the embrace of my current read.

"I think when you make any drink a double, they tend to be stronger," Rob laughed.

His laughter brought my attention back to him, and I started laughing too. Maybe I could turn this around. His blonde hair was swept to the side, and his brown eyes were intense as he took me in. This was about the time I should start swooning. Our eyes should connect, and I should feel that thing, that pulse—but nothing happened.

Zippo!

This was turning into a nasty habit.

"Probably a connection." I took a sip of the Trigger Finger and wondered what on earth made me decide to give whisky another try in my lifetime. I pushed down the shudder and smiled as the sting lingered on my lips.

"I still don't understand how you got out of college without a ring on your finger," Rob said, leaning back in his chair.

Seriously, dude?

I tried not to spit out the whiskey mixture and swallowed the last bit.

"Ha," I belted out. "Who said I want a ring on my finger?"

His brow arched and he leaned forward at the table. "Touché."

"Believe it or not, some women actually go to college to get an education. It was a shock to my great-grandmother as well, so don't feel alone." I glared at him.

Great! How was I going to exit this one gracefully?

"I think I like this side of you," he said, his voice lowering.

"The angry side?" A tiny quake of revulsion ran through my body as he eyed me.

3

He laughed loudly and suddenly his status as Portland's most eligible bachelor became all too clear. I probably shouldn't tell him that though. Nope. I wouldn't do that. He was a co-worker. I had to save face and be polite.

But, man, he was annoying.

"So you're always scurrying off to Seattle on the weekends. Why's that?" he asked, his eyes touching down on mine quickly before scanning the room.

"I have two best friends up there," I said, feeling my phone buzz inside my clutch. I hoped to heaven it was some nonlife-threatening emergency to get me out of here.

"That's right. One was in an accident or something?"

I guess I should be flattered he remembered.

"Yeah. That was Brandy. She was in a motorcycle accident."

"Stupid people do stupid things," he replied, shaking his head.

"Excuse me?" my voice raised. "It wasn't her fault."

His eyes held an amusement that made me uncomfortable. It was like his mission was to get a rise out of me.

"Anyone who wants to ride—"

"Enough," I said, cutting him off. I wasn't going to even bother getting into the fact that the reason she got into the accident was because someone tried to kill her. "The book I left on my nightstand is calling me. Thank you for a lovely dinner." I stood up and tossed my napkin on the table.

"Sit down," he hissed, his eyes were shooting into mine.

I don't know why, but I did. I sat down quickly and leaned in.

"You've done good things for my father's firm. He reminds me of that every day, but don't think I've forgotten just how many times you've turned me down."

What the hell was going on?

"I wasn't in a place to date—"

"I don't care to hear it," he interrupted, his brow arching as a sardonic smile spread across his lips.

Was this guy for real?

My heart was racing as I tried to figure out what was up his sleeve. What I really wanted to do was smack him with my clutch and order an eight-hundred dollar bottle of wine to finish him off.

"We have an account we're trying to get, and we had someone specifically request you take the lead when submitting our bid." He gritted his teeth. I could tell it was extremely painful for him to say the words.

"What company?" I asked.

"The client has asked to remain anonymous until the morning of the presentation," he replied.

"Well, I need to know the brand in order to come up with a decent storyboard and plan. I need to see their failures and successes."

Besides after this meal, I wasn't planning on staying at this firm any longer.

"Listen, you would've been out the door yesterday if this hadn't come to our attention," he said.

"Because I wouldn't sleep with you?" My eyes narrowed.

"Don't be ridiculous. Because you can't see what's good for you. Who is good for you..."

The air got sucked out of my lungs. Did we somehow get zapped into the same era this music was from?

"Every launch that I've taken the lead on has doubled and sometimes tripled sales projections," I replied coolly. "Firing me wouldn't be performance based, and it would cost your firm money."

And because of my splendid performance, I already had wracked up enough in bonus money to carry me through at least a year without additional income.

So take that, turkey.

"On the topic of money..." He grinned. "You do realize that if *we* let *you* go, you aren't vested. You haven't been with our firm long enough to be fully vested in anything."

I earned that money. What was he talking about? I knew their contribution to my retirement plan wasn't vested, but my bonuses? My heart was pounding as I looked at him.

"I didn't think you knew that little fact. It's the fine print that'll always kill ya. So as I was saying, the client expects you to present on Wednesday."

"Wednesday?" I interrupted.

"You have a problem with that?" he asked.

"No. Not at all," I replied through my teeth.

"I've already sent you an email with the details," he replied, as he stood up.

"At least one of the great mysteries of the world has been solved tonight," I said.

"And what is that, sweetheart?" He grinned.

"Why you're still on Portland's most eligible bachelor list for five years in a row."

"If you'll excuse me, I intend to get my Friday night rolling the way it should be. Have a nice evening with your book, Lily."

I swear to the heavens above, I saw actual horns grow out of his head, one on each side. I stayed seated at the table and watched him waddle off. That was right. He no longer glided across the room in my world. He waddled. He waddled because he was a bona fide ass!

If only I could find a new job by Monday. Then it wouldn't matter who needed who in this deal.

I pulled my cell phone out of my clutch and glanced down at the screen. My pulse quickened when I saw the name. The last time I got a text from Ayden, one of Brandy's bothers, was when she'd been in an accident.

My heart was thumping by the time I made it out of the restaurant and hailed a cab. There was never a steady stream of cabs in Portland so this alone was somewhat of a miracle. Maybe, things were turning around. I slid across the backseat of the Prius and gave the driver my address. I stared at the screen as I opened up my text message.

I'm in town through Wednesday and thought if you weren't busy, I could come by at some point and fill you in on a little scheme my sister and Gabby have cooked up. It involves you and I just can't keep you in the dark.

I chuckled and speedily typed my response and hit send.

You don't want to tell me over the phone-lol?

He responded quickly.

With a sister like Brandy, I've learned to never have anything incriminating in writing.

I laughed and the cabdriver looked up at me in the rearview mirror. I texted Ayden back.

Probably wise. But anything they've got planned has got to be better than anything I can get myself into, but I'm all ears. I can make time whenever you're free. xx

It was quiet for a few minutes as I waited for a response from Ayden. I looked out the window as the city quickly blurred into itself. How did I not see this coming? Rob seemed funny and normal at work. There was never a hint he was like this.

Not a hint!

Well, maybe a hint.

The subtle vibration in my lap alerted me to another text.

I could come by tonight or tomorrow. And what is xx?

I smiled and shook my head. Our age gap wasn't that big. He was only a few years older than me but still.

Hugs. xx is hugs!! And as long as you bring a bottle of wine, tonight would be fine. And maybe some takeout. Yeah. Definitely some takeout.

He replied.

Tonight it is then. Can you send your address?

I texted my address and sat up in the seat as the driver parked in front of my apartment building on Park Avenue. And I'll fully admit I chose this place just because it was on Park Avenue. I liked the way it sounded, and I knew I never actually wanted to live on *THE* Park Avenue in Manhattan so now was my chance to say it.

I gave the cab driver a ten-dollar bill and hopped out of the Prius onto the sidewalk. The building was a sleek skyscraper and the interior of the building was just as modern. The views of the city were sensational, and I really loved my cozy one-thousand square foot apartment. It felt like home.

I walked through the lobby toward the elevator and stepped right in.

"Floor nine," I replied to the elevator.

"Store swine," the elevator's virtual voice responded. *Not again!*

"Floor nine," I repeated.

"Or Bye," the elevator confirmed.

I totally embraced technology. Really. I did. But voice technology just wasn't there yet. Between Siri telling me to drive off a cliff and this elevator kicking me out the door, I just wanted a button. Was that so much to ask for?

I started laughing and so did the elevator as I stepped out of the carriage and tried again. I took a leap back into the elevator and faced the intercom.

"Floooorrrr Niiiinnne," I said slowly.

"Nine," the elevator confirmed, and the doors closed, quickly whisking me to home at last.

Finally!

My apartment was pretty tidy already so I concentrated on the important stuff—getting a drink to wipe away the horrid memories from earlier. I poured a glass of red wine and sat on the stool at my breakfast bar, wondering what in the world Brandy's brother felt he needed to tell me. I loved Gabby and Brandy, but having them up north while I was stuck in Portland was starting to get to me, especially if they were up to some shady business that involved me.

I swirled the liquid in the glass and took a sip. Ayden and Mason were both great guys and they were nice to look at, which I loved reminding Brandy about any chance I got. When Brandy, Gabby, and I were in college, her brothers could always be counted on.

There was a knock at the door and my stomach fluttered.

What the heck? Where'd that flutter come from?

I slid off the stool and opened the door.

"I think your elevator's possessed," Ayden said, holding Chinese takeout in one hand and a bottle of wine in the other.

"Tell me about it." I grinned, grabbing the wine from him. "I'll take this. Thank you very much."

"Rough night?" he teased, still standing in the hall.

"Beyond rough. I think it could qualify as torture."

Ayden's blonde hair was mussed up slightly, and he was wearing a black wool sweater that fit across his chest nicely. And by nicely, I mean I could imagine how delectable he must look under the yarn. My eyes dipped lower, and I couldn't help but admire how tight his jeans hugged his thighs. I had no idea who he was trying to impress, but I was thankful for the view.

Oh, good God!

"Are you going to let me in or do I need to hand over the food and deliver my message from here?" His vibrant blue eyes met mine as he was leaning against the doorframe. He looked amused.

A completely puzzling sensation ran through me as his eyes bored into mine. It was a cross between weightlessness and the flu. The wine was definitely getting to me. Or maybe it was the whiskey.

"Oh, yeah. Sorry. I danced with whiskey tonight and—"

His laughter boomed into the entry as he shut the door behind him.

"And you're planning on boogying with the wine?" He followed me into the kitchen and set the containers on the counter. "That's a deadly mix."

"Meh, I've seen deadlier," I teased and shrugged my shoulders, placing my now empty glass on the counter.

"Is that so?" He narrowed his eyes at me and took a step closer as he removed the cartons out of the bag. I reached for the plastic utensils and my arm bumped into his, and I took a quick step back. It felt like all of the air had been sucked out of the room, and I had no idea why. It wasn't like we hadn't been alone together before. Granted, it wasn't in my apartment, and Brandy was usually lurking around the corner or something, but what the hell?

"So you didn't have dinner yet?" he asked, seemingly unfazed.

Didn't he notice the earth just shifted off its axis point for God's sake?

"No. I had dinner. I had a steak dinner, actually."

His grin deepened. "Care to elaborate?"

"By the time I got to the cab, I was hungry again. That's what I get for ordering a petite filet mignon. Besides, I want something good and greasy to take away the bad taste in my mouth from the date from hell." I rolled my eyes and grabbed two plates.

"You were on a date tonight?" The timbre of his voice lowered in a way that told me I didn't imagine the shift in the universe.

I shrugged. "Yes and no. Technically yes. But it was a mistake, and one I won't be repeating anytime soon."

Ayden was quiet while I piled two scoops of chow mein on my plate, followed by cashew chicken and broccoli beef.

"Nice selection," I said, flashing him a smile. I emptied the open bottle of wine into my glass. "If you want to uncork that bottle, the opener's in the drawer right by your left hip."

I wandered into the living room and sat down on the couch with my plate full of food on my lap, and I set the glass of wine on the coffee table. I heard him rattling around in the kitchen as I turned on the television and then happily began forking the noodles in my mouth.

Would I normally be this carefree about loving my noodles in front of a man?

No.

But this was Ayden.

The same guy who has had to scrape me up off the ground. Not that it was a common occurrence, but there was this one unfortunate incident sophomore year where I got a little too excited about beer pong. Brandy and Gabby called for reinforcements, Ayden and Mason, but it had been too late. I was a goner by the time they arrived. I never repeated that mistake again. Although, I was probably well on my way right now...

Ayden sat next to me and again, I noticed a shift. It had to be the wine.

"So what went so terribly wrong that you even needed to eat a second dinner to get the first out of that brain of yours?" He took a sip of wine and his gaze steadied on mine.

"It was a co-worker. I thought I felt something, but once the date happened, I was dead wrong. That's been happening a lot lately. I think I'm taking a hiatus from the whole dating scene. It's just too much." I placed my hand against my forehead feigning exhaustion.

"Interesting you say that," he said, scooping the broccoli beef onto his fork.

"How so?"

"That's kind of what I came here to talk to you about." He took a bite and a few beats went by before he spoke again. "Does Austin Graham ring a bell?"

My heart plummeted as if it was crashing down the side of the Empire State building, and I didn't feel an end in sight so I just sat frozen, staring at Ayden as he waited for a reply.

Two

"They tracked him down, and tomorrow you'll be getting a text from my sister about a ski trip to Utah," Ayden replied.

"Oh, no," I whispered. "Please tell me they didn't contact him."

"I don't know if they've contacted him, but they know where he is."

"I never should have told them about my high school boyfriend," I sighed. "There's more to the story, and I really didn't want to go digging it up again. It was pretty awful."

"Did he hurt you?" his voice as steady as his gaze.

"No. God no. Nothing like that. I probably did the hurting."

I bit my lip and looked at the television where some reality show had couples yelling at one another.

"I didn't even tell them his name."

"Well, you put Brandy down in front of a database and she can find anyone. She should probably scrap law school and go straight into PI work." He smiled and put his hand on my knee and a pulse of heat ran through me. "She really gets off on it."

I put my plate on the coffee table and sat back on the couch while Ayden continued to eat. What were Brandy and Gabby thinking? Just because Austin was my high school boyfriend didn't mean I wanted to hunt the poor guy down. I was sure he moved on. I did...kind of. The funny part was that I wanted to be mad at Brandy and Gabby, but I wasn't. I should've told them the whole story, and then they would never have thought about tracking him down. Never.

I let out a deep breath, hoping it would lessen the tight, achy sensation in my chest.

It didn't.

"So you want to tell me what happened between you and him?" Ayden asked. He shifted on the couch and put his empty plate next to mine. "Maybe if you get it off your chest, you'll feel better."

"You know how high school love is," I laughed, hoping to dismiss it quickly. "Drama filled...where every emotion is at the surface, and every piece of gossip is internalized."

"Actually, I don't," Ayden said. "I didn't mess around with having a girlfriend in high school. I didn't like the idea of being tied down. Mason, on the other hand, switched girls every trimester."

"You didn't date in high school?" I asked, my attention momentarily swayed.

"I didn't say that. I just didn't have a girlfriend."

"You were one of those..." I grinned.

Ayden started laughing and shrugged. "Guilty. So what's up with Austin?"

Did I really want to bore poor Ayden with details?

I glanced at him and saw a trace of amusement behind his eyes and felt it was only fair that I embraced my chatterbox ways in front of him. After all, he was related to the mastermind of destruction. Someone had to pay.

"Austin and I were the perfect match and completely inseparable. We went through a lot and made it through as a couple. I know it was high school and all, but we actually could have made it." I steadied my eyes on Ayden's. I waited for an eye roll or a bit of skepticism to be reflected behind his expression, but it didn't happen. His eyes were kind and welcoming, and there was a bit of something more hidden in his expression, but I couldn't tell what it was. "And what tore us apart was some piece of gossip that I knew wasn't even true. But I used it as my excuse and took off to college early and never spoke to him again. I guess because I wanted to believe it was true so I had an excuse to escape."

"So you were scared and bolted."

"I guess."

"What was the gossip?" he questioned.

"That he'd gotten some other girl pregnant. It wasn't true."

"When you said you went through a lot as a couple?" Ayden questioned. His eyes fastened on mine.

"I've never talked about it to anyone," I said, pushing myself further into the couch. "But we needed each other and got each other through it."

And I never would tell anyone. It was too painful. I had managed to shove it to the farthest place in my mind and bury it under lots of new memories.

He was quiet for a moment and then spoke. "Until you left him."

I nodded and a lump formed in the back of my throat.

I was a mess. Between the whiskey, wine, steak, and Chinese food, I was a ticking time bomb.

I NEVER cried.

I NEVER allowed myself to be vulnerable.

I NEVER talked about anything serious.

And somehow in front of Ayden, all three of my rules were about to be broken. It was definitely the alcohol. Had to be. I was going to turn this around.

"So they expect me to take off from work for a ski trip?" I asked, arching my brow.

"That they do. Actually, I'll be going too. And so will Mason."

My heart sputtered.

"Well, I wonder if I should give them a taste of their own medicine?" I asked. "Especially if you are already planning on coming."

Once he realized I was no longer going to have a meltdown, Ayden's eyes flicked to a lighter shade of blue and his body relaxed.

"How so?" he asked.

"I'm not sure yet, but I'll think of something. Maybe, you'll be my boy toy? We can totally freak out Brandy.

And then I'll figure out a way to ensure I don't bump into poor, unsuspecting Austin."

"Who said I'd be willing to do that?" he chided.

"Just a hunch." I flashed him a grin.

"So you're not going to tell me what—"

"Nope. It's water under the bridge and Brandy and Gabby don't even know. If they did, I don't think they would've gotten this bright idea of theirs," I interrupted.

That was putting it lightly. Why didn't I just tell him? Was I afraid he'd judge me? Was I worried he'd think less of me? I was sure I'd already given him enough ammo over the years to make him skeptical of my decision-making skills. I was even skeptical of them.

"Funny how they assume I can just take time off," I replied. "Although, I probably won't have a job by then."

"What do you mean?"

"Long story. It's not quite the place I thought it was. I love my job and I'm damn good at it, but it's not gonna work out for the long term. The d-bag I went on a date with tonight is the son of the president of the firm. To say he wasn't thrilled that I'd turned him down so many times before tonight would be putting it mildly. I was just lucky some potential account requested me or I probably would've gotten canned this week. What really sucks is all the bonus money I have coming to me. It's almost mine but not quite. If they let me go or I quit before the vesting date, I'm screwed."

Ayden's eyes darkened a shade and he turned to face me. "Lily, this is serious. This is sexual harassment. They can't get away with that," his voice tipped with anger.

"Well, being that this is my first position out of school, I don't want to risk bringing attention to anything of the sort. I don't need that type of reputation in the industry. You know a girl-who-cries-wolf or something. I just want to make it to the vesting date and get the hell out of there—quietly. I have enough money owed to me to carry me through a year, even if I have a hard time finding another job."

"When's the date?" he asked.

"December 23rd."

Ayden nodded and seemed to be contemplating something.

"What?" I asked.

"Just thinking about how far we've come in this world and how far we have to go."

I knew this had to irritate him. Ayden and Mason were so protective of Brandy that any sort of discrimination or unfairness when it came to females drove them insane.

"I know what I'll do," I said, turning the subject back to the reason for his visit.

"Tell me," he replied, the mischief creeping back into his expression.

He was so sexy I had to turn away.

No. It wasn't that he was sexy. It was as if his body was calling for sex, and turning away did nothing to calm the rush of feelings that were inside of me. I had to get back on track and wait for the alcohol to leave my system.

"When she texts me about the ski trip, I'll reply how awesome that'll be, and how I'm going to bring a date!" I gushed.

"A date?" he asked, looking baffled.

Was it my imagination or did I sense a glimpse of disappointment?

"Yeah...You! But she doesn't have to know that part. But it'll totally mess with her."

Ayden laughed, and I scooted forward on the couch as he stood up to get a refill.

"That's evil." He grabbed his glass off the table and made his way to the kitchen.

"Not as evil as hunting down a crush from high school," I shouted.

"Now poor Austin was just a crush, huh?" Ayden's voice echoed through the apartment.

"You know what I mean."

He came back with a full glass and the bottle to refill mine, and he was wearing a huge grin. I stood up and stepped over to him, holding out my glass.

"I don't think any guy could just have a crush on you," he said quietly, as the liquid splashed inside of my wine-glass, and his words rattled around my mind.

My heart stopped, and it felt like the room was spinning. Did I just hear that right? I shouldn't have stood up. But rather than sit back down, I stared up at him and took a sip of wine. His eyes locked on mine, and I felt the energy between us charge up even more. Wine or not, there was definitely something going on here. A few strands of my hair got caught between my lips and the glass, but I didn't do anything to remove it. Instead, I watched his eyes lower to my lips and hoped for a kiss.

Ayden's hand touched my cheek softly as I finished my sip, and he pushed my auburn hair off my shoulder.

His touch made my thoughts dive into murky waters, and I could no longer figure out what was what so I sat down quickly and laughed.

Great! And now I had turned into the Joker.

So I sighed, and then I sighed again.

"Sorry," he muttered.

He sat next to me, and the way he turned made his muscles flex under his sweater in a way that made it impossible not to want to see what was hidden from view. It's not like I hadn't seen him before. I'd seen him in shorts and no shirt many times over the years but somehow this was different.

And that was the problem. I knew exactly how flawless he looked under the sweater. So much so I could imagine my fingers running across his chest, my lips tracing along his neck. Maybe I'd found the perfect combination to turn myself on again? Wine and whisky!

"You have nothing to be sorry for," I said softly, waiting for something more.

"What if the Austin thing actually worked out? You hear about that all the time where people go back to their high school sweethearts and fall madly in love all over again," he said.

His words completely wiped away all the fantasies I was just enjoying.

Damn him! What if he was right?

"I think that's very unlikely. First, he'd have to be willing to speak to me. Second, he'd have to be willing to speak to me and—"

"Let me guess. Third, he'd have to be willing to speak to you." His brow quirked up. "So this is an already known issue?"

"What?" I asked, playing innocent.

"Him not speaking to you?"

"I may or may not have reached out over the years. And yes, silence very well could have been what I heard back." I twisted my mouth into a pile of contorted lips that no longer wanted to participate in this conversation.

I guess that was another little fact I failed to mention to Brandy and Gabby.

Ayden pushed his fingers through his hair and let out a deep breath.

"Well, I actually was going to bring someone, but—"

I slapped my forehead harder than I intended and yelped.

"Oh, my god. That was so selfish of me. I don't know what got into me," I stammered, feeling a blush creep up my face.

Of course, he was going to bring someone. He was gorgeous, wealthy, and available. The wine may have brought my feel-goods back being around the opposite sex, but it completely messed with my sense of reality.

"No. It's not like that. It's nothing serious. I hadn't even mentioned it to her."

For some reason, the word *her* made me nauseous and agitated.

Well, maybe it wasn't the word.

"Ayden, you've done so much just by telling me what's up. Don't worry about it. That's one of the perks you've got being a twin. I'll ask Mason." I winked at him playfully and felt my control slowly seeping back in. Keep everyone at a safe distance, and I would never get hurt. That always was my plan and always would be my plan.

"Nah, seriously. I don't mind. I think it would be a lot of fun. I didn't assume I'd become part of your plan, but I like the idea. I hate being the third wheel. That's the only reason I was bringing someone. But if..." his voice trailed off.

"If what?" I prompted.

"If nothing, actually. I'd love the opportunity to punk my sister. And you never know, maybe this Austin thing will be good for you." He smiled, but the look in his eyes didn't match.

"Now you're starting to sound like your sister," I scoffed, crossing my arms in front of me.

He cringed and laughed as he grabbed the remote and began flipping through the channels. "Can't have that."

"You want me to make some popcorn?" I asked.

"That sounds nice. I think I could get used to making this a tradition when I'm in Portland. *And* you have expanded channels?"

His words sent a streak of happiness through me as I stood up and walked toward the kitchen.

"I have *all* the channels, premium too. Even though I've developed quite the reputation for going out, I enjoy staying home with a good book or movie even more. I just like to throw people off, keep 'em talking."

"Well, it's working," he muttered.

I grabbed the air popper and shook the kernels into the cup. I perched myself up on the counter next to the sink and filled a glass with water, gulping it quickly as the popcorn popped into a giant metal bowl.

As I sat comfortably on the counter, my mind began wandering to the issue at hand. What if everyone was right? What if meeting up with Austin turned out to be a good thing? So many things were left unsaid when I left him. I wasn't ready to say them right after high school, so I did the logical thing and ran. The problem with my plan was that I never realized how stuck in the past that would make me. It was as if I had been left stranded in high school while everyone else moved on in life and grew up.

Instead of maturing, I replayed the images over and over again of the night that changed my life forever. The images that woke me up at night—that made me question what my purpose in life was supposed to be. And the one person who helped me through it all, I abandoned.

Austin was the only person who had gotten me through the most horrible moment in my life, and as a thank you, I ditched him. When I had finally reached out to Austin, it was too late. And that was when I began wearing my flaws out in the open, to protect myself. In college I went wild, or at least it looked like I did. What no one knew was that I was just searching for the one person to make me feel alive again, like Austin did. I wanted to feel that safe and happy again. And to this day, I hadn't been able to find it.

It had all been an act and my best friends didn't even see it. I wished it were different. That I'd responded differently to the pain I felt, but I didn't. By all appearances it looked like my dating life was hooked up to a twenty-four hour revolving door.

The popcorn maker finished popping, and I melted some butter, drizzling it over the corn, and tossed it slightly before salting it. Now wasn't the time to keep going down memory lane.

"Hope you like lots of butter," I called to Ayden.

"How could a person not?" he asked, as I handed him the napkins and took a seat right next to him so we could share the popcorn easier.

Sitting this close to Ayden made me keenly aware of his movements and just his entire existence. I didn't remember the last time when I noticed how a man smelled, but he was intoxicating, a mixture of soap and something woodsy, something Ayden.

"You okay?" he asked.

I laughed and felt completely insecure as he sank his fingers into the bowl and crunched on the first handful of corn.

"Perfection," he said, his eyes meeting mine.

I wasn't sure if he was talking about the popcorn any longer. Or at least I hoped he wasn't.

"It's one of my favorite dinners so I got it right a long time ago," I said, grabbing a few kernels.

"You eat popcorn for dinner?"

"Some nights I do," I confessed. "The hours I keep kind of make my options limited."

His eyes stayed focused on mine. "You're hard to figure out. I'm starting to think the Lily everyone knows isn't the true Lily at all." He grinned as if he'd cracked open some sort of age-old mystery.

I laughed. "Believe me. I'm not that complex. What you see is what you get."

"I don't believe it for a second," he replied. "But someday, maybe I'll get to know the real Lily. Until then,

I've narrowed our movie selection to either the rom-com or a sci-fi movie for the night."

"You obviously don't know the real me at all, because if you did, you'd know sci-fi would win every time," I said, snatching the remote from his fingers, clicking the okay button on *Alien*.

"You're right. I wouldn't have guessed that one."

"*Alien* it is," I said, noticing he wrapped his arm around me as I held the popcorn bowl tighter.

"You know, I'm really happy my sister gave me an excuse to drop by," he said, and my stomach literally dropped to the floor. "Scheming and chilling with you is kind of fun."

He gave me a quick squeeze and took his arm away. We were clearly still in the friend zone and that was okay. That was how it should be.

As the movie started, I felt my body relax against his, and my mind escaped to a land far away from the one we lived in, filled with creatures and exploding things. Just how I liked it.

Nothing too deep.

Three

I was at the office this morning by seven o'clock. The weekend went by in a flash, and I'd spent most of Sunday sketching out some ideas for the new client. I always got lost in a fantasy world when I created campaigns, which was why I loved doing it so much.

It'd been nice to hang out with Ayden. There were no expectations or disappointments. Plus, he accepted my whiskey behavior without judgment, and for that, I was extremely grateful. I didn't remember all of the things that may have slipped out of my mouth, but I knew he wouldn't hold any of them against me.

By Sunday, the idea of seeing Austin again began to creep into my mind, and it was kind of intriguing.

As foolish as it sounded, I'd never been able to shut out those emotions and feelings that he conjured when I had been around him in high school.

High school!

And I'd been spending the start of my adult life trying to replicate them with men who looked the part but didn't fit with me. Something needed to change!

I never received a text from Brandy or Gabby so either they'd had second thoughts or they were ensuring their story had no holes, which might take some extra time. Either way, I couldn't wait to mess with them once I got the official invite.

"Have a nice weekend, Lily?"

I looked up from my laptop and smiled at Tori. She worked in the graphics department and her outfit matched that profession. She had purple eyeglass frames that could be spotted a mile away, and she generally wore layers and layers of clothing that were all mismatched, yet somehow went together flawlessly. If I tried out the look I'd either look like Bobo the clown or a hobo from the 1920's. And I'm deathly afraid of clowns.

I smiled at Tori and nodded, bringing my attention back to her. "Really great. I had an unfortunate little date, but a friend from out of town came over and made it all better."

Her eyes narrowed as she carefully examined me for something more.

"What?" I asked.

"You look different somehow. Like you've met someone. Are you sure the date was a disaster?"

I started laughing. "Positive."

28

Maybe the idea of seeing Austin again did breathe new life into me.

"Well, whatever it is, keep it up. My weekend was absolutely horrid. I spent all of Saturday and Sunday redoing all of the artwork from last week's meeting with Telly's Ale. One minute they want old-school vibe and the next sleek and modern."

"Oooh, that sucks," I replied, noticing Rob walking off the elevator.

Perfect! Just the man I wanted to run into.

Tori followed my gaze and chuckled. "Gotcha. He finally wore you down, huh?"

I shivered and she caught my reaction, which resulted in a chuckle-snort from her mouth and a glance in my direction from Rob.

"Sorry," she whispered. "Hard to believe something that can look that good on the outside can be so god-awful on the inside."

"So you—"

She nodded. "I made it to date two and couldn't handle it any longer. But luck was on my side, and a new hire came on board that distracted him enough to make my getaway painless."

"Who?" I asked, leaning into the desk.

Rob had trundled off to his office so at least I was safe for a while.

"Cindy," she uttered.

I absolutely loved office gossip as long as I wasn't part of it!

"No way! She's so—"

"Prudish?" Tori responded, smiling.

"Exactly."

"Just know it happens to the best of us. I'm impressed you held out so long."

"The date imploded before dessert was even served," I confessed.

Her brows fell in disappointment, and I knew it then...she'd had sex with him.

Poor soul!

"Lucky," she hissed, and turned around, making her way through the sea of cubicles.

For once, I was thrilled that I wasn't the one doing the march of shame.

My phone buzzed, and I saw a new email had come over. This was it, had to be it! The message was from Brandy and the subject simply read 'Ski Trip'. I chuckled as I opened it up and read through it.

Grab your cute sweaters and furry earmuffs! We're headed to the mountains of Utah. Plans are set and there's no getting out of it. Gabby, Jason, and Aaron are coming. And my brothers are coming too! We've got a great place rented for all of us. You can bring your board or skis or rent whatever. I'll send the deets over this week, but put in for December 26th–January 1st so you can get the time off. We'll show this New Year who's boss and maybe you'll even bump into Mr. Right!

Hugs and smooches,

Brandy

I felt absolutely giddy as I hit the reply button. I was so grateful to Ayden for spilling the beans.

You always know the right thing to do! Can't wait! And guess what, girl? I've even got a guy to bring and ring in the New Year. How perfect is that?

Hugs and Smooches back at ya,

L

I started laughing as I set the phone down. My guess was I'd get a message within five minutes, which would give her enough time to consult with Gabby before sending a frantic email back.

I bent under my desk, adjusting the dial on my space heater. I had to get it blasting before my toes fell off. I loved my office and all of the windows that looked over the city, but it made it extremely chilly now that it was December. The heat began wrapping around my ankles, and I sat back in my chair taking everything in around my office. It was an odd sensation knowing that I was going to be giving my notice soon.

The space had really started to feel like my second home. I liked how I had decorated it and had many memories of eating take-out late at night, staring at storyboards spread out all over the place. Beyond the boring décor that was standard in all of the offices, I'd brought in a few photographs of my family and some funky artwork that one of my friends from college had painted. But it would all look just as wonderful somewhere else—of that I was sure.

I picked up the photo of my parents, who had been married for over forty years. My father had his arm

wrapped around my mom's shoulders. I think it was a
church directory photo, and it showed. They loved each
other, but it wasn't a passionate relationship. Not like the
one I imagined for myself or saw with Brandy's parents.
Maybe their relationship held some fire in the beginning, but I didn't ever remember them showing affection
in public. My father was a successful real estate developer,
and my mom worked with him in his office, off and on.
My dad also happened to be the mayor of our small town
for much of my junior high and high school years, which
explained why my dating life always felt like such a liabil-
ity to them. God forbid something might happen that
would ruin his bid for reelection. But if I were honest
with myself, I'd say I outgrew them. They had a very small
view of the world.

I set down the picture and picked up the one of our
entire family. I had my father's eyes, but everything else
seemed to be from my mom. My brother, Heath, was
a spitting image of my father and so was my sister, Ivy.
Their raven-colored hair was shiny and beautiful and
with their green eyes, they were stunning. Our eye color
was the only thing that signaled we were related. My
auburn hair came from my mom, as did all of our name
choices. She liked the idea of naming us all after plants.

I'd been one of those surprises that parents speak
about, so both of my siblings were quite a bit older than
me. My brother had graduated from high school, and
my sister had just entered high school when I was born.
We got along well enough, but it wasn't a really close
relationship. They both followed the paths my parents
wanted for them. Heath had a city council job and my

sister married right out of college. My parents were already proud grandparents, so at least, I was off the hook for that.

Placing the photo back on the desk, I grabbed my notes and flipped through some of the artwork I'd envisioned for a launch. Retro was popular right now and much of the campaign I came up with reflected that. Now, I just needed to get some of the storyboards going, and the launch party details figured out.

I had to stay on track! If I could get the preliminary sketches done tonight, I could send them out to the team to look over tomorrow before our meeting on Wednesday. It was going to be a long night.

My phone dinged, and I saw the reply from Brandy like clockwork. This time it didn't come over on email. It was a text.

What?!?!? How could you not tell your poor, crippled best friend this piece of news? I'm excited to hear all about him, but are you sure he should come? Not that it matters and we have plenty of room.

I laughed as I read the last sentence.

You may be poor but you're not crippled. Nice try. And YES!! Totally bringing him. I'm sure you'll love him like he's your brother! Now off to finish this project. xx

By the time evening rolled around, I was tired, hungry, and grumpy. My office looked like a bomb went off, and my mind felt just as scattered. I sat on the couch, alternating between sipping a cold latte from Starbucks and nibbling on a dried out bagel. My neck was killing me, but I had to finish and get the email sent before I could leave for the night. I grabbed the remote to my iTunes player and turned it up. Something had to keep me going.

It had taken me far longer to get everything organized than I'd planned because my mind kept wandering off...daydreaming about Austin. And the 'what ifs'.

I even Googled him!
Three times!
In an hour!
Twice!

The problem with that—okay, there were a lot of problems with that, I'd admit it—was that he wasn't one of those guys who turned into a troll out of college.

Oh, no! He turned out to be hotter than I remembered from high school. He had that rugged snowboarder look, like he didn't care what he looked like and everything magically just fell into place after a day on the slopes. The last time I had spied on him, he looked good but not this good.

I wasn't even sure why I was getting so amped up about him. It wasn't like my odds were that high that he'd even acknowledge that I existed. His non-communication style already did a good job of that.

I stood up and circled around the corkboards that I had everything pinned to. Maybe I was closer to being finished than I realized. I wanted to capture the winter season in the drawings, and I think I did that. What was lacking was a female presence. How was I going to fit that in?

My phone dinged, and I walked over to my desk and glanced at the screen. It was Ayden.

Stopped by your place to surprise you with a warm meal, but you're not here.

I laughed and texted back.

Nope. I'm not there. I'm here. At the office. Preparing for that presentation I told you about.

The flutter in my stomach took me off guard and he texted back immediately.

Have you eaten?

I typed back.

Starving, but I won't be home for at least an hour.

He didn't miss a beat.

Text me your address and I'll drop it off.

A smile spread across my lips as I thought about Ayden standing at my apartment door with a bag full of food. I knew he was sweet, but I didn't know he was that sweet. I texted him my office address when I had an epiphany. That was what this story needed. The brand bringing people together, friendship at its best. I quickly began sketching out the last scene of a couple huddled together by a fire, enjoying love and laughter.

I started scanning my sketches and notes, organizing them quickly so I could compose the email to the team. I was halfway through when my office phone rang. It was the security guard and Ayden was downstairs with the food. I told the guard I'd be right down and hung up the phone.

The elevator quickly whisked me down to the lobby, and I heard Ayden's laughter bounce along the marble walls as I walked off the elevator. He was joking around with the guard, standing in front of the large counter, holding several take-out bags. His blonde hair was disheveled, and he was dressed in a gray-checked flannel shirt and loose-fit, dark jeans. His blue eyes met mine and a charge ran through me so quickly, I wasn't even sure if it was real or imagined.

"Thanks," Ayden told the security guard, but his eyes never left mine as he walked toward me. "Hope you like Italian."

"I love Italian," I said, but my words sounded more breathy than I expected. And I noticed a glint of amusement flash across his gaze. I walked onto the already waiting elevator and pressed my floor.

"Do you always look this sexy at work?" Ayden murmured, as he stepped onto the elevator.

My hands started sweating, and my entire body felt like I'd walked into a sauna. I could feel his gaze running down the length of my body before I turned to face him.

"You certainly know the right words to say," I teased, pushing my hair back. I knew what I looked like, and it was far from sexy. "I feel like a squirrel who forgot where she put her nuts, and I'm pretty sure I look like that too. But thanks."

He laughed loudly and shook his head, and somehow the space between us narrowed even more. When the elevator doors opened, he placed his free hand on the small of my back and guided me forward. A pulse of excitement ran through me and I chuckled.

"What?" he asked, his voice low.

I shook my head, ignoring his question, and guided him through the cubicles toward my office. It was the only one with lights on, and I was suddenly contemplating how private it was, which was ridiculous.

"We can sit over there on the couch," I said, pointing at the small trail we could follow to get there.

"Perfect. I wasn't sure what you'd want so I got Spaghetti alla Carbonara, Spaghetti with Bolognese Sauce, and Fettuccine Alfredo."

"Sounds delicious. But what are you going to have?" I teased.

"These are incredible," Ayden said, not answering my question as he stopped to look at some of the designs I had piled along the trail. "Great concept."

"Thanks. I'm getting there. Hopefully, the guy will like it."

"I can't imagine him not liking it. I really think you're there." He sat down next to me and placed the bags on the side table, digging out the plastic utensils and paper napkins.

"So what does that girl you plan to bring to Utah think about you delivering food to—"

"I ended it," he interrupted, maneuvering the cartons out of the bag.

"What? Why?" I asked, not expecting the conversation to take a turn like this.

"It wasn't serious. Now which do you want?" He held the cartons out as he avoided my gaze.

"Geez, I'm sorry. I think I seriously do have like a foot-in-mouth disease of some sort. I'll take the Carbonara."

He handed me the carton and smiled. "You don't have foot-in-mouth. I've seen what that looks like first-hand. Mason has it and you're not even close. Besides, that's kind of a legit question, under the circumstances."

Circumstances? What circumstances?

"Thanks for the other night, by the way. I think the whiskey had gotten to me and—"

He held up his hand to stop me. "There's nothing to apologize for. I had an amazing time hanging out. And as hard as you work," he looked around the office, "I can understand why you need to let loose sometimes. I heard you got the infamous email and riled my sister and Gabby up some. Brandy was in full-blown panic mode when you said you had a boyfriend. Nice work."

"I feel kind of bad about that but not enough to stop yet. And I Googled him," I confessed before piling in a bite of the delicious pasta.

Ayden's brow arched. "And?"

"He looks better than I remembered, and I think he's working at a ski resort."

"Would you even admit if you were looking forward to seeing him again?" Ayden asked.

It was like he could read my mind, and it was disarming to say the least. I hadn't expected that question so I stayed focused on spinning my pasta longer than normal as I contemplated my options. I wasn't fond of being overly girly when it came to sharing feelings. I wasn't the greatest about opening up. And I wasn't sure how crazy I'd sound if I said yes. But there was something etching Ayden's voice that made me want to tell him, made me feel it was okay to tell him...like I should tell him.

I brought my gaze to his and nodded. "Yeah. I'm actually hoping I get to at least talk to him."

"Good. Then that makes this whole thing worth it." His voice sounded distant, and he broke his gaze away from mine.

But something was different. Something had changed.

Four

Cindy had gotten an assortment of pastries and placed them on the conference room table. It was hard to look at her the same way now that I knew about her and Rob. I never in a million years would've thought she'd fall for him. He was definitely a leech. I held in a chuckle and continued fastening the boards along the far wall. The team loved my ideas, which was a relief because with so little turnaround time it would be hard to start over or make many adjustments. I glanced through the glass walls that overlooked cubicle life. I decided to keep the blinds open so that the bustle and energy of the office beyond would be felt inside the conference room during the meeting.

I took a step back and looked at everything now that it was laid out and ready for the client. Tori helped spiffy up the artwork and create a more cohesive finish to everything last night. I really hoped there would be another Tori wherever I landed. She was a great co-worker and friend, but she never liked to be in the limelight. She only wanted to deal with her artwork, not the clients.

I glanced at the clock on the wall. I had about ten minutes before the client would be here. That would be just enough time to gather my thoughts and my notes. I walked to my office and sat down at my desk, glancing at the incoming emails and trying to calm my nerves. Even though I enjoyed presenting to clients, my blood always got pumping right beforehand. It was a nervous excitement.

Tori popped into my office wearing a huge lopsided grin. "I'm definitely sitting in on this one with you."

I laughed and pushed myself back from the desk. "And why's that? I thought you hated these stuffy client meetings?"

"I normally do, but wow!"

"Wow, what?" I pressed, grabbing my folder.

"Just you wait."

I walked toward her and shook my head, noticing a wave of women popping their heads over the cubicles to get a glimpse of whoever it was sitting in the conference room.

Seriously?

I rolled my eyes at Hannah, who was in the closest cubicle and had the perfect vantage point, and she just laughed.

"Come on. How often do we ever get eye candy in this office?" she whispered.

"Obviously, not often enough," I laughed, walking by Hannah as she sat back down in her cubicle.

As the conference room came into view, I felt Tori right on my heels and heard her whisper, "I can't wait to watch you try to stay composed during this meeting."

I stopped and spun around, and Tori almost ran right into me. "You know you're always more than welcome to sit in on these meetings, but you're making me more nervous. Knock it off."

"Sorry," she squeaked. But she wasn't.

When I turned back around, I looked through the glass into the conference room to find Rob and his father, Ted, examining the storyboards. On the calendar invite, only Rob replied as attending, but it would figure that his dad would show up to this one too. My gaze fell to the back of the man who was sitting at the table. His dark suit stretched nicely across his broad shoulders, and it looked as if he was engaging in discussions with Rob and Ted already, his head bobbing every so often. His blonde hair was slightly shaggy and that's when my breath caught.

"What?" Tori asked.

"Nothing," I replied, marching into the conference room.

"Wonderful work," Ted said, turning to me. "Mr. Rhodes hasn't even heard your pitch and already loves the graphics and concept."

My heart skipped a beat as I felt Ayden's eyes on me, Mr. Rhodes.

"Thank you, sir. Tori did the artwork and really helped pull the preliminaries together," I said, not turning to face Ayden.

How did I not figure this out? And I had divulged so much to him about Rob's behavior. Mortified didn't even begin to cover the emotions that began pulsing through me.

"Why don't we begin?" Rob motioned toward me and I nodded. His face conveyed everything from the weekend before, and I knew the only reason I still had a job was the potential client sitting at this table.

Tori took a seat across from Ayden and flashed me a grin, putting me at ease, and pulling me out of the spiral I was about to go into. She was dreamily gazing toward Ayden, who didn't seem to notice in the slightest. The reason I knew that was because his eyes never left me.

As I placed my folder on the table, I glanced at Rob and Ted who took a seat at each end of the table.

Ted eyed me and began, "We'll have Mr. Rhodes introduce himself and his brand to you, Lily, and then we'll—"

"Judging by what Lily has put together so far, I think she is more than capable of handling today's meeting," Ayden's voice cut through Ted's, and my stomach dropped to my toes and then shot right back up again. *Wow!*

Tori looked nervously at Ted, Rob, and Ayden before her gaze landed on me.

No one spoke to Ted like that, client or not. Instead of waiting for a response from Ted, I began speaking.

"I'm aware of Mr. Rhodes' brand. The Better brand holds the largest share of natural and organic energy drinks in the category, and he's beginning to take share from the regular energy drinks, which is unheard of. Every line he has introduced has become more successful than the previous. Beat, Enhance, Recover, Restore, and Superior all have antioxidant properties in addition to providing a long-lasting energy boost. The brand thrives on community, and his marketing strategies so far have included targeting college campuses and gaining social media momentum. My guess is that Mr. Rhodes would like to expand past the typical age range of these types of products as his new line is launched. As we all know, the eighteen to twenty-four year olds own this category. If we can branch out and capture the twenty-four plus year olds, there'll be no stopping the Better brand. And I think this campaign will do that flawlessly. I incorporated all of the elements that were given to me, and I think this new launch has endless possibilities. This new line will be a logical next step to expand into the untapped age group."

My eyes landed on Ayden's, and a wicked grin was plastered on his lips.

"Well, I can see you know a lot about Better brands. Now, let's see what our firm can do to help move Better brands forward," Rob spoke, punctuating each syllable. "But I do find it curious how you know so much about Better."

Because I helped build Ayden's brand while I was in college.

"My expertise is in the beverage segment. It wouldn't behoove me to be ignorant of such movers and shakers in the industry, now would it?"

44

Rob's eyes narrowed on mine. "Interesting that you have such passion reserved for this brand."

I caught Ayden's eyes focused on Rob as he spoke and realized it looked as if he wanted to kill the guy. He didn't miss Rob's implications either.

Ignoring Rob, I went on to discuss the campaign, going over the vision for the launch, running through the boards and answering any of Ayden's questions while Ted and Rob stayed mostly quiet.

"Really fresh ideas," Ayden replied, bringing the nodding duo out of hibernation.

"Our firm will be able to handle all of the details you'll need," Rob began. "And I'll personally oversee the entire project."

Ayden leaned back in his chair and his brow arched. It almost looked like he was holding back a laugh. "I don't see how that will work in this instance. But I thank you for the offer. The person who had the vision should be the one executing this launch."

I had to hide my smile, but Tori didn't even bother. She was beaming as she watched the scene unfold.

"We can accommodate that request," Ted began, eyeing me coolly. "About the timeline?"

"The launch party is on the 23rd," Ayden said.

"Of what?" Rob asked.

"December."

The day I get my bonus money. Thank you, Ayden!

"That's ridiculous. The 23rd isn't even two weeks away. I've never seen a successful launch in this short of time."

"All of my launches are built to look like an impulse idea and most of the time they are. If I spent months on the launch, the vigor and buzz would be gone by the time the product hit the shelves. Social media bores easily. If you can't pull it off, I can surely find someone else who can," Ayden replied.

The difficulty of keeping my smile hidden was growing by the second. I had handled all of Ayden's launches over the last couple of years. I had it down like nobody's business, which he knew.

"We'll get right on it," Rob assured him.

"Wonderful to hear," Ayden stood up and buttoned the middle button of his jacket before reaching over to shake Rob's hand.

"Lily, I recognize this is a short turnaround time and right before the holidays so if you need anything reach out to me directly. I'm sure Ted will send you my contact information."

I nodded and felt the familiar electricity run between us as he came over to shake my hand.

But there was a distance between us, one that hadn't really existed before.

"Nice work," he replied.

"Thank you, Mr. Rhodes."

And I watched him turn around and exit the room with Ted and Rob right behind.

"What was that all about?" Tori gushed. "I thought Mr. Rhodes was going to crush those two with his thumb. That was incredible."

"It was, wasn't it?"

She nodded and helped me take down all of the boards.

"Now if I could run across a guy like that, I'd make an exception to my 'no dating corporate guys' rule," Tori muttered.

Funny. I never thought of Ayden as a corporate guy, but I guess he was.

"I'm really impressed with how little time you gave that guy. I don't think I would've been able to keep my eyes off him," she continued.

I started laughing as I pulled the last board off the wall. "I don't think you did keep your eyes off of him."

"Was it that obvious?" She grinned, following me out of the conference room.

"Only if someone spotted the puddle of drool in front of you."

She smacked me playfully and followed me to my office.

"So how can I help? What do we need to get this show started?" she asked.

"I've got a list of contacts that'll work perfectly for this launch. I'll start reaching out to the papers and local magazines. The only issue will be ensuring that I can find a space that's not already taken up by office holiday parties. I'd say the most important thing is to get the art-work to the printers ASAP. Take what we have and doll it up a bit and send me over the proofs. I think if we can get the final artwork to the printer by Friday, at the latest, we'll be set."

"Perfect." Tori gave me a slight nod and headed out of my office, closing the door behind her, right before my phone buzzed.

It was a message from Ayden.

Surprise!

I replied quickly, hoping that the distance I sensed earlier was all in my head.

Surprise indeed. Thank you for that. The 23rd? Genius! I can't believe I didn't figure out the client was you...

A knock on my door interrupted my exchange so I hit the send button and looked up. It was Rob. He stepped into my office and closed the door, glaring at me as he walked to the chair in front of my desk. He'd obviously done the math. The look of disdain was written all over Rob's expression with the realization that the very project that was bringing the firm lots of money was also the reason I'd be getting mine.

"I'm sure my father and I can count on you to see this campaign through. If you need anything, let us know. I see you put in for vacation after the holidays. Unfortunately, I can't approve it."

I could tell there was no *unfortunately* about it. He was delighted to break the news to me. But it really didn't matter because on December 24th, I'd be giving my notice and loving every second of it.

"I understand. It was short notice," I replied.

"My father was quite impressed with your knowledge of Better and seems to be reconsidering your employment here."

Yeah, right.

My stomach was literally churning this morning's latte and lemon pound cake, but I had to tolerate the games. I needed to get to December 23rd. I'd had some reckless moments in my life, but this wasn't going to be one of them.

"That's wonderful news," I replied, looking into Rob's vacant eyes.

"Great. I'll let you get back to work. Again, if there's anything you need, let me know." He tapped my desk and turned around, exiting quickly. I knew there was something more going on in Rob's mind. I only hoped I wouldn't be around to see what it was.

Five

"You guys made the trip," I squealed, as I opened my door to see Brandy and Gabby standing in front of me. They were both holding an assortment of shopping bags, and I knew what they'd been up to while I was at the office.

I think they were feeling guilty about what they had up their sleeves but not guilty enough to confess or call it off. I got out of the way as they piled into the entry.

"Who's running the bakery, if you're down here tearing up the stores?" I teased.

It was almost impossible to convince Gabby to take a day off. In fact, I wasn't sure how Brandy had convinced her to take an entire week off for our Utah trip. They must have thought I was in a dating crisis.

"Girls' weekend," they both sang together.

"When it comes to my Lily, I'd close up shop if I had to," Gabby laughed.

I raised a brow and watched as they made their way into the family room. I had a few candles lit on the coffee table, and the flokati rug I'd ordered had finally arrived and was placed in the center of the room, complimenting the linen color of the couches nicely. The built-in shelves on each side of the fireplace overflowed with books. Even though I had copies of most on my e-reader now, I couldn't bear to part with the paperbacks.

Gabby fell into a chair and Brandy sat on a couch, flipping the television on.

"I love the new chair," Gabby said, crossing her legs and pulling a blanket onto her lap. "It feels like home."

"Okay, what are you two up to?" I sat on the couch next to Brandy and grabbed one of the cream pillows to hold. "You're *never* this nice."

"I'm offended," Brandy said, snatching the pillow from my lap. "This rug is so soft. I love it." She had flung off her shoes, and her feet were buried deep in the shag.

"Can you believe how good she looks?" Gabby asked Brandy. "It's like she's glowing. This new guy must be good for her, whoever he is."

"You went over the top with that one. You're never this nice," I laughed. "Plus, it's Friday night and the fact that you two want to stay in makes me suspicious. And nervous."

"We're all attached so why would we go out and try to meet guys," Gabby said.

"On that note, tell us all about your new guy." Brandy switched the topic.

I had somewhat planned for this so I had my list at the ready.

"He's absolutely amazing. Tall, tan, muscular, loyal, completely hot but adorable…is employed full-time."

As I listed Ayden's qualities, I almost started laughing.

"Sounds like a winner already," Brandy teased. "Employed full-time, huh?"

"You'd be surprised. Around here that is a *big* deal," I laughed. "He's absolutely gorgeous, and he snowboards so that should be perfect for our little getaway."

Brandy and Gabby traded nervous glances and Brandy let out a sigh.

Were they cracking already?

"First, we aren't kidding about how good you look. There's something about you that's really refreshing to see," Gabby said.

"But we do have something to confess," Brandy continued.

"You didn't really come down to visit me?" My brow arched. "You only wanted to come to my town for no sales tax?"

"No, we did come to see you. But you may not want us to stick around after we tell you what we did," Brandy said.

They were cracking!

"Let's order pizza first," I said, reaching for my phone. I knew once they'd made up their mind to tell me about their Austin plan, it had to have been driving them nuts. Once they could get everything off their chests, they'd start to feel better. But I wasn't ready for them to feel better yet. Nope! I wasn't that nice. "You want chicken and spinach pizza, Thai pizza, pepperoni? And we have to have a salad. Maybe a Greek salad or we could do the chop-chop. Their chocolate brownies are to die for."

"You know..." Brandy narrowed her eyes at me.

"Know what?" I feigned innocence.

"She *does* know." Gabby nodded her head. "The little snot. Who told you?"

"Told me what?"

"You know what," Gabby said.

"What kind of pizza do you want?" I tried again.

"Was it Mason? He can never keep his mouth shut," Brandy huffed.

"I bet it was Aaron. He didn't seem too pleased," Gabby mused.

"What on earth are you guys talking about?" I glanced at my phone, wondering if I should text Ayden that his sister was about to give in and tell me everything. I hadn't actually heard from him since Wednesday, and with this, I'd at least have an excuse to reach out.

"We tracked down your high school boyfriend," Brandy said, at last.

Even though I knew it was coming, my heart still did the stop and 'oh my gosh' routine, which was annoying. I didn't want to give away that Ayden had come clean so I just stared at them, waiting for either one of them to continue.

"That was why we planned a trip to Utah," she continued.

"You didn't have his name."

"Do you think I'd let a little thing like that stop me from possibly finding my best friend's true love?" Brandy asked, completely deadpan.

"Listen, what you guys have done is sweet but very misguided. There was more to the story than I told you. And I recognize that's my fault, not yours. But I actually have tried to reach out over the years and he's never responded. So you better get ready to just enjoy a lovely ski trip and nothing more."

Brandy and Gabby looked at each other and then turned their attention to me.

"He responded to us," Gabby said.

"What do you mean *responded* to you?" I asked. My pulse began racing as I thought about what just rolled off her tongue. It was one thing to track him down but quite another to contact him.

"Aaron and Jason have been against this idea from the beginning—"

"For good reason," I interrupted Brandy.

"They knew they couldn't convince us to give up our idea, but they thought the least we could do was make sure Austin wasn't married with five kids." Gabby had pressed herself into the chair as far as she could go.

"And?" I asked.

"He's not married, not by a long shot," Brandy answered. "He responded to our email and said he'd love to see you."

"Well, that's not exactly how he said it." Gabby's brow raised at Brandy, but Brandy didn't continue so Gabby took over. "He kind of implied he was looking forward to meeting *all* of us."

"Okaaay?" I prompted. "That seems normal enough."

"It was kind of in a flirty way," Brandy finished for Gabby.

I noticed just how close Brandy and Gabby had become recently. Living in Portland away from them definitely put a bit of wedge between me and them. Maybe I should look for work in Seattle once I gave my notice. They were like my family, far more so than my blood relatives.

"He's single. It's not illegal to flirt." I found myself already making excuses for him, and it wasn't like I even knew who he was any longer. We'd both gone our separate directions.

"He thinks you're single because we thought you were when we emailed him," Brandy replied. "And I think I'd like pepperoni."

"Me too," Gabby agreed.

"The pizza can wait," I muttered. "I want to hear what you guys thought could come of this. I want your idea of what a happily-ever-after would be in this case."

"Our hope was that you wouldn't know any of this was happening. That you were going to arrive in Utah. We'd all have a wonderful group dinner and when we went to leave for the evening, he'd be standing across the room and you'd see him. And he'd see you," Brandy's voice trailed off.

"And then both of your eyes would lock on each others, knowing it was meant to be," Gabby sighed. "Ridiculous. I know."

"I've known about your plan for an entire week," I confessed.

My cheeks began to get warm, and I felt overly anxious for some reason.

"I'm gonna grab some water. Do you guys want anything to drink?" I asked. I needed to regroup, and I didn't want to admit that their foolish ideas of how love worked, also matched mine for the last week.

"I'm fine," Brandy responded.

"Me too," Gabby agreed.

I went to the kitchen and filled my water glass and took huge gulps as I fought with myself over make-believe scenarios. This type of reminiscing was detrimental. It was one thing to wonder where people landed in life, but this took it to an entirely different place, a place that wasn't even grounded in this world, let alone this universe. But I had to love them for trying.

Feeling hydrated and a little more centered, I walked back into the family room. Neither of them had spoken a word since they'd unveiled their vision for me and my happily-ever-after. There was just an awkward silence.

"The truth of it is," I paused, "I've dreamed that would be my fairytale ending too," I replied.

Gabby's mouth fell open.

"Since I found out about what you two were up to, I've Googled him countless times and spent my nights imagining that we'd reconnect, and all would be forgiven, and he'd fall madly in love with me all over again. And I feel absolutely insane for having those thoughts cross my mind. I blame you both completely. It's entirely unlike me and even my own bullshit detector's going off," I said. "But then I think back to the connection we shared in high school. It was so intense, and I've spent the short amount of time that I've been an adult hoping to find that again."

"Well, maybe you can't find it with anyone else because Austin's the one," Brandy offered.

"Do you really believe in just one?" I asked.

"I do." Brandy nodded.

"You?" I asked Gabby.

"Yup. Now that I have Jason."

"So I have two hopeless romantics trying to plan my future. This is so not going to work out well," I sighed.

"Especially since you're going down to Utah already attached," Brandy said, nodding in agreement.

"About that." I picked up the phone and dialed the pizza place. "I'm not seeing anyone. I just wanted to drive you two mad. And it looks like it worked."

As I was ordering the pizza, Gabby and Brandy were whispering nonstop about who could have told me about their master plan and how dirty I played it. I couldn't help but love these girls. We didn't talk behind one another's back. Nope. We just did it right in front of each other. I hung up the phone and curled my legs underneath me on the couch.

"Pizza'll be here in fifteen minutes," I said.

"Why won't you tell us who ratted us out?" Brandy scowled.

"I always protect my sources."

My mind drifted to Ayden, and I wondered what he was up to tonight. And then the trip flashed into my mind with a jolt. The jig was up. I needed to text him. I got up from the couch and walked to my bedroom, leaving Brandy and Gabby to their guessing game.

My comforter was pushed down to the foot of the bed, and the sheets had been stripped off my bed and were in the washer, but I crawled on top anyway. The mattress fabric was kind of scratchy so I propped my elbows on my pillows as I typed my text out to Ayden.

They let the cat out of the bag. Fully admitted everything about the trip. Just wanted to let you know so you still had time to find someone to take with you, third wheel and all. Also, all is on schedule for your campaign. Thanks again for everything. You're the best. xx

I hit the send button and decided to wait a few minutes before leaving my room. I didn't want to get out there and have a text from Ayden flash on my screen. That would be a dead giveaway.

I thought I'd already mentioned that I wasn't bringing anyone. Glad you got them to confess. I have full confidence in the campaign. No need for updates.

Huh...

Was he like cutting off communication or just trying to make me feel like he trusted me with his account? But I already knew he did. He had for the last couple of years. I stretched out on my mattress completely perplexed. Maybe he was with someone. After all, it was a Friday night. Did it matter? Why was I worried about his text?

Okay. Well, I don't want you to be upset if everyone's paired up and you're not. You were very clear that you didn't want to feel like a third wheel. I just don't want to be to blame. That's all.

I let out a sigh after I sent the text and began to crawl off the bed. Surprisingly my phone buzzed.

Curious?? Sudden interest in my dating life.

Well, now he was just twisting my words and my intention.

Not curious at all. Just wanted to make sure you had the opp to bring someone if you so choose. I have hung around your sister enough tonight to believe in happily ever afters and I wanted everyone to have one.

He immediately replied back.

How much whiskey and wine did you have tonight?

The nerve! I have had absolutely none! I quickly typed my response.

Zilch. Thank you very much. Shouldn't you be out finding some hot chick? It's a Friday night!

His reply took only seconds.
Again with the dating life...What am I to think?

Oh, he was annoying! I wrote my response as I walked halfway down the hall to Brandy and Gabby.

Think what you will. But I have my sights set on a completely unattainable guy because that's how I roll. Have a great night.

His response flashed on the screen.

Oh, not to worry. I plan to.

What the heck was that supposed to mean? I marched into the family room just as the doorbell rang.

"See? There's that glow again," Brandy laughed, pointing at my face.

"Whatever. Who wants some beer with their pizza?" I asked, opening the door. I almost didn't recognize my regular pizza guy who was standing with the three boxes of pizza I'd ordered. He had buzzed his hair off. He was always cute, but this new hairdo threw me off. I wasn't sure I liked it.

"Having a party?" he asked, smiling.

"Nope. Just me and my two best friends." I handed him the cash and smiled. "These smell delicious. Thanks for bringing them over."

"That's what we do," he laughed. "Have a good night."

"You too." I shut the door and heard Brandy and Gabby in the kitchen already grabbing the plates and beers for us all.

"Get enough pizza?" Brandy laughed.

"I figured we'd be able to snack on it all night," I protested.

"A pizza for each," Gabby muttered. "There must be something more going on that you just haven't told us."

"Like what?" I asked, placing a slice of each kind on my plate.

"Whenever you're confused over guy stuff, you tend to eat a lot of pizza and drink a lot of beer," Brandy said, grabbing a couple slices of pepperoni.

"Actually, she just eats a lot of anything. Does this Austin thing have you that wound up?" Gabby asked, following us back into the family room.

"Possibly. I don't know. A lot of stuff's going on. I'm giving my notice on the 24th, after I finish a project for Better," I began.

"Wait. Ayden took his campaign to your firm? Didn't you just normally moonlight for him?" Brandy asked.

"Yeah. But I have to say this came at the perfect time. Remember the co-worker who I thought was beyond amazing?"

They both nodded.

"Well, he wasn't just a co-worker. He was the son of the boss."

"Not again," Brandy slapped her forehead.

I ignored her and continued, "I finally said yes to him and last weekend we went out. Little did I know that he was holding a grudge this whole time because I kept turning him down. First of all," I paused to take a sip of beer and a bite of pizza. "I never turn someone down who I'm interested in…so why did I do it this time? And then the one time I do play a little hard to get, it comes back to bite me in the ass. The only reason we went to dinner was for him to tell me that he wanted to fire me, but a potential client had specifically asked for me."

"That client was my brother?" Brandy asked.

"Yep. Thank God. Needless to say, without your brother, I wouldn't be getting any of the bonus money that's owed to me because of their vesting schedule and all. Anyway, I owe him a lot. I had mentioned to him what happened," I said, realizing I was saying too much.

Gabby's eyes narrowed as she began studying me.

"The long and the short of it is that once I get my bonus money, I'm out of there. I've even been thinking about moving up to Seattle, maybe…"

"Seriously?" Gabby had snapped out of her contemplative mood as excitement radiated from her.

"So you don't hate us?" Brandy laughed.

"Not at all or maybe I'll be moving to Utah soon. Who knows?" I teased.

The room fell silent.

"Kidding!"

Brandy and Gabby started laughing as a new text rolled over my phone. It was from Ayden.

Not sure this is the guy you really want to meet up with again.

I scrolled past the message and saw a picture of a blonde guy somehow making out with two really cute females. At the same time. I couldn't see the guy's face, but I knew who it was.

I texted Ayden back quickly, hoping Brandy or Gabby wouldn't ask who I was messaging.

So what? He's single!

I didn't hear anything else from Ayden the rest of the night, or the rest of the weekend. And I was fine with that. Really fine with that.

Six

Today was the day—the 23rd of December, and the day before I was going to give my notice. I was completely exhausted, but I was also totally excited about the prospect of leaving. I was enthralled with the idea of the unknown. It seemed really appealing. Plus, the last week was pure torture. Rob appeared whenever and wherever he could, trying to complicate things, but Tori and I managed to pull through. Unfortunately, it was at the cost of completely missing the holiday season but whatever. I wasn't really in the mood anyway.

I glanced at the clock in my bedroom and sighed. The launch party was less than two hours away, and I still needed to get ready. My hair was wet from the shower, and my energy level was completely zapped, but I'd have to put on my bubbly persona and celebrate our accomplishments. My last accomplishment at the firm—weird!

I hadn't heard much from Ayden since my comment about Austin being single. We communicated some about the launch party and campaign, but that was about it. Our communication level was probably just back to where it was before he divulged his sister's secret plan. But I did miss the deeper friendship that seemed to be taking off between us. I liked being able to tell him just about anything without judgment. And if I were to be completely honest, a knot had formed in my stomach, and it had been tightening each day that went by when he hadn't sent a text.

Lame, I know!

I had no idea if it was because of the picture of Austin or the actual text from Ayden. Or maybe it was the combo. But something was definitely bothering me enough to make falling asleep at night impossible. I was usually one of those people who fell asleep as soon as my head hit the pillow but not lately.

I looked in the bathroom mirror as I began blow-drying my hair straight. I'd definitely need to put extra concealer on underneath my eyes to ensure I didn't look like the living dead or the undead living or whatever the hell it was.

Once my hair was as good as I could get it and lying flat, I quickly applied my makeup and secured my hair back on the sides with barrettes. My phone buzzed, and I picked it up quickly to see a message from Brandy come across the screen.

Can't wait to see you tomorrow night. I've already started cooking for Christmas Eve! Have fun tonight and drink as much as you can on your almost ex-firm's nickel. Good luck tomorrow!

I chuckled and quickly sent a reply back. I was really looking forward to spending time with Brandy and everyone for the holidays. My parents were in Paris for Christmas, and I didn't feel like going to my sister's in Chicago. Our family wasn't that close. Well, actually my family was really close with each other, just not with me. I always felt like an outsider.

I began looking through my stack of shrugs and shawls when my phone buzzed again. This one from Ayden.

Look forward to seeing you tonight. Thanks for all of your hard work on this campaign.

My heart did a flip and then a flop before I texted back.

Thanks! I had fun working on it. Look forward to seeing you too. And thanks again for everything.

I grabbed an ivory satin shrug and slipped into it before checking myself in the mirror one more time. All set! A car had been waiting for me downstairs, courtesy of my firm. I was going to miss my corporate credit card! Once I finished locking everything up for the evening, I hurried downstairs and into the cold night air.

The driver opened the back door of the sedan for me and I slid onto the seat, adjusting my dress along the way. I had picked a cocktail dress that was a bit slinkier than usual, but it was the color I was going for. I wanted to match the blue theme of the party, and this one did that.

"How are you this lovely evening?" the driver asked. "Off to an office holiday party?"

Hey! That's right. This firm didn't even throw a holiday party! Definitely time to ditch the place.

"Nope. Off to a work-related party. It's for the launch of a new energy product. Should be fun," I said, glancing out the window as we took off through the city.

The trees lining the streets were wrapped in twinkling white lights, making the sidewalks look as if glitter had been sprayed everywhere. The holiday scenes in the window displays were so festive. Some windows had stacks of sparkling packages and snowflakes dangling, and other windows were more subdued, with only a hint of something dazzling edging the glass. After all, Portland was the hipster capital of the West, and nothing was meant to look like too much fun.

"So do I really need to drop you off at the park? Won't it be kind of cold for a party?" the driver asked.

"Yup. It really is the park. We were able to rent out the acreage and place a huge tent overlooking the waterfront. It's completely heated so we should be fine," I assured him, as we wound our way through the downtown corridor.

"That must've cost a fortune," he said.

"It wasn't cheap, but I bet the drink bill will be worse," I laughed.

He pulled up to the curb, and I took a deep breath as I thought about this being my last event working with the firm.

"Miss, you enjoy yourself, and you have the number to text when I need to pick you up?"

I nodded as he got out of the driver's seat and came around to let me out of the sedan.

"Thank you."

I turned around to take in the scene. It was perfect. A bright, blue carpet was leading from the sidewalk all the way through the silver trees. We were able to create a canopy from the branches, which led to the white tent. As I walked along the path, I stopped every so often to adjust some of the signage or move the samples closer to the walkway. But it looked sensational.

When I stepped inside of the tent, I was in awe. This was a production I was proud to be a part of. It was a good way to exit. The blue color scheme was continued inside of the tent with tiny mirrors attached to the ceiling, reflecting the blue and white lights that bounced in several directions. The dance floor was silver with the logo etched in the middle. And on top of every table, there were miniature replicas of all of Better Brand's products, along with silver and blue vine sculptures shooting toward the ceiling of the tent.

"Stunning," Ayden's voice surprised me.

I turned around to face him and couldn't help but admire how good he looked tonight. He was dressed in a tux, but I noticed the edge of the pocket square matched the blue that was displayed everywhere, kind of like my dress.

"It is stunning. I think the blue reflects the purity of the product nicely. The feel of rejuvenation and…"

"I wasn't talking about the décor," he murmured, interrupting my rambling nature.

I arched a brow and watched him make his way over to me through the scattered tables and chairs.

"You've got to be the king of hot and cold," I muttered.

"How so?" he asked, only a few feet away from me now.

I shrugged. "So no date tonight? You usually always come with someone attached at your hip," I teased.

"Interesting."

"What?" I asked, glancing at the table décor and then back at him.

"There you go talking about my dating life again." His smile was infectious. The way his lips curled only slightly was adorable.

"It was only a comment based on past experiences. Nothing more," I laughed, glancing at where the DJ was setting up.

"You know, this might be crazy..." He bit his lip as he thought about what to say, or how to say it, which for some reason was really sexy. "But what if we don't judge one another on our pasts?"

"I wasn't judging you," I replied.

If there was one thing in life I didn't do, it was pass judgment. With the devastation and turmoil I used to feel because so many passed judgment on me through the years, I wouldn't be the one pointing the finger. Ever. Hence, the Austin kissing two females at once reaction being so void of emotion.

Ayden rubbed his fingers along his chin as he contemplated what else to say. It was hard not to notice the stubble along his jawline, and I suddenly felt flushed from my toes to my head.

"Can you quit doing that?" I asked.

"Doing what?"

"The whole contemplative thing. It's confusing," I lied. It wasn't confusing. It was just sexy as hell.

"I'll try a different approach," he began. Dropping his hand to his side, he slid his fingers into his pocket, and my gaze fell to exactly where it shouldn't have.

Damn him!

And then he didn't say anything. He just stood there, taking in the scenery. Was that his new approach? What was his approach? Why did he stop speaking? I couldn't handle it.

"So you and Mason and your parents will be going over to Brandy and Aaron's, right?" I asked.

I cringed as the words left my lips.

"Yeah, *I'll* be there," he said, smiling.

He caught me!

Feeling slightly frazzled and at a loss as his eyes stayed connected with mine, I placed my hands on a chair and squeezed tightly.

"Good. I'm gonna go check on everything and make sure it's all in order," I mumbled, turning away from him.

"What was that?" he asked.

"I'm gonna go check on some shit." That was the best I could do? Why were things suddenly turning awkward around him? I saw Tori wave at me from the entrance, and I beelined toward her. Her gaze left mine and fell along Ayden's body before she gave me a quick squeeze.

"So how does he like everything?" Tori asked.

"He seems to be happy with the launch." I had hoped the flush I was feeling had already dissipated, but I wasn't sure it had the way Tori was eyeing me.

"He should be," she replied, pointing toward the waterfront.

I hadn't even noticed the view, and that was the entire point of planning the function here.

"True. Listen, I wanted to tell you something tonight," I began.

"I think I already know," she said, glancing at Ayden.

"No. Nothing like that. What would ever give you that idea?" I asked, tapping her shoulder.

"The way he's looking at you. But my bad. So what's up?"

What? How was he looking at me?

Wait.

Enough.

Back to the task at hand.

"I'm giving my notice tomorrow," I sputtered.

"That was my second guess." She nodded.

"Really?" I asked.

"Yeah. The way Rob was putting you through the wringer..." She shook her head in disapproval. "I was surprised you made it through this campaign."

I knew it was bad, but I didn't know it was horrible enough for others to see.

"Yeah, well. I had my reasons to see it through."

Tori's expression softened and she grabbed my hands, pressing them together. "Well, I'm going to miss you like crazy, but I completely understand. And if you need references or anything, I'm your girl. Do you have a place you're going?"

I shook my head and gave her a quick hug. "Thanks. I'm sure I'll need to take you up on that offer. It's actually kind of exciting not knowing what's happening next. Now let's make good use of our open bar. Shall we?"

The music began playing, and I heard the crowds begin to descend outside the tent. After the bartender made our drinks, we walked along the blue carpet to ensure everyone was in their places, handing out the samples. The line to get in was huge and everything was going according to plan. I was worried being so close to the holidays might create a bit of an attendance issue, but offering free food and drinks seemed to be pulling in the corporate buyers.

Tori and I had handpicked the male and female models passing around the samples, and I had to say, they looked hot. We found a place to sit as people began piling in. As I was looking around the tent, my eyes landed on Ayden, who was chatting up one of the female models, and my stomach tightened a tad.

Only a tad!

Tori followed my gaze.

"He's into blondes, huh?" she asked.

I shrugged. "Guess so."

"I didn't tell you what my best friends planned, did I?" I took a sip of my ale.

"No. Do spill."

"They hunted down my old high school boyfriend, and now, we're going on a ski trip to where he lives so they can force us to interact."

"And I thought I had some crazy friends." Her eyes were wide. "Are you okay with this?"

"Kind of. Don't judge me, but I think I've been hung up on him. Thinking that I would never find that kind of love again…It makes dating almost impossible. I'm either on the search for the impossible or forcing things that aren't natural."

She nodded. "You're so not alone on that one. Do you know how many people I hear who are hung up on their first loves?"

"No. Tell me," I laughed. "Because I feel like a complete freak about it."

"Well don't. I see it all the time on Yahoo." Her eyes grew solemn. "It's a serious issue."

"Yahoo?" I laughed. "Well, I wasn't thinking it was serious, just problematic."

"Is he hot?"

I nodded. "Yeah. Complete snowboarder-surfer type with that certain something that says you know you want me. Or at least according to Google images."

Tori laughed and took a sip of her drink. "Well, it sounds like it will be fun, whatever happens."

"I just want closure, one way or the other, so I can put it to rest and shelve the should've-would've-could've syndrome."

"One piece of advice," she replied.

"What's that?"

"Sometimes we'll never understand the reason for certain things in our life, but there's always a reason if we just follow our heart and quit questioning everything that's led us there," she paused. "Wherever *there* is."

I nodded and let her words settle over me. Things in my life did always seem to happen for a reason, even if I had no idea what the hell that reason was until months or years later. Just look at Ayden showing up to have our firm work on his launch.

"Thanks for that," I said, watching Ayden and the model exchange numbers. "That's very easy to forget."

Tori followed my gaze to Ayden. "Maybe Mr. Rhodes came into your life now because—"

I put my hands up. "Let's not get ahead of ourselves. He just exchanged numbers with model number 43."

She started laughing and turned toward the DJ as the lights dimmed. "People are already starting to dance."

"Success," I said, trying to be heard over the music.

Tori grabbed my hand and pulled me onto the dance floor that was now pretty packed with people holding an energy drink in one hand and beer in the other. I let the music drift over me as I closed my eyes and danced, enjoying the sense of freedom that I was about to experience by turning in my letter of resignation. Things were going to be okay, very okay. Tori let go of my hand, and I opened my eyes just as I felt another hand glide along my waist, causing a spike of electricity to run through my body. I wasn't facing him, but I knew who it was.

"Okay if I dance with the person in charge of yet another successful launch?" Ayden murmured, leaning his mouth toward my ear.

I shuddered as his lips lingered so closely to my neck. Feeling his breath scatter across my skin made me light-headed. I could no longer blame the whiskey and wine as he wrapped his arms completely around my waist, pulling me into him.

"I suppose," I said breathlessly.

"Good," he whispered, as I felt his firm body pressed against mine with each step we took together. I enjoyed the way he was holding me, and I didn't want to turn around and face him and ruin this moment because I wasn't sure it would ever happen again.

"You really are stunning," he said, as he began to spin me around, but I shook my head.

"Let's just stay like this," I replied, pressing my back into his chest more as his arms were wrapped around my waist. I knew I should be concerned with how my behavior looked, dancing with a client. But I didn't care anymore. This was where I was meant to be, at least in this moment, because everything happened for a reason.

Seven

The party had slowed, and Ayden and I were sitting near the back corner of the tent, watching everyone enjoy themselves as we cooled off from our last round of dancing. Things had been going wonderfully. Ted and Rob made their appearances and slipped out almost as soon as they came, which was like a dream come true. It was a lot of fun hanging out with Ayden. Or at least it had been until he brought up Austin again and the picture. I'd been biting my tongue about the exchange of numbers between him and the model so far, but it was really hard to do since he kept trying to paint Austin as a complete d-bag. No one was perfect.

"Oh, come on. I'm sure I could find some dirt on you. Or were you just one of the lucky bastards that didn't get photographed by one of your buddies making out with some hot chick?" I laughed. "Or worse?"

"You've got a really warped sense of reality, Lily. How men should behave," he said, his blue eyes fastening on mine.

"Well, hello, Mr. Serious," I said, laughing.

"You know what I mean." His expression took me off guard, and I looked away quickly. "Not all guys are assholes."

"I never said any of them were," I replied, my gaze falling back on his.

"That's exactly what I mean," his voice lowered and his blue eyes darkened. "You put up with shit you shouldn't have. You're better than that, Lily."

I felt the heat from his gaze as he waited for me to respond. But what was I supposed to say to that? I did happen to run into my fair share of scumbags, yet I was always the one making the excuses for them. I guess I felt it was my fault for falling for them in the first place.

"Listen, I'm not going to start picking on some guy I dated in high school who I know absolutely nothing about once he hit drinking age. Having a conversation about him in any sort of context is actually embarrassing because I doubt he's in Utah giving me the time of day. I left him in a cowardly way. He deserved better than what I gave him. So maybe in some instances, I do deserve better, but when it comes to him, he deserved better."

Ayden pulled his chair closer to mine, and I felt the cool touch of his fingers as he enclosed my hands, bringing them toward him, not moving his gaze from mine.

"I know you haven't told anyone what it is that you two experienced that makes you think you should carry around this guilt, but maybe if you did confide in someone, it would make you feel better. I'm not saying I'm that person, but I think someone should be."

My heart fluttered into overdrive as I realized I was on the verge of admitting something to him that I hadn't told a soul about. Ever. The only people who knew what we went through were Austin, me, and our parents. That was it.

I let out a deep breath but felt the weight still pressing heavily on my chest.

"I want you to be happy, Lily. Whether that's with Austin or some farmer in Montana, but the only way that can happen is if you forgive yourself and let go," his voice was steady and comforting. "Whether we know what the reason is or not, everything always happens for a reason."

I started chuckling, and his expression turned to complete bewilderment. "Sorry. I've just heard that phrase twice tonight."

"Maybe the universe wasn't sure you heard the first time." A smile broke onto his lips and the tension began to fade. He brought my hands up to his lips and gave them a soft, gentle kiss, and somehow, it felt like the most passionate kiss I'd ever experienced.

And it was on my knuckles!

A few moments of silence passed between us as I let what happened settle over me. It was just a quick kiss on the knuckles. I was sure he didn't think anything about it. I was sure of it. Besides, he had someone's number in his pocket. This was a complete friendship kiss, and if not, I knew exactly what would kill that switch. I crossed one leg over the other and noticed his gaze drop and run up my leg. Maybe the kiss wasn't so innocent. Who knew, but I was on the verge of finally telling someone about my past—not the candy-coated version, either—and that ought to stop whatever thoughts were getting miscommunicated.

"So, Austin and I only had a few more months before high school graduation. It was like constant party mode. For once in my life, I no longer cared about school. I was all about friends and parties. Having fun was my one and only concern. And most of that fun included Austin and someone else. Someone I cared deeply for, my first boyfriend."

"I thought Austin was your first boyfriend?" Ayden asked.

I shook my head. "My first boyfriend was actually Jake. We'd gone together from sophomore year on. He taught me what love meant. We did everything together, but senior year things started to change. He started to change. I wasn't sure what to make of it, but at that age I took everything personally. I thought it was me, but then he distanced himself from his other friends. When he backed away from his friendship with Austin, I knew something was wrong. By the time he broke up with me, I completely expected it, but it didn't make it feel any better. I still hung around Austin and all of our friends, but Jake always had some excuse not to show up. Since he'd broke up with me, I thought he didn't want to hang out with our friends because I was there, but that had nothing to do with it."

Sliding my elbow onto the table, I propped my cheek on my hand and gauged Ayden's reaction. It felt so natural telling him about me, my history. Ayden's eyes were focused solely on me and the curiosity behind them was genuine. So was the kindness. I could do this. What I couldn't even divulge to his sister, I could tell him.

"Austin and Jake had been best friends since grade school so when Jake wouldn't even hang out with him, I got concerned. We tried talking to his parents, but they dismissed our concerns completely," I continued.

"Austin kind of took over in my life. He became the person I confided in when Jake stopped taking my calls. He was there for me when I tried to get over my first love. And those last couple of months in high school were pretty magical. It was like he took all of the pain away from Jake. At first, we were uneasy about seeing one another since we were all friends, but our emotions called the shots by that point. I had become completely Austin crazy. But I still wanted Jake in my life or anyone's life, but he just wouldn't step out of his shell." I swallowed the lump that started forming in my throat.

Ayden's jaw tensed as he watched me begin to move my finger in a continual circle as if that motion would help me get through what I was about to confess.

"He needed help. Jake needed help and I failed him. Austin and I both failed him. When it happened, when I found him, Austin was with me. I had started getting kind of random texts from him. I didn't understand them, and sometimes they were just links to odd cartoon sites or random bits of pop culture references. They usually happened late at night so I thought he was just partying too much with a crowd I didn't know or something." The hollowness began to spread throughout my body as I spoke. "He always loved to sneak alcohol everywhere. If someone needed it for a party, he was the man. I actually never asked how he got it, but he always did."

I felt buried with guilt and grief, knowing I'd hid my truth, my history.

"I didn't know he was battling so many demons, so much pain. Austin and I had just gotten out of a movie and were walking to his truck when I got the text from Jake. It was cryptic...Cryptic enough to understand his intent. I'll never forget those two words. *I'm done.*"

"Oh, god," Ayden whispered.

"I showed Austin the text, and he told me to reach out to his parents immediately, which I did. But they weren't in the state. I got another text from him apologizing and telling me he loved me. By the time Austin sped into his driveway, I was already jumping out of the car. From the moment I grabbed the hidden key under the rock, to climbing the stairs, everything went into slow motion. It was dark inside the house. I yelled for him, but all I heard was the running water upstairs. Austin and I climbed the stairs two at a time until we finally reached the bathroom. He was in it. The water had overflowed the tub. His body was fully submerged. All I remember was Austin pulling him out of the water, trying to revive him. I fell to the floor, crying, holding Jake's hand, begging for him to come back to me, to us. His parents had called the police on our way over to their house. There was a blur of medics and police. I remember watching the emergency personnel working on him, but nothing they did helped."

Ayden's hand was on my knee, and he was slowly shaking his head as the story I'd never shared with anyone finally had a listener—the listener of my choosing.

"Austin was holding me in his arms, sheltering me from seeing Jake's body as they tried to revive him. Austin became my rock. He got me through the last weeks of school. I didn't even want to bother showing up. I was fine with just throwing in the towel. But he was there every morning, helping me to get ready, driving me to school, walking me to every class. He'd take me by my favorite ice cream place on the way home and sit with me, either helping me with my homework or doing it for me. And it wasn't like Austin wasn't hurting. That was his best friend, but he helped me through it. My parents just wanted me to forget what I saw. And all of the texts I had gotten leading up to his death kept taunting me, showing me how selfish I'd become. That was all I could focus on. I mean, how could I not realize my ex-boyfriend was suffering so much? Austin was the only person who kept me on track. He continually reminded me of my dreams, told me Jake wouldn't want me to throw everything away."

"There wasn't any jealousy as I mourned. Austin understood the place Jake held in my heart. I felt like Jake's demons became entwined in my soul—in my life— as if they were going to start guiding me. My parents were tired of my relationship with Austin and didn't recognize that if it hadn't been for him, I probably wouldn't have graduated. And all Austin wanted to do was shelter me, protect me. I was a wreck. Every night, I woke up with nightmares, the images of Jake in the bathtub. Some nights, Austin would sneak in through my window and stay with me, just holding me." I took a sip of water and watched Ayden's expression change to questioning.

"Your parents?" he asked.

"They were too worried about how everything would look come election time. They didn't want it to look like I was in any way involved with Jake or his activities. He had gotten involved with drugs. We think that's when he started to break away from us all, and we just didn't know it. It came out that his blood-alcohol level was off the charts, and one of my father's platforms was lowering teen drinking. You can imagine how that went down in the household. I was falling to pieces, and all they carried on about was how we looked from the outside. Things got very dark for me. Then came the rumors that Austin got some chick pregnant, and I bolted away to college without ever telling him goodbye." The tears that had been balancing on my lower lids finally spilled over, and I closed my eyes, dabbing them with a cocktail napkin.

I felt Ayden's arms wrap around me and pull me into him, and I finally let the pain escape.

"Was it true?" he whispered.

I shook my head. "I just couldn't do it anymore. I couldn't run from my nightmares because he shared them with me. He reminded me of Jake, reminded me of everything I did wrong and nothing I did right to save

Jake. I felt the only way to start over was to leave him and the memories behind."

"I understand," he replied, running his fingers through my hair to comfort me, and it did. He did. And there were no expectations of anything in return. We were quiet for a few moments before he said anything more. "Lily, you did nothing wrong. Those were Jake's demons. You couldn't have done anything. You need to let go of the guilt."

"I hope to someday," I whispered. "Thanks for listening."

"That's what friends are for. I'm here anytime you need me."

I slowly freed myself from his embrace and looked into his eyes. "I really mean it. Thank you."

"I know you do. And I can now understand why you're willing to take it easy on Austin. It makes sense. What you guys experienced together is unfathomable and changed you both forever. I get it."

I nodded.

"I'll be there for you, no matter what happens. No matter which direction things go. You know that, right?" he asked.

"I do."

The party was now nonexistent and the surroundings were in takedown mode. I glanced over at Tori, who was giving directions to the staff, when my eyes caught the blonde model now eagerly waving at Ayden. I followed her gaze back to his and my stomach clenched.

"Well, I'm gonna take off," I replied. "And I guess I'll see you tomorrow up north."

I spun around before Ayden could give me some lame excuse, and I just waved behind me as I quickly texted the driver to take me home.

Everything did happen for a reason. Now I just had to figure out if I had to bother trying to ever figure out what the reason was.

Eight

'd given my notice this morning—Christmas Eve or not—and drove up to Seattle for the holidays. Between that and talking to Ayden last night, it felt like my world had been reinvented, and I'd barely even done anything. Somehow I'd managed to pack everything for our Utah trip and haul it with me so I could take off from Seattle with everyone. I just stepped inside of Aaron and Brandy's home and instantly felt at ease.

"We are so grateful to you for not killing our daughter for coming up with this crazy idea." Brandy's mom gave me a quick hug and laughed as I caught a funny look from Mason who was in the family room. He was talking to someone quietly, but from where I was standing, I couldn't tell who it was.

"Well, I'm not going to make any promises until we make it through the trip," I laughed.

"Am I really in trouble?" Brandy asked, pulling Aaron behind her.

I gave her a big hug as Aaron waved at me and picked up my bags of presents. He followed Brandy's mom out of the foyer, leaving us alone.

Brandy was dressed in a pale blue cashmere sweater, and her hair fell softly around her face. She looked really beautiful and strong. Strong was the most important with everything she'd been through.

"Seriously, am I in trouble? Because you know Gabby is equally at fault," she teased.

"No. You're not in trouble," I laughed. "But you better have some backup activities planned for me that don't include a long lost boyfriend."

"Noted. Gabby and Jason are on their way over, and I've got a ton of appetizers spread out so you better be hungry."

I followed her down the hallway, bringing Ayden into view. So that was who Mason was talking to with such serious intent.

Mason's eyes followed me as I walked past him and his brother. His brow quirked, and a grin spread across his lips.

"What we're chopped liver?" Mason asked, throwing his hands in the air.

I started laughing and gave Mason a huge hug. He was just like his brother, like exactly, since they were identical twins. But I could always tell the difference from the moment I'd met them. Plus, they dressed completely different. Mason was in a t-shirt and baggy jeans, while Ayden was in dark green sweater that hugged his chest and shoulders—enough of skimming Ayden's chest already!

And fitted jeans that hugged everything else.

Okay, now I was done.

Mason let go of me and Ayden came in next for a quick squeeze.

"Long time no see," I said, as Ayden wrapped his arms around my waist. The hug was completely different than his brother's, more intimate. Or was it in my head?

"Too long," he murmured, tucking his chin down slightly by my ear.

Definitely not in my head!

He let go and I caught Mason watching us, shaking his head. I pushed Ayden away playfully, chuckling.

"See what I mean? You're very complicated," I teased.

"Ayden complicated?" Mason belted out. "Yeah, right. He's about as deep as a kiddie pool."

I couldn't help but widen my grin as Ayden thumped his brother on the head.

"Lily, I made your favorite cheese dip," Brandy hollered from the kitchen. "Get your butt in here."

"That's why you're my BFF," I laughed.

"Is that all it takes?" Ayden asked.

I rolled my eyes and started toward the kitchen.

Every single surface was covered in Christmas décor, and I loved it. Brandy was definitely allowing herself to feel at home at Aaron's house, and I was so happy to see it. On my way to the kitchen, I leaned over to check out a tiny North Pole village and laughed as I saw Brandy and Aaron's heads cut out and pasted on Mr. and Mrs. Claus.

Brandy was done for.

And so was Aaron.

"Thanks, for making my favorite cheesy concoction in the world, Mrs. Claus," I said, scooping the dip up on a chip.

She froze.

"You saw that?" She turned bright red and crinkled her nose.

"Uh, yeah. It's right in plain sight. I'm surprised Ayden or Mason haven't seen it yet."

"And let's hope they don't. I don't want to hear about it all through the holidays and then on our vacation," she warned, her brow furrowed slightly.

I threw my hands up vowing not to tell.

"So are you really okay with meeting up with Austin?" she asked, her tone turning serious.

I nodded. "I am. Totally."

And thanks to last night, I was.

"How are you feeling? You look like you're doing really well," I told Brandy. I knew she didn't like any of us to concentrate on her health and recovery, but I was so proud of her for overcoming so many obstacles that had been thrown her way since the accident. Not to mention all of the legal stuff that followed.

She turned around and smiled, holding a gingerbread cookie. "The pain is almost non-existent. Sometimes it sneaks up on me and slows me down a bit, but that's life. Even though I was determined to be skiing or snowboarding on this trip, my physical therapist has convinced me that a fall this year would be detrimental to my recovery. And we all know that if I'm propped up on either one of those contraptions, I'm bound to hit the ground."

"That sucks," I replied. I knew she'd see through me if I played like it's no big deal, but to Brandy it was. She never wanted to miss out.

"It does. But next year, he promised I can fall down as much as I want." She took another bite of the cookie.

"Well, good! We can get ourselves prepared for that." I eyed her cookie and she handed me one.

"They're from Gabby's bakery," she confirmed.

"I'd hope so," I replied, biting the head off the gingerbread man.

I heard laughter coming from the family room as everyone's attention was trained on National Lampoon's Christmas Vacation, but then I felt a large hand settle on my shoulder from behind just as I was about to swallow.

A wave of energy ran along my arm and I tried not to look affected.

"Hey," Ayden whispered. "Can I talk to you for a sec?"

I traded awkward glances with Brandy and nodded. "Sounds serious."

"It is. It's about Brandy's Christmas present," he said, his expression not giving anything away.

"Then by all means go get it sorted," Brandy commanded, gesturing for me to leave the kitchen. "I don't want hiccups getting in the way of my gift receiving."

"Right, because that's what this holiday is truly about."

I followed Ayden out of the kitchen and into the study.

"So what's up?" I asked, reclining on the leather sofa. Ayden took a seat at the far end of the couch, which seemed a bit odd. Maybe, it really was about Brandy's present.

"I just wanted to let you know that I'm actually bringing someone with me to Utah," he said, running his fingers through his hair. My heart fell, but I managed to keep my face in the full upright position. They always say that's good for crash landings.

"Sweet," I replied, keeping my gaze on his. I didn't want to show even a flicker of disappointment, but I couldn't hold my snarkilicious in. I needed to offer just one jab. "Is it the blonde from last night?"

His eyes fell to the rug and his jaw tensed.

Oh. My. God. It was. That backfired.

"Yeah, actually it is. I dated her years ago. She started traveling a lot for her modeling career so things—"

"Ayden, I promise. You don't have to justify it to me. I think it's great. Plus, she's gorgeous," I interrupted.

He bit his lip and continued to stare at the floor.

Awkward much?

"Shouldn't you be happy about not being the third wheel? I know that was some sort of fear you had." I smiled, still waiting for him to look at me.

Still nothing. What the hell?

"Okay, so I think that's fabulous, and I'm sure she'll be a lot of fun to hang out with," I continued.

Lies, lies, all lies!

"I'm sorry. I..." He finally began to speak and what did I do? I cut him off.

"There's nothing to apologize for," I assured him. I stood up and sat right next to him on the couch. "Your friendship means the world to me. I've opened up to you about things I've never uttered to anyone. I get it. You're a guy and—"

His eyes flashed up to mine, and I felt my chest tighten. He pressed his lips together, his hand falling to my knee as his eyes focused on mine.

"I don't think you do get it, Lily. I saw the way you looked when you spoke about Austin. I don't want to get in the way. There was something there, like you said. You guys shared something. I don't want to be a distraction. And I know myself more than I'd like to admit. I'd make sure that I became a distraction. This is too important for you to have me screwing it up. That's why I'm bringing her." The pained look in his eyes was impossible to miss.

I don't know why I always thought my actions would numb the pain or divert a catastrophe because they never did.

They always complicated things.

Closing my eyes, I leaned in close to Ayden, and I softly kissed him. Not on the lips, just across his jawline. But I felt it, his body tensed and an overwhelming current ran between us. I leaned back and slowly opened my eyes but not before realizing his were still closed as if he had to commit this moment to memory. I touched his cheek, but he grabbed my hand, his eyes now open and locking on mine. We shared this moment in silence, our eyes taking each other in, as if it was our farewell of what could have been before we even started.

"I've been there before...when you think the mistakes of your past will define you. But they don't," he finally replied. "You may still have that connection with Austin. You probably do, actually. And it's worth fighting for. And if you decide that's not what's best for you, then you're going to need space to move on, mourn once and for all. I refuse to get in the way."

"You've got it all figured out, don't you," I muttered.

He didn't reply. Instead, Ayden stood up, leaving me in the study to analyze what the hell just happened. Besides the obvious, which was that I threw my two cents in and complicated the matter, he was letting me go. But I was never his in the first place.

The front door opened and Gabby and Jason came in, carrying trays of goodies. I jumped up and ran over, praying for a distraction, which I got all too quickly.

"Merry Christmas," Gabby sang, as I hopped in front of her, taking two of the trays off her stack.

"Merry Christmas," I replied, smiling at Jason as he watched Gabby glide through the entry. That was the kind of love I wanted—the complete adoration of another type of love.

Was that too much to ask?

Possibly!

"I've got a little something for you that will hopefully calm your mind about our little excursion," Gabby whispered.

"Oh no," I muttered back.

"Seriously, I think if you weren't excited about it, you will be now." She placed the trays down on the kitchen counter, and Brandy gave her a big squeeze.

"Did you get my gift drama out of the way with my brother?" Brandy asked, as Ayden was grabbing a soda out of the refrigerator.

"I did. He was just worrying about nothing."

Ayden avoided my gaze as he walked out of the kitchen, not saying a word.

Gabby was digging around in her purse until she finally found a piece of paper, which was folded up in a tight square. She handed it over to me, and I quickly unfolded it, my heart pounding as I saw Austin's name up top.

"It's an email from him. I wanted Austin to know that this was entirely our idea, and you had nothing to do with it and were beyond mortified that we'd done this. I also made it clear that out of all the years we'd known you, you'd only mentioned him once. You know, I was trying to make it sound like you weren't one of those chicks pining for their old boyfriends nonstop," Gabby rambled.

"Thanks for throwing me a bone," I laughed, my eyes falling to the message.

Hey–

No sweat. I'm actually glad you reached out. I'll admit, it was a little weird at first, but I feel better knowing it wasn't her idea.

I looked up from the letter and scowled at Gabby.
"How is this supposed to make me feel better?"

"Keep reading. You'll see," Gabby said.

I don't know what all she's told you about us, especially given she only mentioned me once. I've been a dick over the last several years not responding to her letters, and it would be nice to be able to apologize to her.

I broke my gaze free from the letter, "Again, this isn't really helping me feel at ease about this whole thing."

Brandy and Gabby traded looks and I continued reading.

This message is somewhere between my tenth and twentieth attempt at emailing you back, and it's not any easier so I'll get straight to the point because everything I want to say just doesn't come out right in print. I do want to see her. Please tell her fall or fly, I'm by her side. She'll know what it means. I've got a reservation under my name for drinks at seven o'clock in the bar at the Lodge.

A. Graham

Fall or fly, my stomach tightened as I reread his words. The words he told me every single day after Jake's death to make me get out of bed. I swallowed the lump down and wiped at the tears that were threatening to cascade down my cheeks.

"Oh, sweetie. Don't cry," Brandy said, wrapping her arms around me.

"Maybe, this was a bad idea," Gabby said.

I shook my head taking in a deep sniff. "No, it was a brilliant idea. And I should have done it myself a long time ago."

"What's going on in here?" Ayden's voice wary.

"Do you mind if he sees it?" Brandy asked, glancing at the paper.

I shook my head, and Brandy grabbed the paper from my hands and shoved it over to Ayden.

Those words had haunted me from the moment I'd left him. They were responsible for every guilty, regret-filled thought that plagued me every single day since I was eighteen, and Austin knew it.

Letting out a sigh, I glanced over at Ayden as he continued to read. I needed this trip more than Brandy and Gabby ever could've imagined, whether it was for closure or new beginnings. I was ready to take the beating.

Ayden's gaze slowly lifted to meet mine and a warmth spread through me as I saw concern fill his expression. I bit my lip and nodded, answering his silent question.

I was going to be okay.

"What's going on, you guys? Why does Ayden seem to understand the letter more than we do?" Brandy asked, crossing her arms.

"I haven't been completely forthright about every-thing. There's some stuff I need to tell you about Austin."

"And my brother already knows?" Brandy asked bewildered.

"Yeah, the poor guy got an earful last night at his launch party," I said, dismissing the importance.

I saw Ayden's shoulders drop out of my periphery, but I couldn't worry about it. I needed to straighten myself out first.

"It didn't occur to me that there was more to the story," she said nervously.

Ayden handed me the letter back and our eyes connected, but this time there was no hiding the turmoil that my action caused.

And for that I was very sorry.

Nine

"This is so awesome," Brandy gushed, popping her head over the back of the leather seat. "Do you realize how big these seats are? And we get special food?"

I had to laugh. Leave it to Brandy to be excited about airplane food. We had just boarded our plane, and Aaron surprised Brandy with First Class seats for all of us. She was so cute about it. I wanted to squeeze her cheeks.

"Seriously? They serve a choice of salmon or steak salad for lunch?" Brandy continued. "This is way better than peanuts or pretzels." Aaron slid his arms around her waist and flipped her back in the seat to a fit of giggles.

We were lucky to have her in our lives.

Gabby rolled her eyes and laughed as she removed a blanket from the sanitized package and spread it over her lap. She leaned her head against Jason, and I glanced quickly out the window as I watched the food cart get loaded inside. First Class had already been called and now all of the regular seats were loading. Mason and Ayden weren't here yet. Somehow, someone's alarm clock didn't go off, or I didn't quite hear the whole story about who was picking up who, but they'd just gotten through security so they'd be here soon.

Once I told Brandy and Gabby the entire story about Austin and me, they were completely beside themselves for setting this trip up, but I promised them it needed to be done. If I didn't want to go, I would have put a stop to it. I think they only felt slightly better about the whole thing. The truth of it was that I wanted to quit speculating about a boy from high school. If I just get it out of my system, I should be able to move on. Or at least that was the plan.

I leaned my head against the seat and then that little pesky voice in my head couldn't leave well enough alone and chirped. "And maybe you'll fall madly in love all over again."

Right, on a ski trip where neither of us have spoken for years.

"You look like you're deep in thought," Ayden's voice brought me back to reality.

I turned to face him and my cheeks warmed. I was certain he knew what I was busy daydreaming about, which only made it worse. His hair looked like he jumped in and out of the shower within a two-minute time period and he'd forgot to comb it. I suspected he was the culprit

KARICE BOLTON

of tardiness. It was hard not to grin as I watched him secure his carry-on in the compartment above; his body stretching and my eyes wandering.

Gabby started laughing, bringing me out of my daze, and I watched her raise a brow from across the aisle. Was it obvious? I rolled my eyes and grabbed one of the magazines I'd bought at the gate.

Flipping the pages, I pretended to be completely enthralled in the fashion hit-and-miss section when Ayden sank into the seat next to me. A light scent of soap and something Ayden drifted over, and I couldn't help but think back to that weekend he came over. The very thing that he came to relay turned out to be the very thing making my emotions bounce all over the place.

Ayden's body began to pulse forward, and I started laughing as Mason sat behind us, thumping his brother's seat with his feet.

"This is why I don't do family vacations any longer," Ayden said, loud enough for his brother to hear.

"What are you gonna do about it?" Mason laughed. "Mr. Bigshot, huh."

As Ayden sat in the chair, his body kept bumping forward as he tried to look at the magazine I was scanning. His smile was so infectious—I couldn't imagine sitting anywhere else. If nothing else, I'd be in a good mood by the time we landed in Salt Lake City. I loved how Brandy's family was so close. She and her brothers were the exact opposite of mine.

"Completely hideous," Ayden said, shaking his head.

"Come on. Your brother's not that bad," I said, laughing as our eyes connected.

"I wasn't talking about my brother." He pointed at the page in front of me where some actress was dressed in a sheer pink jumpsuit with a corset visible underneath.

"You better start getting used to high fashion, you know," I teased. "Dating a model and all."

His smile fell slightly, and he moved forward to grab something out of his bag that he'd slid under the seat in front of him. He pulled out two books and handed me one. He ignored my comment and focused on the book he'd just given me.

"This one's for you. I haven't read it, but I saw it at the bookstore, and it sounded like something you'd like. It's a mystery. I saw a lot of those on your shelves at home. Hope you haven't read it yet."

My heart literally melted on the spot. And I realized how very difficult it was to keep him in the friend zone.

"This was so sweet of you," I said, admiring the cover. "And no, I haven't read this one, but I love the author. I can't wait to start it. Thanks. What do you have?"

I reached over and picked up his novel.

"I'm on a historical kick right now. This guy writes with incredible detail. By the end of each book, I felt like I lived through whatever time period he wrote about."

"I never took you for a reader. Like a *real* reader," I said, grinning.

"Are there fake readers out there?" he joked.

"You'd be surprised. To get people into bed, there are a lot of fake talents floating around out there."

"I didn't know reading was a talent, but I'll take it." His laugh was cut short as the flight attendant began her demonstration on how to survive a plane crash, and I couldn't help but laugh as I watched her gaze move back and forth between Mason and Ayden. It was like her brain was participating in some sort of high stakes ping-pong match of hotness. I glanced at Ayden who didn't even seem to notice her fascination, which resulted in a pulse of satisfaction racing through me.

"So when's..."

"She's getting in tomorrow," he replied, cutting off my question.

How'd he know who or what I was talking about?

"That's cool." I was the one who picked out that particular model and didn't want to admit that I couldn't for the life of me remember her name. "So does model chick know how to ski or snowboard?"

Real mature.

"She skis. Sammie skis." He opened his book and held it in his left hand.

Samantha! That was it. Shouldn't have a problem remembering it now that it rolled off his lips.

I didn't like how it rolled off his lips.

My mind drifted off to the rooming situation, and I tried to remember how many bedrooms this place had... was it four or five?

"I wonder since Mason and I are the singles of the group, if we'll have to bunk up," I joked.

"That would be fine with me, doll," Mason's voice sounded from behind.

I started laughing. "Is that how you start out your moves? With doll?"

"Only on the special ones," he joked.

"I'm honored." The plane began moving down the runway, and I wrapped my fingers around the armrests. Even though I wasn't scared of flying in the traditional sense, I hated taking off and landing. Everything else was fine, and I didn't require meds before boarding like my mother so I'd say I was doing pretty well.

Ayden caught my reaction and smiled. Lowering his hand over mine, I felt the tension of the moment slip away as quickly as it came. Once we were in the sky, we both began reading. Everyone else was plugged into the movie players, which kind of made it like our own little soundproof box. I found myself reading the same sentence over and over again as my mind kept drifting to Austin.

In less than eight hours I would be meeting him for drinks, and I'd know the course of our relationship. Would we be merely acquaintances or would a friendship resurface? Would I go back home with more understanding or resolution? The thought of seeing him was suddenly terrifying as my mind wandered to all of the "what if" scenarios surrounding our history. Had he forgiven me for leaving? Would he be able to forgive me? Did he care? Did I screw him up as much as I did myself?

"That must be an intense page," Ayden said softly.

I looked over at him and laughed. "Lots of big words."

He closed his book and placed it on the tray. "You're going to be okay. When he sees you, all will be forgiven. No one could possibly stay mad at that face."

I turned in my seat and my eyes narrowed as I studied him. "How do you always know what's bothering me?"

"Just lucky, I guess."

"What if I meet him and nothing changes? I go back to Portland and am still as screwed up as I've always been. All these years, I've been able to blame my choices on my past, and what if the problem is really just me?" I laughed, but it didn't sound very funny.

Ayden turned slightly in the chair and lifted up the armrest between us.

"You're not anymore screwed up than the rest of us, Lily."

"Oh, but I am," I assured him.

"I'm not exactly sure what you're referring to, but the Lily I know is a passionate free-spirit who embraces friendship fiercely."

"I'll give you that. I'm an awesome friend, but I suck at romantic relationships. That's what I was referring to." I smiled, and I knew he knew it too.

"You don't see a ring on my finger either," he laughed, wiggling his ring finger.

"Doesn't mean you suck. You just haven't found that special someone."

"So why can't you apply that same line of thinking to yourself. You put so much pressure on yourself," he whispered, as one of the flight attendants walked down the aisle.

I couldn't explain it to him, what it was like to feel numb time and again. And how I so desperately wanted the numbness to fade. Besides we were on our way to a ski vacation, where he would eventually meet up with Sammie, and I would do who knows what with what I was about to discover.

"Maybe you just haven't found the right person. Or maybe you did and he's in Utah."

"Now onto the most important question of all," I said, grinning

"And what is that?"

"Are you a member of the mile-high club?"

He wriggled his brows, and I couldn't help but burst into laughter. "I'll never tell."

Without the armrest separating us, I leaned against him and began reading again, this time flipping the page and allowing myself to bury my mind into someone else's world.

Ten

"**C**an we just stay here forever?" Brandy asked, as we all piled into the grand foyer of the condo.

Besides the fact that the snow began falling once we reached Deer Valley, the lodge was stunning and our condo was spectacular. This was turning into a perfect getaway.

The foyer was two stories high and exposed beams jetted from above in a sunburst pattern. The wall to my left was covered in built-ins for snow gear and straight in front of us was the great room. This would be a wonderful refuge if things headed south on me this week.

"Kudos to whoever picked this place out," I replied, following Jason and Gabby down the hall.

Gabby stopped and took a bow just as I looked around the great room. A large leather sectional framed the room along with several overstuffed chairs, and a huge flat screen was anchored above the fireplace. The room opened to the kitchen, which was just as grand as the rest of the condo. Dark granite countertops covered the rustic, lower cabinets, and the breakfast bar was large enough to fit six chairs.

Ayden came up behind me and set his hand on my shoulder, sending a prickle of electricity down my arm. "This is all fine and dandy, but we need to figure out the bedroom situation. That's where we'll see what's up," he said.

For some reason, hearing Ayden mention the word 'bedroom' messed with me. I closed my eyes and rolled them simultaneously at my pitiful reaction.

"There are five bedrooms," Gabby replied, but her voice went up an octave on the word bedrooms.

Oh, no. There was a catch.

"Two of the bedrooms have an adjoining ensuite. The other three share two main bathrooms," she said.

"That's no big deal," I said, shrugging my shoulder.

"One of the bedrooms has bunk beds. Two of 'em. Twin size." Brandy took over for Gabby. She raised her brow and twisted her lips as she looked at her brothers. "Since we set poor Lily up for this trip, I think it's only fair she gets one of the rooms with a bathroom. Aaron and I'll take one without. But I think it's rock, paper, scissor time for the two of you."

"I'm fine with it," Ayden said. "Bunks for me."

"What about Sammie?" I asked, turning to him. "Are you claiming top or bottom bunk with her?"

Brandy and Gabby laughed, but Mason's expression was one of complete bewilderment as he looked at his brother. Ayden smiled and dropped his hand from my shoulder as I turned to go get my bags from the entry, but he didn't say anything.

"So, Lily's got a date at seven tonight," Gabby called out, as everyone followed my lead. Like they didn't know.

"But it might be a really short one. As far as I know, it's drinks only," I said, in an attempt to brush off some of the anxiety that was building at a rapid pace. The moment the plane had touched down in Utah, it felt like I'd drank two Red Bulls and six cups of coffee. Even my hands shook if I held them out for more than a second.

"How about we go out for drinks and then I'll cook a dinner for us tonight?" Ayden offered, reaching for his bag. "That way you won't feel pressure, one way or another, with Austin. I'll make sure to make plenty in case you come back late and hungry."

I dropped my bag and smacked him in the arm. "Not funny."

"But it could be accurate..." Brandy laughed.

"I can't have the Rhodes siblings ganging up on me in my condition," I said, picking my bag up and walking down the hallway.

"Condition?" Brandy asked, following right behind me.

"Yeah. Condition. Look at this." I held out my free hand, which had a slight tremor to it.

"Shit. You weren't kidding about freaking out," Brandy muttered.

"Yeah. I've been playing it cool, but now my body's betraying me. By the time I see him tonight, I'm going to have to sit on my hands."

I peeked into the first bedroom and laughed. "Found your bunks," I called to Ayden.

The room was bright blue with a ski mural painted on the far wall. There was a teddy bear placed on each of the bottom two bunks. It looked like a bedroom Mason and Ayden would've shared when they were ten. "If this doesn't call out for sexy time with your girlfriend, I don't know what will."

Brandy peeked her head in and started laughing. "Yeah, if you have Sammie by the end of the trip, I'll be impressed."

I glanced at the bathroom and then another bedroom, which looked far more traditional. I could see the entrance to the ensuite as well. "I think this is my stop," I said, admiring the room. There was a fireplace at the end of the bed and an entrance out to the shared patio, which was covered in snow, but there was a trail leading to a Jacuzzi and fire pit that could also be accessed from the great room.

I dropped my bag in the bedroom and followed everyone as we all checked out one another's bedrooms. They were amazing and I actually felt bad for Ayden. He definitely got stuck with the kids' bedroom. But not bad enough to switch with him.

I trundled back out to the great room and noticed a ladder in the far corner, leading to a loft. I climbed the steps quickly and saw an old pinball machine tucked in the back and an old Miss Pacman arcade standing next to it. There were large beanbags spread out in front of another large television with a PS4 hooked up. Very cute.

As I was climbing back down, two large hands gripped my waist and lifted me off the last three steps.

"What did you find up there?" Ayden asked, not putting me down immediately.

"A place I'll probably be hiding out in for most of the trip," I said. "Now put me down or I'll kick you where it counts."

"Whoa," Brandy laughed as she stuck her head around her brother. "You better do what she says."

He placed me gently on the ground as if I weighed no more than a ragdoll, which was definitely not the case, and he quickly climbed the ladder.

"Nice. PS4," he nodded with approval, and I felt a slight stir in my tummy.

"We need a *Call of Duty* tournament before the trip is up. That's all I'm saying," I replied.

Brandy nodded in agreement. "Guys against girls."

Ayden came back down the stairs, and his eyes caught mine. I saw a bit more pleasure than I expected to see reflected in them, and I was suddenly without words.

"There are two bars in the lodge," Gabby said, coming into the great room. "Maybe, we should hang out close in case Lily needs us for anything. I mean we wouldn't like spy on you, but we could hang out in the other one, just in case."

"That's a good idea," Jason said, coming up behind her. He nuzzled her neck, and I looked away as if I was witnessing something too personal. But instead, my eyes bounced over to catch Ayden looking at me, and my heart did a nosedive.

"Well, whatever floats your boat. I'm going to go unwind by taking a shower or bath or two before I have to meet Austin." I felt Ayden's gaze on me as I left the room, and I wondered what in the world he was thinking about since his old girlfriend would be flying into town tomorrow. There was something behind his eyes that I recognized or wanted to recognize as something that was obviously off the table.

I walked down the hall and into my bedroom. Opening up my suitcase, I grabbed a pair of jeans and a fluffy sweater and carried them into the bathroom, where I was more than thrilled at the sight of a Jacuzzi tub. Tossing my clothes on the counter, I turned on the faucet for the tub and poured some gel under the streaming water. The room smelled of citrus and lavender as the aroma drifted from the tub. Stripping off my clothes, I stepped into the water, and the bubbles shifted as I slid into the tub.

My mind wandered to Austin and all of the questions I hadn't let myself worry about very much...like what if he hated me and was going to take this opportunity to tell me so in public. Or what if he didn't even show up?

As the warm water settled around my body, my thoughts drifted to Jake. My chest tightened as images of him flashed into my mind. Would our conversation turn to him? Did I want it to? It had been two weeks since I'd had any nightmares about Jake, and I prayed that they were behind me—that the worst was behind me. It was as if the moment I knew that I'd be facing Austin again, my subconscious began to settle down. But I'd been through stretches before where the nightmares stopped, but it had only been temporary, a couple weeks at the most, and then they came roaring back. But maybe making things right with Austin was the key to letting go and forgiving myself.

I felt warmth trickle down my cheeks as I let the guilt flood through me for the millionth time. I'd spent so many years clutching onto the memory of what Austin and I had shared that the numbness that followed seemed almost welcome. It was a relief to not feel the sorrow and fear of losing someone ever again... until I realized that it was impossible to categorize emotions and everything became numb. I couldn't be dead to sorrow, but be alive for love. Instead, I just felt dead to all emotion. I really didn't want to think what would happen if seeing Austin again didn't help to resolve things. I wondered just how disappointed I was going to be when the meeting with Austin was a bust. Tiring myself out from endless circle talk, I closed my eyes and drifted to a peaceful place.

"Lily. Lily," Gabby's voice bounced around my brain for a moment until I realized where I was at and that the freezing water wasn't part of my dream.

"What time is it?" I asked.

Gabby was standing beside me as I twisted in the tub, trying to gather what few bubbles remained.

"You've got forty minutes," she said, as she turned and walked away.

I shot out of the tub and dried off before glancing at my reflection. Somehow, I think I looked better before the bath.

Great!

I dressed quickly, but I took my time with my hair and makeup. I was no longer in the in-between stage of nervousness and excitement. Now, I was just petrified and my belly felt like a swarm of butterflies had taken over. I dabbed gloss on my lips and let out a deep breath before I walked to the kitchen for a glass of water. I heard everyone upstairs in the loft playing PS4 and laughing.

As I turned the corner into the kitchen, Ayden's voice surprised me. "You look beautiful." He was unpacking grocery bags and putting things away, but he managed to stop long enough to make me feel better. Something about him always made me feel better.

"Thanks," I said, running my hands along my jeans nervously. "So what wonderful meal do I get to look forward to when I come running from the bar?"

He laughed and shook his head. "Something tells me that you're going to have a wonderful night. But, I'm making enchiladas."

"I had no idea you liked to cook," I said, sitting at the counter as he put the groceries away. I had ten minutes and it was only a five-minute walk to the lodge. I didn't want to arrive early.

"There's probably a lot of things about me that might surprise you," he said, grinning.

"I don't doubt it."

Mason came into the kitchen, searching the bags and the floor for something.

"Dude, where'd you put it?" His gaze met Ayden's with a panicked expression.

"Beer's in the entry. I only had so many arms," Ayden laughed.

I watched Mason shuffle off to the entry and Ayden's eyes met mine once more. "If you need anything, text me," he continued.

I nodded. "I will."

He leaned across the counter and his lip curled slightly. I found myself leaning toward him. His hand reached around something, which he slammed in front of me.

"You might want to try that mix of whiskey and wine again tonight. It seemed to work wonders on you that one night..." he murmured, pushing a shot of the brown liquid toward me. "Bottoms up."

Eleven

I walked along the mostly cleared path toward the main lodge; the frigid air slapping me in the face with each new gust of wind. By the time I opened the doors to the lodge, my hair felt like it had been whipped around in its own personal blizzard. Quickly smoothing my hair as I stepped into the warmth of the lobby, I glanced toward the bar. There were quite a few people already inside, warming up from a day on the slopes. My eyes explored every male who was standing, sitting, leaning, walking, talking, only to come up empty-handed. No Austin.

A wave of relief washed over me as I started toward the bar. I wasn't quite ready to see him. My mind raced with thoughts of backing out as I beelined toward an empty table in the far corner, overlooking the patio. I sat quickly in one seat, and then realized I couldn't see anyone coming in, so I switched seats, but not before a low, gravelly voice met my movements.

"Lily? Is that you?" his voice was pure seduction, and my body froze as all of the memories came rushing in—all of the firsts we shared.

Hearing his voice—the familiarity of it—did something to me I wasn't expecting. It made me shy. I spun around slowly as I felt the burn in my cheeks. My lashes lowered as I mustered the courage to see the man I ran away from so many years before.

As I turned to face him, my voice completely lacked the confidence I'd grown to rely on over the years. "Austin?"

Our eyes met and an awareness of one another melted the rest of the bar into oblivion. I suddenly felt like I was eighteen again, and he was protecting me from myself and from my parents. And like I'd done so many times before, I wanted to run into his arms, but I couldn't. I wasn't that girl any longer and he wasn't that guy.

I shook my head in disbelief and smiled at my apparent lack of words as the shyness took hold. I owed Austin so much, and yet, I couldn't think of anything to say.

Instead, I stood in place, staring at him. And he let me. His blonde hair looked like he'd just ran his fingers through it, and the stubble along his jawline accentuated just how strong his features had become since high school.

High school!

He was dressed in a pair of loose jeans, and a white button-down stretched across his broad shoulders nicely.

The smile he wore seemed genuine, but I was so tightly wound, it didn't help.

"It's good to see you," he said, reaching out to hug me.

I took a step forward as his arms wrapped around my body, almost crushing me as I took a deep breath in. He smelled exactly like I remembered, a mix of spice and outdoors. "It's so good to see you too," I murmured, as my head pressed against his chest. "It's really nice of you—"

"Hey, I should have done this a long time ago," he interrupted, dropping his embrace. "But let's not get ahead of ourselves."

Austin flagged a waiter as he motioned for me to take a seat, which I did. It was like I had this sudden urge to obey him.

"Mr. Graham, would you and your guest like a drink this evening?" the waiter asked.

How often did Austin hang out at this bar?

I glanced at Austin and Ayden's words floated through my mind. Maybe I just needed a little help to make this easier. "I'd like a Jack and Coke."

"Impressive," Austin laughed. "I'll take the same."

The waiter nodded and wandered off the way he came. I glanced back at Austin, wondering when on earth my sentences would start forming. This was so unlike me.

"You have really great friends," Austin said, his eyes locked on mine. "They really care about you."

I nodded. "They do. They mean well. They didn't know."

"Didn't know what in particular?" he asked, his stare anchoring me in the chair.

"About how we ended. What I did."

"Well, what is there to say?" He shrugged. "It's all water under the bridge."

I nodded, grateful that the waiter was already delivering our drinks.

I looked over toward a large group of people sitting by the fireplace, and an ache for my friends arose in my chest.

"So what have you been up to since graduating?" he asked.

I felt his gaze on me, studying me as I avoided his stare. I had imagined a lot of ways that our conversation would go, but this wasn't one of them. I never imagined it would be this awkward.

"I worked for a large PR firm in Portland. It was a great place." My gaze met his and I blushed.

"Then why's it in the past tense?"

"Just time for me to move on." I pressed my lips together as he narrowed his eyes on me, his lip curling only slightly.

"I've got an idea," he said, his eyes sparkling with mischief.

"What's that?"

"How about if we start completely over. I'll go over there." He pointed toward the entrance and smiled at me. "And then I'll make my way through the bar, and it'll give you a chance to get used to the idea of me coming over."

My cheeks felt like they were on fire. I wasn't someone who got overwhelmed. And I was overwhelmed.

I flashed him a grateful smile and took another sip of my drink.

"I think that sounds like a plan. But maybe hang out in the lobby for a minute or two to add some intrigue," I proposed.

He stood up quickly, his eyes still focused on mine as he took a sip of his drink. Maybe I wasn't the only one who felt on the spot. "This reminds me of that time in drama class with Mr. Hener when he made us do the scene over at least a hundred times."

I couldn't believe he remembered that. I started laughing as my mind drifted back to that day. I'd already roped Austin into joining drama with me, and I promised him he wouldn't have to do anything besides paint on sets and nail wood together. But I was oh so wrong. Before I knew it, he was cast as Romeo and couldn't convince Mr. Hener that he'd made a mistake. I was Juliet so I was fine with the whole thing. I secretly loved every second I got to play opposite Austin. It was just another excuse to spend every moment with him. But the day before the play was to open, our rehearsal was pure torture, and Mr. Hener sent Austin out into the lobby to regroup before we ran through the final scene. The warmth from the memory calmed me as I grinned at Austin.

"The things we do for love," he teased. My heart immediately stilled. Not waiting for a reply, he turned around and walked out of the bar with ease and confidence, scooting between women and chairs.

I caught the attention of the waiter and ordered a glass of wine. My gaze fell to the lobby where Austin was sitting on one of the benches, looking at his phone. And magically, my nerves began to settle and excitement began to pulse through me. Things would be okay.

I heard Gabby's laughter echo through the space and watched as my friends walked through the lobby to the pub across the way. Ayden fell behind and quickly glanced around before following everyone into the other pub. I wondered if he was looking for me, but I shoved the thought aside as I watched Austin stand up. He slipped his phone into his jeans and started making his way through the bar again for take two. And miraculously, this second time around I felt more settled.

"Lily?" he asked, his eyes focused on mine.

I couldn't help but giggle as I stood up. "Austin?"

"And scene," he said, sliding his hand horizontally in front of him.

"That's much better," I confessed. "I'm surprised you remembered that from drama class."

"Oh, I majored in drama in college." He smiled, leaning back in the chair.

"You did? I thought you were going into…" my voice trailed off once I realized that he was joking.

His eyes danced with that familiar spark I remembered from so many years ago, and it was hard not to enjoy his company. Just like I remembered, just like I hoped.

"Jerk," I teased, feeling the unease from earlier slip away. "So did you major in business?"

He nodded. "And I tried to convince myself to go on to an MBA, but I just couldn't stand the thought of any more school."

"I hear that," I sighed. "But sometimes I think I should."

"Life's short," he replied, his gaze focusing on mine. "Unless you really want to spend a couple more years in school, I wouldn't bother."

The familiarity of his gestures and movements created a sense of relief with each passing second.

"So even though I know you'd love to bum around on the slopes all day, what is it that you do?"

"Bum around on the slopes all day."

"Seriously?"

Austin sat up a little straighter and combed his fingers through his hair, almost nervously. "My grandfather owns this resort, and my father never had any interest in running it, and now my dad's looking at retiring anyway...So it seemed logical."

"You run this resort?"

He shook his head. "A lot of great people run the resort. I just oversee certain aspects of it."

"But your title is?" I prompted.

"Vice President."

My parents would absolutely die if they knew the boy they chased me away from would soon be the president of a high-end resort. It gave me some sort of sick satisfaction, but my stomach knotted as I thought about how easily manipulated I was at eighteen.

"And your grandfather is the President?"

He nodded. "I don't think he'll relinquish the reins anytime soon. He loves his job too much. And I've still got a lot to learn, but he wants to keep it in the family. But back to my original statement, I do ensure I'm on the slopes every single day." Austin's grin offered me a promise of something I didn't understand.

"That must be nice."

"It is. It really is. I'm a lucky man." He leaned forward to be heard. The voices in the bar elevated several clicks, and it was getting difficult to have a conversation.

"You want to do dinner?" he asked. "I reserved a room upstairs."

"Excuse me?"

He started laughing. "A private dining room overlooking the slopes, Lily. Not a room in the lodge."

My cheeks flamed, and I started laughing at the misunderstanding.

"God, I missed that laugh," he said, flagging down the waiter.

His statement snapped me back to reality, but I barely heard Austin giving instructions to the waiter to transfer us upstairs. I glanced at him, fighting the urge to empty my soul out to him, ask for forgiveness, and pretend that everything was okay. That I never ran from him, that I never hurt him.

"Ready?" he asked.

I nodded, standing up from the table as the waiter grabbed both of our drinks.

Austin gestured for us to follow the waiter, and he gently placed his hand on my back, guiding me through the bar. His touch triggered a part of me that I'd hidden for so long, a vulnerability that I had worked hard at dismissing.

"You look even more beautiful than I remember," he murmured, as we worked our way toward the stairs.

We walked up the steps, and I was speechless when we reached the small room. There was a table set for two, with a vase of lilies in the middle. A twinge in my chest surfaced as more memories flooded through me. Every single day from the moment we started dating, Austin brought me one lily stem. Some days, he would have it waiting in my locker, on my desk in class, on my doorstep...

Austin pulled out the chair, and I took a seat as the waiter placed my wine glass in front of me and Austin's drink in front of him. He handed us both menus and left us to decide.

"The lilies are beautiful."

"Thanks. I had our florist come up with something," he said. "She thought it was clever with your name and all when she came up with the lilies."

My heart sunk at his admission, or maybe it was over the fact that I was placing so much importance on these little things, clinging on to any kind of sign that our history was as important to him as it was to me.

"They're lovely." I pushed down the ridiculous lump that was forming, and I opened up the menu. "What do you suggest?"

I sat frozen, staring at the menu, while I allowed myself a moment to regain control and reason. And I had to patch up that nasty bit of vulnerability. It just didn't work well with my personality.

"The filet mignon is the best in Utah and the pork chop with apple chutney is excellent," he replied.

I closed my menu and glanced up at him to catch something I wasn't expecting, something calculating and cold behind his expression. I took another sip of wine and wondered if we could order a bottle.

"So have you had any serious relationships?" he asked, his brow quirking up slightly.

I almost choked on my wine, but somehow managed to swallow it quickly and regain my composure. I wasn't expecting this line of questioning quite so soon, especially paired with the expression that was still on his face.

I shook my head and set the glass down.

"Nothing in college?" Austin looked surprised.

"Nothing serious."

I was never so relieved in my life to see a waiter as I was in this moment. Ordering a chopped salad and a filet, I handed my menu back to the waiter and wondered what Austin was searching for from me. What kind of answers he wanted to hear.

"I find it hard to believe you escaped college with not even one serious relationship to your name," his voice lowered, and I felt extremely confused and uncomfortable.

"I dated plenty, but there was nothing I would consider serious." I pressed my lips together and stared at him. His blue eyes darkened as his hands steepled on the table.

Deflect! Deflection was my specialty. If it had gotten me through with two nosey best friends, it could certainly serve me well now.

"Since my dating life seems of such interest, how about you? Did you have anything serious through college?"

He let out a sigh and my heart sank. His expression softened slightly as he looked at me. "No. You pretty much ruined me for other women."

Wait. Like in a good way or a bad way? Or was there no good way with that statement?

"I didn't expect you to be so charming, Lily," he continued.

Me? Charming?

"I had it in my head to tear you to shreds, make you pay for—" he stopped himself. "But I just can't do it."

I let out a slow and steady breath at his admission.

"I understand. What I did was wrong and there hasn't been one day that's gone by that I don't regret my decision."

"You were my world, Lily," his voice lowered. "I didn't understand how you could just leave like that. I thought we had something deeper."

I emptied my wine glass just as the waiter appeared with our salads.

"We'd like a bottle of the pinot noir," Austin said, pointing at my glass.

"Absolutely," the waiter replied.

"I don't know how I could either. I don't know if I thought you'd come running after me or if I really didn't want to be found," I replied.

"I knew you didn't believe the rumors or you would have approached me about them, getting a girl pregnant." There was something commanding in his voice, something that made me doubt my decision to be here tonight. "That's how well I knew you, Lily."

"You know me better than anyone ever has," I confessed, my gaze connecting with his.

"No. I *knew* you better than anyone ever has. I don't know you at all now." His words stung, but I knew I deserved far worse.

"I want to know why you ran."

"I ask myself that all the time," I whispered.

"And what answer have you come up with?" his voice softened only slightly. "I know your parents hated me with a passion, but please don't tell me they were the reason."

I shook my head. "They weren't the reason, Austin. I was afraid of losing you. After losing Jake, the thought of you leaving me consumed me. I didn't want to go through that twice."

"But you lost me by leaving." He didn't seem convinced.

I nodded. "It was on my terms. When Jake died, it suddenly made loss seem real. But the truth of it was, I lost him months before. I was barely holding on when he left me until you made me laugh again. You helped me get through every single day."

"I remember."

Austin saved me and I thanked him by fleeing.

"Everything between us happened so fast after his death, and I knew that we were headed to different colleges, different states. When you offered me the promise ring, I didn't want the heartache of falling deeper in love with you, only to lose you. Only to have you leave me once you fell in love with someone else at your new college. I know it makes no sense. I can see that now, but I wasn't right in the head after Jake's death. Nothing I did made sense. I'm not asking for you to excuse my behavior. There's no excusing it, but I want you to know that I'm deeply sorry for what I did to you, what I did to us."

Austin's phone buzzed and he glanced at it. "Sorry. I wouldn't normally grab it, but it's my son."

My jaw dropped as he answered his phone and began speaking quietly, telling his son good night before hanging up and glancing at me.

"So the rumors *were* true?" I asked.

His gaze steadied on mine.

"Partially."

Twelve

Shock rolled through me as his admission settled in a place deep within my soul. My gaze fell to the table while I tried to sift through the many emotions drilling into me. Anger, confusion, and disgust were the top three that rattled me enough to keep me silent. For the last several years, I'd been carrying the burden that I ruined something perfect and close to my heart. I held Austin up as the ideal relationship model, which seemed completely unattainable, as I tried and tried again to recreate it. But apparently, the reason I could never find it was because it was unreachable, impossible. I reached for my glass of wine and drank enough to numb the betrayal. I had wasted how many years searching for that kind of love when it didn't even exist in the first place?

I chewed on my cheek nervously and felt the fury finally begin to make its way to the surface. "Ever since I left you, I've been suffocating from guilt and remorse. Instead of accepting what we had as special, I searched for it everywhere with men who did nothing for me. But apparently I was wrong. I was on a pursuit for something that was impossible. I was the fool. Every man that I dismissed over the years because they weren't you..." I couldn't even finish my statement and just shook my head, bringing my gaze to meet his.

I recognized the intensity in his eyes as he waited for my silence. The heat behind his expression made my words seem inconsequential, like he'd been waiting for me to confess my love for him this entire time. But it didn't change anything between us. The facts were still what they were. I left him. And he got someone pregnant.

"Lily, I didn't cheat on you. I never would've done that." I saw the fierce loyalty that I'd come to love in high school reappear, but I wouldn't fall for it this time. Those drama classes had paid off far more than I realized. The phone call was all the proof I needed.

"But you have a son," I stated, raising a brow.

The waiter appeared, refilling my glass and taking our plates away.

Austin nodded.

"With her?"

"When you left, I was heartbroken. I didn't think love could hurt like that. I didn't think love was supposed to hurt like that, but it did. I never thought you'd believe the rumors," his voice lowered.

"Apparently, they weren't rumors," I said sharply.

"They were rumors. I didn't even know Christy before then. I mean why would I? She went to the other high school in our town." Hearing her name roll off of his tongue so easily made me cringe. It implied a closeness I hadn't expected even with the recent revelation.

"Your parents are very influential," he continued.

"Why are you bringing my parents into this?" I snapped, never before feeling a need to protect the family that had valued position in society over love, loyalty, and family. I knew this about them already.

Austin's brow arched and he ignored my question. "Like I said, I never even knew who this Christy chick was, and then all of a sudden, she's the reason I lost the person I cared about, and as it turned out, so did Christy. Your parents made sure this rumor turned into more than just a rumor."

"What did my parents do? Lock you two in a room together and throw away the key?" I scoffed.

But no matter how angry I was at Austin, I knew what he was implying. I'd seen it pan out many times before during campaigns. The dirt my father's team was willing to dig up and fabricate against any other candidate always ensured my father's victory. I just didn't understand the connection between my boyfriend and some eighteen-year old at another high school. And then Austin continued and it all made perfect, maddening sense.

"Christy was the daughter of the candidate running against your father in the next election. My father and grandfather contributed a significant amount toward his campaign, not your father's."

"I had no idea," I muttered, my heart crushing like it was going to implode. I wished beyond anything that I had more faith in my parents, but I didn't. I believed Austin. I only wish I'd believed him when it counted.

"It got nasty, and we didn't even realize the connection until it was too late. Christy's summer was full of horrible Facebook posts and tweets. Kids in town jumped on it and tormented her. She did an amazing job of ignoring it, but unfortunately her boyfriend began to believe some of the things people were saying and posting. It was so bizarre to see it unfold the way it did."

I tried to remember anything that my parents might have mentioned from that time, but they kept silent about it. My father had won the election, that much I could recall, but at what cost?

"Do you know how many nights I laid awake wondering what our lives could've been, if things went the natural course, without interference?" he asked, his eyes darkening a shade. "I loved you."

I dipped my gaze, shaking my head. *Loved, past tense.*

"Once my parents realized what was going on, they attempted to expose everything because I was being portrayed as such a creep, but I didn't even care about what I looked like. I never paid attention to that stuff. I didn't even have a Facebook account."

My heart sank as my mind swirled around all of the components—the mess I'd left Austin in—all because he had cared about me, but I couldn't understand how he had a son. How did that fit into the equation?

"But anything I thought I faced was nothing compared to what Christy went through." His jaw tensed and he took a sip of wine. "You can imagine what kinds of things were said about her. What kinds of things your father said about his opponent and his family. I didn't even know the girl in the beginning, but I was concerned about her. She shut down her Facebook page, Twitter account, all of it. But that didn't stop the pages that were still actively going about the topic. It even continued after the election. She had a somewhat positive outlook about it and could joke about all the fourteen year olds who trolled her, but I knew she was hurt."

My stomach tightened as I nodded my head slightly. I knew exactly what my father's team was capable of. He had a lot of money thanks to real estate, and he enjoyed throwing it toward buying elections.

"When you left, you took a piece of me with you, a big piece. I wanted someone to fill that void, Lily. I wanted to be close to someone again."

My eyes locked on his, understanding that same endless search. Austin's expression hardened as he ran his hands through his hair.

"Christy wasn't even pregnant. But her boyfriend didn't care. He left her."

I recognized the same Austin I knew so many years ago as his voice filled with compassion talking about the events that forever changed his life and mine. It wasn't my time to speak. It was my time to listen to the pain I caused; the problems I created all because of a choice I made, the choice to run away from love and life, my life.

"Christy and I got close, Lily," he said softly. "I'm not going to lie and candy-coat it. I was there for her when she needed it most, and she was there for me when I needed that void to be filled. What I didn't understand was that it couldn't be filled."

A lump formed in the back of my throat that I fought with all my might to force back down. He deserved to find that someone. I shouldn't mourn something I so freely tossed aside. I lost that right many years ago.

"It was our first year at college when she got pregnant." A smile spread across his lips and I had to look away.

"I'm so..."

"Lily," he interrupted. "My son is the greatest gift I could ask for. I wouldn't take anything back. Nothing." His eyes held me in place as the words landed firmly in place. "Carter showed me what is important in life, what love truly means. Christy and I weren't meant to be together. I didn't love her like a man should love his partner and she didn't love me, not like that. We both came into each other's life for a reason and that reason was to bring Carter into this world."

"I don't even know what to say," I uttered.

"You don't have to say anything. I just wanted to tell you my truth. You haven't been the only one searching all these years. I wanted to see it in Christy, that kind of love you and I had. I wanted to believe that she would fill the void you left, but she didn't. She couldn't. All of those letters you sent, I kept every single one of them. She actually found some tucked in a drawer, which didn't sit well for obvious reasons."

"Please, forgive me," I whispered.

"I forgave you the moment you left, but I couldn't forget you no matter how hard I tried." He slid his hand across the table, and his fingers ran across my hand, sending a warm and familiar sensation through me. "I'm sorry for being an ass."

"You weren't," I murmured. "I'm the one who should be apologizing."

I felt his gaze on me and looked up to meet the heat in his eyes.

"Where do we go from here?" I asked.

He shook his head and smiled. "I honestly don't know."

He released his hand and leaned back in the chair just as our dinners were placed in front of us.

"So you and Christy?" I glanced down at my plate, trying to make my question sound casual.

"We parted ways before Carter was even born. She knew I hadn't gotten over you, and I couldn't pretend any more. Christy deserved better and she found it. We take co-parenting seriously. I was in the room when he was born, and I've been there ever since. And it will always be like that."

My heart warmed with his acknowledgment of responsibility and love. And it represented growth so much deeper than what I had demanded out of my own life. It was literally like I was stagnant, a buoy bouncing up and down in the same spot, waiting to be set free. But what would it take?

"I've felt stuck in life, and I've never done anything to change that," I confessed. "Hearing everything you've done and been through makes me feel foolish."

"Don't do that," Austin said softly.

"What?"

"Put yourself down. You did that after Jake's death and it killed me. That wasn't your fault, just like this isn't your fault. Everything happens for a reason."

His words chilled me to the bone. What was it with this message pounding me from every angle, especially when my life was built on one mistake after another? I obviously wasn't getting the point, whatever the point was.

"I don't know what the future holds, but I'm really happy to have you sitting in front of me now. It feels right."

I nodded and reached for his hand. "It does feel right."

"And you're even more gorgeous than I remembered, and I can tell you my memory of you was pretty damn hot," he laughed.

I didn't know how he did it, but that one little statement put me at complete ease as the Austin I knew finally began to show himself to me, the carefree guy I had fallen in love with so many years before.

"I was thinking the same thing. But Google kind of told me what to expect before I made the trek." I smiled and took a sip of my wine.

"You Googled me?" His brow arched as he smiled in satisfaction.

I bit my lip to hold in my laughter, forgetting what that used to do him.

"Do you have plans for tomorrow, during the day?" he asked, his eyes raked over my shoulders, flooding my mind with confused expectations that I decided to no longer try to understand.

"We were leaving it kind of loose in case," I stopped myself, blushing.

"In case?" His lip curved slightly.

"I haven't had the greatest track record."

He started laughing and picked up his fork. "Don't let it get cold, or I can't stand by my claim that it's the best steak in Utah."

"So about tomorrow?" I prompted, cutting into my steak.

"I have a vendor meeting in the early evening, but I'd love to take you out on the slopes during the day," he offered.

"I would love it, but don't expect much. I haven't had the luxury of getting to spend my days on the slopes," I teased.

"It's never too late to start." He took a drink of his wine and so did I as my mind oddly wandered to everyone back at the condo, eating Ayden's enchiladas, and enjoying one another's company. I was no longer sure of what my expectations were with Austin, but enchiladas sounded good right now, and I missed the family I'd built around me to get me to where I needed to be. How could I be such a confused person?

"Everything okay?" Austin asked.

"Sorry. Just kind of overwhelmed with everything and nothing at the same time. If that makes sense."

"It does," he said. "But how about if we lighten up the pressure and just enjoy one another's company while you're in town and maybe get to know the people we've become rather than the people we used to be."

Smiling, I took a bite of the meat and enjoyed the best steak in Utah.

"Well?" he asked, eyeing my plate.

"It's melt-in-your-mouth delicious," I said.

"I'm glad to hear it," he laughed. "But that wasn't what I was referring to."

I rolled my eyes and chuckled. "I think it sounds like a perfect plan. Thanks for giving me a chance. Something tells me you were vacillating."

"I'll confess there was a part of me that..." his voice trailed off.

"That what?" I prompted.

"That wanted to make you pay," he said.

His honesty took me aback, but I appreciated it. I actually needed it.

"I kind of sensed that. And I'd braced myself for it."

There was a comfortable silence between us as we ate our meals.

"I don't think I can do another bite," I said, pushing my plate away.

"That's good because I don't think there's another bite to be had." He smiled and wiped his mouth with a napkin. "I always appreciated that about you. You weren't one of those girls who acted like they never ate."

"Nope. Definitely not one of those." I thought back to my night with Ayden and the steak dinner, Chinese food combo. "And if I'm having a particularly stressful day, I resort to two dinners."

His eyes widened at my admission. "Well, it doesn't show."

"If I have to eat twice as much, I have to work out twice as much or else it does show. I surpassed the freshman fifteen and went straight for thirty before I realized that equation."

He laughed. "That's probably the real reason I'm on the mountain so often. I'd rather eat and drink whatever I want than miss out."

The waiter asked if we wanted any dessert and we started laughing, especially once I said I did want dessert.

After we both ordered something sinfully delicious to end on, Austin's expression shifted and his voice lowered. "The worst part of not talking to you was not knowing how you are, how you've been doing."

My chest tightened with his directness. I knew where he was headed.

"Have your nightmares gone away?" he asked, his eyes probing.

I dropped my gaze and shook my head. "They're less frequent, but I still get them."

He nodded. "It always killed me that I couldn't take away your pain. I always felt inadequate."

I gasped and shook my head quickly. "Austin, if it hadn't been for you, I don't know that I would've survived. Those nights you'd sneak into my room and just hold me? Those were the nights that showed me I could survive, that I needed to survive. That's why leaving was the most inexcusable thing..."

"But you had to do it." His eyes fastened on mine. "I know you think you were running because you were afraid of losing me and maybe that's part of it, but I think it was because I reminded you of him. If you left me behind, I think you thought you could leave Jake behind and the nightmare he passed on to you."

My heart started hammering as I thought about what he said. He was right. I wanted to escape everything that reminded me of that night, but I could never escape it.

"I never called Jake's parents," I whispered.

"They knew you loved him, Lily. They knew we all loved him and we would've done anything to help him... if we could have helped him. But he made that decision. Jake made his decision, and it didn't include any of us. Don't hold onto the guilt. He wouldn't have wanted that."

And that's when it hit me. Therapists always said there were five stages of grief and after this many years I just now realized I was still stuck at the first stage. I was in *denial* and I *isolated* myself from everyone I loved and who reminded me that he really was gone. I looked up at Austin and the tears sprang to life. He was right. I ran to isolate myself from the pain, to deny that he ever left us. Even when the nightmares woke me, I was content to remain by myself, to harbor my secrets, and never share my burden with others. I put myself in complete isolation, even with Gabby and Brandy, my two best friends. I only showed them the side I wanted them to see.

"I'm so angry at him," I said, as an odd mix of relief and fury finally spread through my system. I finally said it, admitted it out loud. I finally hit stage two.

"So angry," I repeated.

"You have every right to be," Austin whispered, reaching across the table for my hand. "I know I was.

I was furious with him. I blamed Jake for everything, including losing you. It took me a long time to get over it. Carter actually helped me to see that there was more to life than death. More to life than loss."

I used the napkin to blot away the tears as Austin squeezed my hand.

"Thank you, Austin."

"I didn't do anything," he assured me.

"You've done more than you can imagine." I nodded.

We both ate our desserts in silence, and I wondered if there were any more enchiladas back at the house waiting for me. I certainly hoped so because tonight was nothing like I expected it to be, but then again that's how life always seemed to be. I needed to get back to my friends and show them the whole me, not just the side I wanted them to see. And I needed to inform Ayden that his theory about whiskey and wine was seriously flawed.

Thirteen

Brandy and Gabby opened up the front door before I even made it to the top step. Snow was falling outside and the warm glow from inside called to me. I enjoyed spending time with Austin, but now I needed my family and that's who was inside waiting for me. Even though these people weren't blood, they were my family and tonight's revelations only strengthened that line of reasoning. I could imagine everyone huddled around the fireplace or playing games in the loft, and I got excited at the thought of being with them.

"How did it go?" Brandy asked, glancing nervously at Gabby before pulling me inside.

"It went really well, surprisingly well," I confessed. I tossed my hat and gloves on the bench and hung my jacket in the closet.

"That's so cruel," Gabby said.

"What's cruel?" I asked innocently, grinning.

"You know what." She scowled at me. "I want details, woman. Details!"

"Is the belle of the ball *finally* home?" I heard Ayden's voice float down the hall and my cheeks warmed. "My sister wouldn't shut up while you were gone. She even went snooping in the bar to find you."

Brandy spun around and smacked him hard, really hard. "You promised you wouldn't tell." But she turned back to me, and her brows rose as she waited for my reply.

"We met in the bar and it got too loud. We went upstairs so we could hear each other," I began.

"Upstairs?" Ayden questioned.

"He had set up a special dinner in a private dining room," I corrected.

"I'm out," Ayden said, jogging toward Mason who was now climbing the steps to the loft. "Too much info."

Gabby watched Ayden leave, and she smiled a smile that made me wonder what she was thinking about.

Instead of me trying to figure out what just happened, Brandy pulled me into the great room, and we sank into the overstuffed chairs while Gabby brought over seltzers for us.

"So you guys had dinner?" Brandy pressed.

I nodded. "I have no idea where things will go from here."

I heard all the guys upstairs howling with laughter as explosions sounded. They were obviously enjoying themselves in the land of *Call of Duty*. Gabby rolled her eyes as she heard Jason betting on something and then things got far too silent in the loft. The guys were plotting, which never led to good things.

"Okay, so was there a connection?" Brandy asked.

"He felt really familiar, and I liked that sensation. I missed being around him all these years. That part wasn't a surprise. At first, it was awkward, but he made that feeling go away. He's a really sweet guy."

"Regardless of what my brother pulled up online?" Brandy asked.

"He showed you?" I asked, completely mortified.

"The two girls he made out with? Yeah. It made me doubt our plan," Brandy confessed.

"Austin's single and he's been through a lot, a lot more than I realized. Besides, we've all had our wild moments."

"You don't say," Gabby teased.

"Okay, maybe some of us more than others." I rolled my eyes.

"So are you going to see him again?" she asked.

I nodded and took a sip of seltzer before answering. "Tomorrow. We're going to go boarding."

"Sweet," Gabby said, dropping onto the couch. "So you won't kill us when all is said and done."

"No. It was good for me," I acknowledged. "And he's not shabby to look at either."

"That's the old Lily. I was wondering what happened to her," Brandy laughed, but I noticed Gabby try to hide a chuckle, which struck me odd.

"He has a son," I blurted out.

"Wait. What?" Gabby asked, leaning forward. "So the rumors were true?"

"No. They weren't true, but it was far messier than I realized. You know how I've mentioned that my parents manipulate people and situations?"

They both nodded. "To say that's what happened is putting it mildly. Since I never stuck around to find out any of this, apparently my father didn't like the competition he was facing in the elections the year I left. The girl I heard the rumors about turned out to be the daughter of the other candidate. The short story is that she was bullied and pelted with nasty rumors online and that kind of led Christy and Austin to meet each other. And they dated in college…"

"Christy was the girl in the rumors and now he has a son," Gabby repeated.

"Do you believe him? That he didn't get with her until after you left?" Brandy asked out of the blue.

"Yeah. I felt he was being genuine. I think. Why'd you have to ask that?" I laughed. "But whatever. We're just getting to know each other and who knows what'll happen. Besides, I don't think now is the time for either of our past dating escapades to be outed."

Gabby's gaze flashed to the steps where Jason hopped to the floor from the loft. Gripping his phone tightly, he walked through the great room toward their bedroom, avoiding Gabby.

"Everything okay?" Gabby asked, standing up quickly to follow.

"Everything's fine," Jason called behind him, as he shut the door to the bedroom.

"What the hell was that all about?" I asked, as she sat back down, almost embarrassed.

Gabby's gaze fell to the floor and she circled her fingers on the couch before raising her eyes to meet mine. "I don't know, but I'm starting to get really worried about things."

Brandy and I hopped out of our chairs to sit next to Gabby. "What do you mean?" I whispered. "What kinds of things? Where'd this come from?"

"I didn't want to bring it up during the holidays or on the trip but..." Gabby's voice broke.

"What's going on?" Brandy asked, her hand on Gabby's knees. "Do my brothers need to kick his ass?"

That got a laugh out of Gabby, but when her eyes met mine again, tears lined the edges. "I don't know what's going on. Ever since he got in touch with his aunt and found out about his sister, things haven't felt right."

"You should have told us," I said, giving her a hug. "But I'm sure it's okay. He's probably just trying to digest everything. Has he mentioned more about his family?"

She shook her head. "No. That's part of the problem. Anytime, I try to ask him about what he's found out or how I can help or anything...he just clams up."

"I'm even beginning to wonder if it really is about his family or if everything has been too good to be true and..." The sound of the door opening down the hall, made us all still and Gabby quickly wiped away her tears.

Jason grabbed a few beers out of the fridge to take upstairs for the guys. "What's up with the silence? Shouldn't you guys be pestering poor Lily about her date?" Jason teased.

"It wasn't a date," I corrected.

"That's not what Ayden said," Jason laughed.

I wondered what he did say...

"So what was so important that you had to take a *Call of Duty* break?" Brandy asked, staring straight at him. She was never one to dance around a topic...that was for sure.

"There was a problem at the shop," he said, walking over to where we were sitting. He looked relaxed, too relaxed, and gave Gabby a quick kiss on the cheek.

"At this time of night?" Brandy dug. "Seems highly unlikely."

Jason just shrugged and walked up the steps, carefully balancing all of the bottles for the players waiting upstairs.

"See?" Gabby asked, defeated.

"I'll pester Aaron and see if I can find anything out," Brandy said softly. "You're right. Something feels off."

I glared at Brandy as Gabby's eyes filled with worry. She didn't need to make Gabby feel worse.

"I'm sure it's nothing bad. It's probably just family stuff that maybe embarrasses him or maybe he doesn't even know what's going on yet and doesn't want to burden you," I offered. "I mean I wasn't the greatest at telling you guys everything about my past and look where we are now. And you're my best friends of how many years?"

"I think I'm going to go with Lily's assumptions right now. They make me feel better," Gabby laughed.

"Well, we're here for you, girl. No matter what," Brandy said. "And I'll let you know what I find out."

"This is exactly what I didn't want to have happen. Now come on, tell us more about Austin," Gabby said, smiling. "Tell me this. Did you feel *it*?"

"Umm. I think so. I mean I don't know," I stumbled over my words.

"You don't know?" Brandy asked, her gaze quizzical.

"I think there was too much stuff that needed to be sorted before I could even let my mind go there."

Gabby pressed her lips together, and I could tell she was wondering the same thing as me. What if *it* didn't come?

"So are there any enchiladas left?" I asked, switching the subject.

"I thought you had dinner?" They both asked at the same time.

"I did. But—"

"Oh, no. Not again," Brandy laughed as she stood up slowly. "You're in really rough shape if you need two dinners."

"It's a two-alarm emergency," Gabby laughed.

I watched Brandy slowly make her way to the kitchen, and I wondered if she was hurting. I hoped she wasn't, but there was something about the way she moved that told me things weren't painless.

"Do I smell enchiladas?" Ayden called from the loft as she set a plate of enchiladas in front of me. "If I do, heat me up one too."

"Heat it up yourself," Brandy hollered back. Regardless of what she hollered, she grabbed an empty plate for her brother, and I thought about how nice it must be to have that kind of connection to a sibling.

Ayden was already in the kitchen by the time Brandy grabbed the steaming plate out of the microwave and placed it on the counter.

"Another rough night with the two-dinner thing?" Ayden laughed as he grabbed the plate from Brandy.

Oh my God! He didn't just say that, did he?

Brandy gripped the plate tightly, not releasing it to Ayden. He didn't even realize what he'd just implied as he continued to pull on the plate.

"What do you mean another two-dinner night?" Brandy asked, her brow arched. "How would you know about that?"

Ayden's expression turned completely playful while mine turned beet red. It felt like my cheeks were on fire.

"Can I have the plate?" he asked, tugging both the plate and Brandy toward him.

"Not until you tell me what other time you've experienced Lily's two-dinner number?" Brandy scowled, and I just stared at my own plate of enchiladas, refusing to look at her.

"I didn't experience it," he laughed. "I just heard about it."

"Liar." I felt Brandy's eyes on me, and then the next thing I knew I was giggling uncontrollably.

Ayden let go of the plate Brandy was gripping and sauntered over to where I was laughing and sat next to me, picking up my fork and digging in.

"You were the one who told her?" Brandy asked, setting the plate on the counter. "Traitor. An absolute traitor. And I thought you were the trustworthy brother. I never guessed it was you. Never thought for a moment."

I could see the mischief in her eyes as she reprimanded her brother, and all I could think about was my vanishing enchilada.

"When did this happen?" Her lips were puckered, trying not to laugh as she pestered her brother for answers.

"I'm pleading the fifth," he said, finally relinquishing my fork.

"You owe me at least half of your enchilada," I said, watching him move swiftly into the kitchen to steal the plate from his sister who was now far too curious to care.

"That weekend I was in Portland," Ayden said.

"One of those better be for me. These are to die for," I said, smiling, avoiding the topic of conversation at all costs.

"I feel out of the loop, and I hate feeling out of the loop," Brandy said, turning to face her brother.

"There's no loop. There's no story. I learned two things that night about Lily. One, if she's having a bad day, she's a two dinner girl. And two, wine and whisky is an interesting combo for her. That's it. End of story."

I froze at his admission and Brandy slowly turned toward me. Ayden couldn't hide his smile, and I suddenly saw why Brandy always had the urge to slug him.

"You needed a two-dinner night when you found out about our plan to hook you up with Austin?" Gabby asked, her voice completely sympathetic.

"No. I needed it before then," I assured her. "Ayden showed up the night I had my awful date with Rob."

"Well, that makes me feel a hundred percent better. I didn't want to be responsible for one of those," Brandy laughed.

"No. You were responsible for the two-breakfast morning the next day. Ayden had to go all over town to find eggs benedict for me," I teased.

Brandy's eyes looked like they were about to fall out of her head when Gabby started cracking up. It was Ayden's turn to be frozen in position and I loved every second of it.

"Kidding," I chided.

"I don't think you deserve one of these," Ayden joked, moving his plate away.

"I think she deserves as many as she wants after that one," Gabby said, applauding my work. "It's hard to make Brandy hyperventilate like that."

I glanced at Ayden and noticed his gaze was on me, and there was something behind it that I recognized from that night. He walked over to where I was sitting, and I felt a current between us again. I shifted away slightly at the thought of what it could mean or what I wanted it to mean.

But then my mouth betrayed me.

"By the way, your observation about me and whisky and wine is incorrect. It did diddley tonight," I whispered, as Brandy and Gabby started hauling out the chips and dip.

His eyes fastened on mine and a charge ran down my spine. "What were you expecting the combo to do tonight, Lily?" His voice rumbled its way through me and I had to catch my breath.

"I wanted it to do that," I mumbled.

"What?"

"You know what," I breathed.

"No. I really don't."

Brandy turned around and plopped a bowl of chips on the island as Jason, Aaron, and Mason came into the kitchen.

"What was the hoopla about?" Mason asked, leaning in between Ayden and me.

"I found out who can't keep a secret," Brandy said.

"So who's your favorite brother now?" Mason grabbed a chip and crunched right next to my ear.

"Obviously you are," Brandy teased.

"Then my work here is done," Mason said.

"When's Sammie getting in tomorrow?" Gabby asked. Her eyes steadied on mine, and I flashed her a return smile.

"Can't remember," Ayden said, shrugging his shoulders.

"You can't remember?" I asked.

"Afternoon or something," he replied, avoiding my gaze.

Mason placed his hand on my shoulder and started to speak, "I thought—"

"So are we ready for Operation Ice Cube?" Ayden asked, interrupting his brother.

I looked at Brandy and Gabby just as Aaron and Jason scooped them both up. I started laughing, but the next thing I knew, Ayden had me locked in his arms as Mason ran to the sliding glass doors and opened them up.

"Where are you taking us?" Gabby squealed, pounding on Jason.

"Let me go," Brandy seconded.

I was wriggling and shifting so violently in Ayden's clutch, I wasn't even sure how I remained secured so tightly in his arms.

"You better not," I screamed, as I watched Mason peel back the hot tub cover.

"Or what," Ayden murmured.

My head and hands rested on his chest as I felt everything go into slow motion. First Jason plopped Gabby into the steaming hot tub, and then Aaron did the same. Just as Ayden dangled me over the water, I reached my arms around his neck and held on tightly, bringing the front of him into the hot tub too. As soon as my body hit the warm water, I let go. But it was too late, Mason, Jason and Aaron had already pushed him in and we were all dying of laughter.

"Is that all you've got?" I shouted.

Brandy, Gabby and I huddled in the far corner, splashing water on the fully clothed men, drenching them completely.

"I do declare, we are the winners," Brandy feigned, placing her hand against her forehead.

Ayden stood up in the hot tub, and his clothes clung to his body as he crawled out of the water. My heart literally skipped a beat as his eyes met mine, and all I could do was look away as the guys delivered our towels.

Fourteen

I had just finished braiding my hair and was dressed for a day on the mountain when I heard the hum of a coffee grinder down the hall. I hoped whoever was out there would be making enough for more than one. Austin was going to be here any second, and I'd love to get some caffeine streaming though me before I left the house. Reaching for my knit cap, I pulled it on my head before trundling down the hall to a wall of closed bedroom doors. We were all up really late after the hot tub incident and I'd be sleeping too, if I didn't already have plans. The smell of coffee brewing led me into the kitchen, where Ayden was standing. He had his back turned toward me as he faced the kitchen window.

Damn him!

He was dressed in a loose pair of green, plaid pajama bottoms that hung low around his waist, and he had no shirt on. My eyes slid along the length of his long, lean back, stumbling across every muscle, every curve of his body. He turned on the water and rinsed his hands while I stood staring. I wanted to quietly sneak back to where I came from—the safety of my bedroom—but my feet wouldn't cooperate. My breath caught as he turned around, his eyes running along the length of me. He didn't smile. Instead, his gaze lingered on my mouth, creating a lightning bolt of confusion in my chest.

That was the problem with Ayden lately; everything around him caused me to feel sensations that were far too powerful to be real. And they were all extremes.

"Coffee?" I barked, attempting to break my gaze from his chest.

A faint smile traced his lips as he reached for an empty mug and poured me a cup of the steaming brew.

"Rough night?" he asked, as he handed me the mug of liquid.

"No. Why would you ask that?"

"You seem a little skittish...so when's your lover boy gonna be here." He took a sip of his coffee, as a smirk landed on his face. It was like he was taunting me, pushing my buttons to get a rise out of me, and I had no idea why.

"He's not my lover boy and there's a lot more to him, to his story, than I care to tell you about."

"Why's that? Afraid I won't approve?" His brows quirked up slightly.

"Since when have I ever wanted or cared about getting your approval?" The liquid stung my lips as I took a sip, but I didn't let the pain show.

Ayden shrugged and leaned against the counter, allowing his torso to stretch...which inadvertently lowered his pajamas...which *made* my eyes dip as I followed along his abdomen to where the elastic met the fabric. It was totally not my fault.

"You. Are. Trouble," I mumbled, as I heard his laughter from across the kitchen.

There was a knock at the door, and I spun around excited to see Austin and start my day in the snow.

"Have fun with Austin," Ayden called.

"Same to you about what's her face."

I opened the door and my breath caught at the sight of Austin.

His snowboard pants and coat covered up most of his body, but there was something in his eyes that startled me, an intensity I didn't recognize from the night before. His wavy hair hung loosely under his cap, flipping up on the edges.

"You look beautiful," he said, kissing my cheek.

A pulse of joy settled over me as I felt his gaze on me, and I quickly closed the door behind me, ready for my day with Austin, a day I'd been waiting years for.

"You don't look so bad yourself."

He handed me a lily and grinned. "Sorry for being an ass last night. I did tell the florist to use lilies, and I don't know why I lied about it. It wasn't her idea. It was mine." His board was propped on his shoulder. "I guess I just didn't know which side I wanted to show you."

"How many do you have?" I laughed, as I followed him back down the steps toward the lifts.

"Enough." He held out his free hand and I took it in mine, glove to glove.

"Well, I think I like this one you settled on," I confessed as we walked along the snowy path. "Do you suggest I go snowboarding or skiing?"

"Have you ever tried snowboarding?" he asked.

"Yes, but it is more of a sitting-down endeavor where I turn my snowboard into a sled to make it down the mountain."

His laughter churned the familiar longing I'd held onto for so many years, and I glanced at him, at his smile.

"Have you ever had lessons?" he asked.

"No. I'm self-taught, which is why I'm a master at it."

"How about I teach you today?" Austin's eyes flicked to mine as we stood in front of the rentals. "I bet it'll only take a few key pointers, and you'll be sailing upright down the mountain."

"I hope you're right," I said, nodding. "But I'm game."

I started toward the building, but Austin slammed his board into the snow and anchored me next to his equipment. "I've got this. Just keep an eye on my board."

"Thanks."

I watched Austin trudge through the snow and into the rental building as I let my mind wander. Would I be able to make it down the mountain in one piece? I dug my phone out of my jacket and quickly texted Gabby.

He's teaching me how to snowboard.

It didn't take long to receive a reply that made me laugh.

Are you nuts? People our age don't just decide to show off their snowboarding skills on a date.

I smiled as I typed my reply.

Since when did we hit the age of eighty? I'll be fine! I've wanted to get the hang of this for a while. And I am a snowboarder! I even have my own board at home. xx

She replied back.

I forgot to ask if you were doing dinner with him tonight?

I bristled a little at the question. Not because of the question but because of my answer.

No. He's got a meeting.

I got another quick response.

Sweet. You're ours tonight then!

Followed by another one.

*I'm taking my girlfriend back from you.
Go have fun with Austin and quit texting...Jason*

That was the Jason I knew and the one I loved. Whatever was going on between them or with him couldn't be anything bad. There was no way. But the way he snapped last night at Gabby was so unusual. I slipped my phone back in my pocket and fought down the tinge of worry that threatened to destroy my perfect image of those two.

"Got you a hot chocolate," Austin's voice warmed me up immediately, and I quickly forgot what I was worrying about.

"Thank you," I said, taking the cup from him. "I protected your board. No one even dared look in my direction."

I reached for the boots he was holding, and he motioned for the bench a few feet away. "I can put your snow boots in the locker."

"Thanks." I untied one pair of boots and swapped them out for the other. Austin jogged back toward the building to lock up my snow boots, while I tightened everything up and readied myself for a day full of bruises and more bruises.

There wasn't a cloud in the sky, and it seemed like the perfect day to hit the slopes, especially with the fresh coat of snow the mountain got last night.

"Ready?" he asked, his eyes filled with anticipation and something else I didn't want to get my hopes up for.

Austin grabbed both our boards and took off toward the ski lift.

"You don't have to do that," I called.

"You need to save your energy for everything I've got in mind for you."

My mouth fell open as we strapped ourselves onto the boards.

"That came out wrong," he laughed.

"That's too bad," I teased, looking up quickly. He was less than a foot away from me, but it felt far closer as our eyes locked.

"Is it?" His expression darkened, and I immediately realized the connection we once shared was accessible. It still existed if I let it.

"So my job today is to make sure you get down the mountain—"

"Alive?" I interrupted.

"Well, for starters. Alive would be good, but I was thinking that if by the end of the day, the lily is still intact then my job's complete."

"How about this? If the lily stays intact, I owe you dinner. If it falls apart because of faulty teaching techniques, you owe me dinner?" I challenged.

"Dinner tomorrow night?" he asked.

"Yup."

"Sounds like there's no real loser in this deal," he replied, a grin surfacing on his lips, as we took a moment to adjust everything and get situated before we loaded onto the ski lift.

He took the lily from my gloved hand and unzipped my ski jacket.

"You'll crush it," I protested, as he gently placed the stem along my chest, the bloom poking out.

He zipped up my jacket, allowing the blossom to peek out.

"Nah, it'll be fine as long as you don't fall flat on your face."

"No promises," I muttered, following him toward the lift.

The ski lift operator motioned for us to take a seat on the next lift so we quickly walked over, dragging our boards with one foot attached, and waited for the bench to bump the back of our legs, signaling us to take a seat. The lift swayed gently as we took off toward the top of the mountain, leaving the village behind.

"It's beautiful," I whispered, looking at the snow-tipped trees as our lift sailed us up the mountain.

"It is."

I felt his gaze on me as I continued to look below, and I felt the same shyness from last night return.

"You doing okay?" he asked, his gloved finger touching my cheek to get my attention.

"Totally. It's just so peaceful here and that's exactly what I need right now." I turned to look at Austin and noticed his blue eyes taking me in. "I've been thinking a lot about what you told me."

"About what in particular?"

"My parents. My family." I bit my lip and looked over his shoulder as the bench wobbled slightly. "They've disappointed me so often in life that I've come to expect it. But hurting people outside of our own family is just so wrong."

"Politics is a nasty business."

I laughed, "Is it really supposed to be a business though? What happened to that whole public servant thing?"

"Well, that went by the wayside a long time ago." He placed his hand on my knee as our lift continued to usher us up the mountain, and I felt the importance of our history finally present itself. I took a sip of the hot chocolate and welcomed the warm drink. "Don't blame yourself for their behavior."

"It makes me question everything about my father. If he's willing to play that dirty just to remain a mayor of some tiny town, what would he be willing to do for money, for his business?"

"Power makes people do odd things. But I wouldn't read too much into it. Politics is very different than business. I doubt he'd stoop so low in business," he laughed.

"I'd like to think better of my father." I nodded, spotting the tiny house in front of us where we'd be let off. "But I don't. I feel like I never understood their motives, and I never wanted to be like them. How horrible does that sound?"

"Remember that apartment building where he evicted everyone?" Austin asked.

Oh, my god! I had totally forgotten about that.

"I remember," I sighed. "That was horrible. He evicted all of the low-income families because the laws changed, and he could charge more rent if he booted everyone out. He only gave them thirty days notice and most of them had nowhere to go. I remember him talking about how that year alone he'd make an additional quarter million with that move."

"You're nothing like them."

"That's very sweet of you, but how do you know? A lot has changed since we last saw one another."

"Your friends are amazing. They care about you tremendously, and no one who has friends like that could be anything like your parents. Birds of a feather..."

My cheeks reddened as I looked away. "I hope you're right. But enough of that, though. I'm here to be taught how to save a lily and make it down a mountain."

The ski lift slowed marginally at the last incline, and I felt my board touch the hardened snow as I stood up ready to ride down the little bank with Austin right next to me. But just as I stood up and Austin glided down the slope, my glove stuck on the railing of the lift, not letting me detach. Before I fully understood what was happening, I was holding on for dear life with my body dangling from the lift as it continued to soar through the air and head back down the mountain. I heard Austin yelling at the operator to turn off the lift, but I kept sailing back down the mountain with my board attached to one foot and both hands holding tightly onto the railing. People hollered for me to jump, while others commanded me to hang on. I couldn't gauge how high or low I was from the mountain so I just hung on until the lift finally sputtered into stillness.

"Lily, let go," Austin hollered. His voice was coming closer, and I looked down at the snow bank beneath me wondering if he really meant it. "You're only about six feet up, it just looks worse. The snow bank will cushion your fall."

Was that a good thing?

The lift swung back and forth and I decided to just go for it. I glared at the man in the booth who didn't feel a need to turn off the lift before I found myself in this predicament. He was grinning. Of course he was.

I closed my eyes and let go of the lift, and within a second, my butt sank into the snow, and Austin was helping me up and out. Humiliated, horrified, and embarrassed were far too gentle of terms to describe how I was feeling.

Who dangled from a ski lift on a date?

"Are you okay?" Austin asked, breathless from his jog over, lifting me from the pile of snow and placing me in front of him, dusting the snow off my shoulders.

I nodded. "My ego's bruised more than anything. Or, at least, I hope that's the case. I usually can make it off the lift. I promise."

"It was kind of cute. You know, after I realized you weren't going to die." Austin's eyes dipped down to my lips and he laughed softly. I felt a familiar pool of warmth swell through me as I wondered if he was going to kiss me. Did I want him to kiss me?

"Well, the lily is still perfectly intact. I'm impressed," he said, grinning, as relief spread through me. "Do you want to ride the lift back down and call it a day? I'd totally understand. We could grab lunch."

"No. I have no intention of riding that thing back down. I'd rather sled down on my snowboard at record speeds. But seriously I'm fine. I promise."

He helped me back up the mountain and told me to stay put while he went to the booth where the operator was sitting.

It didn't sound like things were going well for the person inside the shack as Austin went off on him for not stopping the lift sooner. My heart rate finally began to slow down as I watched Austin make his way back to me.

"I'm so sorry that happened. He should've cut it the moment it made its way around the corner." Austin touched my chin and smiled.

"I'm just bummed I lost my drink," I teased. "So show me your stuff, ski bum."

We walked over to a clearing, and he strapped himself in and I did the same.

"So stopping is a problem for me," I revealed to Austin as I stood up ready for my lesson. "And so is turning."

He started laughing and slid into position in front of me. He held out his two hands and motioned for me to grab on.

"You're going to go backwards?"

He nodded and began slowly pulling me down the mountain. "Keep your knees bent and your weight equally distributed. Do you feel your back edge digging into the hill?"

"Yeah."

"Okay, so flatten your board so it's not digging in."

"Eeek." My board started gliding down the hill quickly as Austin guided me along the mountain.

"Now dig your back edge in again," he said.

I came to a slow stop and looked up at him. His gaze sent a flurry of emotions through me, none that I recognized.

"Nice," he muttered, guiding me along the mountain, giving instructions and helping to avoid collisions.

I'd finally gotten to the point where the nose of my board was pointing directly down the mountain without a wave of fear rushing through me. This was definite progress. By the time I was two-thirds down the mountain, I hadn't fallen once and I was starving.

"Ready for lunch?" Austin asked, as we made our way toward a ski hut.

"I'm ravenous. This takes a lot more work than just sitting on it and riding it down." I unstrapped my board, and secured it in the pegs, and Austin did the same.

"This place has great nachos," he replied, holding the door open for me.

"Awesome."

We found a table for two, and Austin went to grab our food while I carefully pulled out my flower and placed it on the table. I watched Austin as he stood in line, talking to a couple in front of him, laughing and looking so carefree.

I heard a female squeal and followed the sound to see a petite brunette, wearing a pink plaid snowboard jacket and white pants, jumping up and down. She was waving in Austin's direction, and I quickly glanced at him to see if there was a connection.

And there was.

A huge grin broke onto his face, and he motioned for the female to walk over to him.

And she did.

She ran over and jumped into his arms as he spun her around, laughing. My stomach knotted, and I looked down at my flower, feeling completely inadequate and pathetic. Not a combination I enjoyed.

I glanced back up at the cozy couple and caught Austin's look before he turned to order our food. At least, I think it was our food. At this point, I wasn't sure if he'd forgotten who he was actually here with. As I watched the two wander off toward the drink dispenser, I wondered if

I could make a clean getaway, ride my board back down to the village and slip away into our condo.

"Lily," Austin's voice took me off guard. "I'd love for you to meet a friend of mine, Stephanie."

I looked up to see the brunette standing at the edge of the table, her eyes dropping to the lily on the table before meeting my stare. Her gaze turned icy as she offered me her hand.

"I've heard so much about you," she replied, with a phony smile.

Fifteen

ustin brought over two trays of food while Stephanie pulled up a chair to sit at the table. She narrowed her light brown eyes on me as I slid the lily to the edge of the table so nothing happened to it.

"Your friends planned this for you?" she asked. I couldn't help but stare at her upturned nose as she glared at me. "And you had no idea?"

"Yup. They came up with this idea all on their own. Thankfully, one of my best friend's brother clued me in beforehand though." I reached for some nachos and watched as Austin sat down, not really intervening or seeming to notice how uncomfortable things were as Stephanie continued to stare at me.

"Seems odd that they'd track someone down that you knew all the way back in high school." Stephanie grabbed an olive off the nachos and tossed it in her mouth before she flashed a smile at Austin. "Did they get tired of you talking endlessly about him or something?"

She giggled and glanced at Austin who was either acting oblivious or actually was oblivious. "I mean he is quite the catch, if someone could get him to settle down." Stephanie ran her hand along his arm and I cringed.

"I only mentioned him once. My friends are just too sweet for their own good," I replied. "But yes. He was a very nice person in high school so I'm sure he's just as caring now."

"Caring, huh?" Her brows shot up.

"I am a man with many sides," he replied, his eyes catching mine.

"You seem to be," I laughed. Turning to Stephanie I asked, "How'd you meet Austin?"

"We met in Montana last year. I was on a ski trip and so was he. As it turned out, we only lived about ten miles away from each other here in Utah."

"Small world," I said, eating the nachos quickly and hoping for a way out of here. Things felt very awkward. She seemed to be very possessive and Austin was still completely oblivious. I didn't want to be caught in the middle of this whole thing.

"Neither of us are relationship-type people." She eyed me. "So we bonded immediately."

"Is that so?" I asked Austin.

"Pretty much." He wiped his mouth with a napkin, but I saw amusement flicker in his eyes, like he was enjoying this far too much.

"Well, that makes three of us," I said, patting Stephanie's hand. "Relationships just get in the way of a good time. At least, that's my motto."

And it was.

My emotions burned inside of me as I watched Austin become yet another person. This one was far too sure of himself and tricky. I really had been holding onto some foolish notion about what Austin was going to be like, which was completely unlike me. He wasn't the same person. We weren't the same people. And watching him unveil yet another side of himself was really tiresome.

"Hey, I'd like a beer. Do either of you want one?" I asked, hopping up.

"I'd love one," Stephanie said.

"I've got some Fireball in my jacket," Austin laughed. "But a beer might be nice to kick off the rest of the afternoon. My treat."

He motioned for me to sit down as he stood up and went toward the bar in the far part of the cafeteria. Part of me wanted to follow him and ask all sorts of questions, but the other part of me told me not to care. What did I expect from a guy I'd only seen twice in twenty-four hours since high school? He was a player? So was I. Was this news?

I sat down and eyed Stephanie whose emotions for Austin were getting the best of her, regardless of whatever game she was willing to play with herself.

"I hope you understand what you're getting yourself into," she cooed.

"Excuse me?"

"You'll just be another temporary distraction for him."

"Are you always this friendly to Austin's old acquaintances?" I asked, feeling the old Lily settling right in.

"You aren't just an old acquaintance," she replied tartly. "And we both know it."

"If you aren't into relationships—"

"Don't go there," she hissed. "Austin's a great guy. Amazing. And if he's not ready for a relationship than neither am I."

Ready? If he was anything like me, he'd never be ready. I actually felt sorry for her. She was willing to roll the dice on the waiting game.

"You might be waiting a very long time," I said, taking a sip of iced tea as the realization of everything settled over me.

Her expression remained unchanged, and I felt the power shift between us. I was no longer the one on the other end of the firing squad. I was in self-preservation mode, which I always settled into nicely. It was too uncomfortable being exposed anyway.

"We are only friends with the occasional benefit," she said sharply.

"It's not my business." I held up my hands in defense. "Honestly, whatever you guys have going is seriously none of my business."

"You're telling me, you and your friends flew all the way out here, and you have nothing you want to get out of the deal?"

I shook my head and settled into the seat. "I'm content where I'm at."

Apparently, that only made her angrier. Maybe, she was making my self-revelation into something more, like overconfidence? Relief spread through me when I saw Austin make his way through the crowd. Maybe he would make it stop!

"Thanks," I said, grabbing the beer from Austin's tray as Stephanie did the same.

He just nodded and sat down as if he was enjoying the show.

"You want to board down the mountain with us?" I turned my attention to her as she took a sip of the beer. It appeased her, at least marginally.

"I don't want to interfere," her voice syrupy.

Austin's gaze shifted to mine and I smiled. This was turning into a mess. I was completely confused. I wanted to like the guy sitting in front of me. I enjoyed his company. No. I enjoyed his company until Stephanie came into the picture. Now, I couldn't figure out which Austin was which. I liked the one I knew in high school, and the one who was helping me down the mountain. But this one sitting at the table wasn't one I was too fond of.

"The more, the merrier," I lied.

"But you came all the way to Utah to spend time with Austin."

"Wasn't a concern a few minutes ago, why let it be one now?" I laughed, grinning at Austin.

"Lily," a male voice boomed. I turned around and saw Ayden walking toward me. A huge wave of relief went through me until I saw that his date had arrived. Sammie was right behind him as they made their way to our table.

I stood up quickly and gave Ayden a hug as he reintroduced me to Sammie.

"Thank you so much for letting me crash your trip," she said, her fingers lacing into each other. She looked completely nervous and endearing all while being wrapped in a beautiful model's body. It was impossible not to instantly like her.

Ayden took a step forward and glanced at the table and then back at me, his expression falling as he looked into my eyes. I saw a twitch along his jaw as he watched Austin and then Stephanie—together.

"Um, this is Austin," I said, motioning toward Austin. "And this is Ayden, my friend."

"This is one of the friends that hunted Austin down?" Stephanie looked completely enthralled with Ayden and my stomach knotted.

"Nice to meet you," Austin replied, barely glancing at Ayden.

"Same. And you are?" Ayden's gaze was fixed on Stephanie.

"I'm one of Austin's friends. I just ran into him, and we all decided to have lunch together."

"Really. A group decision?" Ayden looked at me, knowing I was anything but pleased with Stephanie's added presence.

But what could I do?

"Are you going up again?" Sammie asked me. I could tell she felt the tension between us all as well. So why was everyone else clueing into this predicament other than Austin. "You could ride along with us."

I nodded. "You know, that sounds like a wonderful idea. You don't mind if I'm a third wheel?"

"You're not a third wheel," Sammie replied, giving me a hug.

Stephanie sat with a smug expression on her lips as Austin stared at me, completely bewildered.

"Have fun," I said, grabbing the lily and tucking it back into my jacket. "And I'll be sure to report back about the condition of the flower."

I turned around and started through the restaurant with Ayden and Sammie when I heard Austin's voice calling after me.

"You don't have to go to him," Ayden said, his voice low.

Sammie glanced up at Ayden and then back at me. "It's true," she replied. "What he pulled seems pretty shitty."

I glanced behind me and saw Austin sitting there by himself. Stephanie was nowhere to be seen, and suddenly I felt like I was back in high school. Maybe I wasn't the only one stuck in life.

He held up a hand and gave a slight wave and apologetic smile, and I stopped. What was I doing?

"Guys, go ahead. I don't want to ruin your fun and I'd like to hear what he has to say," I replied, not looking at Ayden.

Sammie gave me a sympathetic smile, which made me feel completely pathetic as I turned and walked back toward Austin.

I pulled out the chair and sat down, staring at Stephanie's empty seat. "So where'd your friend go?"

"I asked her to take off, and I'm so sorry for being such an ass," he replied.

"Okay, so are you now reverting back to the Austin from this morning because the new one you just showed wore me out."

"I deserve that. I know."

"You deserve more than that."

"True."

"What is your deal?" I asked, pulling out the flower and placing it on the table.

"I don't do relationships."

"Yeah, I think your girlfriend-non-girlfriend sent that message loud and clear. And if you'll remember, I don't either."

He reached his hand across the table and grabbed mine. "Listen. No more tricks like that. No more games. I promise what you see is what you'll get. I don't know what came over me. And honestly, she is just a friend. There's nothing romantic with her."

"Keep telling yourself that," I replied.

"I don't have feelings for her."

Was that supposed to make me feel better? Instead, it made me feel sorry for her.

"Just like I told her, it's none of my business. Your relationships are none of my business. If you run into any more *friends* on the mountain, you don't have to chase them away. I may not choose to spend my vacation hanging out with strangers, but I really don't care. You've lowered my expectations tremendously during lunch today, which is exactly what I needed."

The look in Austin's eyes was like a wounded animal, and my chest tightened as I watched him. The complete arrogance from only minutes before was completely wiped away as he watched me.

"I deserve that. Listen, I'm sorry. This is just a lot for me to handle. I thought I was fine with seeing you again, but it's shaking up all of the old resentments and feelings that I wasn't expecting. All I can do is apologize and hope you'll let me show you the real me."

"I keep waiting for that to happen, but you keep changing it up on me," I laughed nervously. "And I honestly don't think I can keep up any longer."

"From this moment on, no games. I promise. Just trust me. I don't want you leaving Utah thinking I'm a complete creep," he continued.

"Just a partial creep?"

"No creep at all."

"We'll see about that," I laughed, as I grabbed the flower and stood up. "Well, let's get back on the hill so that I don't forget what you've taught me."

He nodded, standing up and making his way over to where I was, and he slid his hand along my waist, and I kind of liked it. Even with everything.

"At least, I'm learning some good snowboarding techniques," I said, as we walked outside.

"I'm more than just a snowboard instructor," he said, grabbing his board off the stand.

"Only time will tell, my friend," I teased. The uneasiness from before slowly dissipated as we walked to the mid-mountain ski lift. I anchored my butt on the seat as we were whisked up the mountain.

"I will make it off the lift this time," I vowed.

"Only time will tell," he replied.

I rolled my eyes at him and wondered if I was making things a bigger deal than they were. What was I expecting him to do? Yell at Stephanie and make a scene?

He wrapped his arm around my shoulder and pulled me into him as I watched the hillside glide by. I couldn't deny the familiar sensation that his embrace aroused, or how his body felt against mine. Maybe, that was what was holding me to an idea that there was something more behind his charades. But matters of the heart were never easy, and the same man that helped me through everything years ago was still inside. I just had to dig him out and make him stay.

His lips pressed against my knit cap, and I felt the slightest of kisses on top my head as we came to the unloading area. He released his arm from me and gave me a quick nod.

"You've got this," he said, standing up as his board hit the snow.

I quickly followed and guided my board down the tiny hill and out of the way, landing next to him with great satisfaction and relief.

"Nicely done." He grinned and adjusted his goggles.

"Thank you. It's because of your superb teaching skills."

His eyes met mine, and I didn't detect any of the game playing I'd experienced earlier.

"Ready?" he asked.

I nodded and slowly followed him across and down the mountain, working on stopping and turning. Every so often, he would stop and wait for me or give me pointers, but I could definitely tell I had improved tremendously. He flagged me over to a snack bar and I followed. We'd been on the mountain another couple hours and I'd already mustered up quite the appetite again. Quickly releasing my feet from my board, I followed him over to the line.

"I'm buying," I said, jumping in front of him. "What do you want?"

"I'll take a polish dog and tots." His smile anchored me in place as I remembered back to the many times before when that same smile stopped me in my tracks, made me forget myself and my problems.

"Do you remember that one time we went camping?" I asked.

"When we almost floated away in our tent? Yeah. Hard to forget," he laughed, as I placed our order and paid.

His laughter sounded right—not like earlier today—and I hoped I could make it last this time. I liked this side of Austin. It was the Austin I remembered.

I walked over to grab some napkins and was pleasantly surprised to feel Austin's arms wrap around me and tug me into him.

"The best part of camping was getting to spend time with you," he whispered.

"Even though all of our stuff was drenched, you didn't want to go home," I laughed. "You put our things in the car with the heater on full blast to dry the stuff out, rather than just call it quits."

"It was worth it, wasn't it?" he asked, as he spun me around in his arms.

I looked up into his eyes and nodded. "Yeah. That was a special time."

I felt the familiar ache in my chest as my mind drifted to the memories I had spent so much time forcing out. I ruined what we once had and now expected things to fall magically into place? Who was I kidding?

"Remember when we went hiking and got lost?" I teased.

"We weren't actually lost," he confessed.

"What do you mean? We went in circles like three times."

"That's because I kept telling you to go the wrong way so we could spend a little more time together."

"Are you serious?" I smacked him just as our order was called.

"Take a seat and I'll go grab everything," he said, grinning.

And for once, this felt right between us. But I couldn't help but wonder if that was enough? Was having a sense of history enough to anchor two lives together?

"Small world," Stephanie's voice interrupted my peace as she plunked down in front of me.

All I did was sigh as I glanced over at Austin. "So it looked like you two were getting cozy. I thought that wasn't what this was about." Her brows furrowed as she waited for a response.

I didn't say a word, but watched as Austin quietly walked up behind her.

"He's not ready for a relationship. Anyone who meets him knows that. But I'll do my damndest to be sure I'm the one there when he's ready. You got that?"

"Is that so, Steph?" Austin's voice shocked her back to reality. "I had no idea I was so easy to read."

He placed the tray on the table and stood next to me. "I think it's time for you to get back on your board before you make even more of a fool of yourself."

"You didn't hear what she said to me first," she hissed, standing up so quickly the tots tipped over on the tray. I quickly rewound what just transpired and realized I hadn't said anything. But it wasn't worth giving her a rebuttal.

"It doesn't really matter what she said to you. I heard enough." His eyes fell to mine, and I realized the games had finally ended.

Sixteen

"So is it everything and more?" Ayden teased, as everyone else settled in the kitchen, laughing and talking over one another, while Ayden and I were setting the table for dinner. I hadn't expected that line of questioning, joke or not. I glanced up at him and grinned.

"Things feel really..." I stopped myself.

What did things feel? Familiar and comforting, possibly? Not out of this world, but that wouldn't be very realistic...

"Things are great," I said, placing a fork at the head of the table.

Ayden stopped moving along the table and his eyes steadied on mine. "I wasn't sure with everything this afternoon—"

"You mean everyone?" I laughed. "Yeah, that wasn't the highlight of my day. But things got tremendously better after she left."

Ayden's jaw tightened as he dropped his gaze. "How so?"

"He apologized, and when she reappeared again on the mountain, he stuck up for me." Once I uttered the words, I felt completely embarrassed. That really wasn't that praiseworthy of behavior. "Anyway, he's been pretty honest with me, and I'm surprised he's even talking to me. I'm just taking things one step at a time and enjoying his company. Sooo, that's the Austin update." I felt completely awkward talking to Ayden about today's events, and I wasn't sure if it was because he could see through me or if I felt judged, which was something we both promised we wouldn't do.

"And you're enjoying his company?" Ayden's voice was husky as he shifted the place setting.

"Yeah. Very much so."

"Lasagna, baked ziti, hot dogs, and potato salad coming up," Gabby's voice rang out as she carried a large dish into the eating area.

I started laughing. "Hot dogs and potato salad?"

"Sorry. It's me," Sammie said, grinning and raising her hand as she walked into the eating area. "My appetite's been off recently."

Brandy and Gabby started laughing, and I realized I was completely missing some inside joke thanks to a day with Austin.

"Let's eat," Ayden said, clapping his hands so loudly I jumped. "Little nervous?"

I rolled my eyes and sat down in the chair closest to me as Jason, Mason, and Aaron carried in the rest of the food. Brandy followed behind holding two bottles of wine and placed them on the table while everyone took their seat.

"I think hot dogs sound like the perfect appetizer," I said, grinning at Sammie. Ayden sat next to her, which was only logical, but watching the care he took with her took me by surprise, and I looked away quickly. It felt like I was intruding.

"So did we scare Austin away?" Jason laughed, hopping back up from his seat. "I forgot the garlic bread. Be right back."

"Nope. He had some vendor meeting tonight." I scooped up a big spoonful of ziti and plopped it on my plate and grabbed a hot dog. Never too old to try new things, I guess.

"That's too bad," Mason replied, grinning. "I was kind of hoping he could be our entertainment for the evening."

"You're as bad as your brother," I laughed.

"No. I'm way worse," he laughed, and I glanced at Ayden who was talking quietly with Sammie.

"Thank god he had a meeting then." I scowled lovingly at Mason.

"We heard there was some female with you guys?" Gabby asked, obviously unimpressed.

"Female?" I laughed. "Yeah. There was an extra *female*. And you heard that from Ayden, I assume."

"Nope. Sammie filled us in," Brandy replied.

"What'd I do?" Sammie asked, breaking away from her conversation with Ayden.

"You told us about the SWF hanging around Austin and Lily," Brandy replied.

"That I did, but I don't think I used Craigslist terminology," Sammie said, decorating her hotdog.

"That seems really rude," Brandy replied, looking at Gabby for backing.

"It does. We didn't haul you down here to be mistreated."

"Guys, I wasn't mistreated. She's just some friend of Austin's who happened to be grabbing lunch at the same time as us so she took a seat," I assured them.

"If it was no big deal, then why were you ready to bolt?" Ayden smirked and I wanted to punch him. He really could see right through me.

"Okay, well. She wasn't a very friendly friend. And she seems to feel she's got ownership rights on Austin once his lease is up, but—"

"You're making excuses for a guy that..." Ayden started.

"Sshh." Sammie motioned for Ayden to calm down. "Love is a complex emotion."

"I'm not in love with him," I spurted out. "He's just a friend."

Surprised by my own reaction, my cheeks warmed as Ayden's gaze met mine. A flicker of intensity shot through his eyes as he watched me, and a slight smile tucked behind his lips. I felt that charge of electricity run between us and immediately became flooded with guilt. My eyes broke from his, and I glanced at Sammie. Whatever feelings were churning up inside of me were completely inappropriate and uncalled for. I was sure I was misreading Ayden's expression.

"You guys make a really cute couple," I said, hoping to switch the topic away from me.

Deflection time!

"Oh, we aren't a couple," Sammie said, her eyes wide as she stared back at me. "We're just friends."

"I thought you guys dated?" I asked.

Ayden scooted back from the table. "Anyone want some more water? I'm gonna go grab some."

Everyone shook their heads as we all stared at Sammie, except for Mason. Mason just continued to shovel food in his mouth with a big dopey smile.

"Been there, done that. Won't be doing it again," she laughed. "Don't get me wrong. He's a great guy..."

"What?" I asked, unable to hide my surprise.

"Completely platonic," she said, giving me a quick wink.

My mouth betrayed me by plastering a smile on my lips. "Well, never say never," I offered.

"Oh, I don't think my soon-to-be baby's daddy would be all too thrilled with that kind of surprise."

My eyes fell to her flat stomach, and her empty ring finger before rising quickly back to her gaze.

"You are..." I replied. "But you don't..."

Sammie smiled. "Three months along. This was my last time to snowboard before it became unsafe so I thought it would be a fun trip. Plus, it would keep my mind off the fact that I miss my guy, Mario. My fiancé is over in Italy settling some affairs before he comes over and we start nesting."

"Wow. You look amazing."

"It's the hotdogs. They do wonders for the complexion. All the preservatives. But I haven't been able to wear my engagement ring since my fingers bloated up last week. I don't know if they'll deflate or not," she said, glancing down at her manicured hand.

Ayden came in with a freshly-filled glass of water and slid back onto his chair.

"So when did you tell Ayden the good news?" I asked. My brow arched at Ayden as he stiffened in his chair. Mason started laughing. Twins could be so annoying.

"That party you hired me for, actually," she said, patting his shoulder. "And thanks by the way. That was kind of my last hoorah before the baby."

"You were perfect for it. It was my last hoorah at the firm too," I laughed.

"Oh, yeah. Ayden mentioned that," she said, her gaze shifting playfully to Ayden.

"So, how did Ayden and you meet?" Jason asked, completely amused with the situation.

"Oh, you don't want to hear about that," Ayden said, as he grabbed a slice of lasagna and placed it on his plate.

"Oh, but I think we do," Brandy agreed.

"I'll second that," Gabby laughed.

"Well, the table has spoken," Sammie laughed. "Sorry, buddy."

I looked down at my plate and felt a pulse of excitement and jubilation course through my veins. For what in particular, I wasn't sure.

"We really don't have to go into details," Ayden replied, staring at Sammie. His lips were pressed together, and he turned in his chair to plead with her. But he was going to lose. Sammie had already made up her mind. I really liked her!

"You're only making us want to know the story even more now," I hushed Ayden.

"So when I was still in college, some guy propositioned me to try out modeling," she began. "It wasn't really modeling but whatever."

Please tell me that wasn't Ayden. This sounded far too creepy.

"I was on campus and apparently there was some underground fighting club that needed girls."

"To hold up the cards," Mason interjected.

I glanced over at him and he shrunk into his seat and laughed. "Not that I'd know."

"Like Fight Club?" I asked.

Sammie laughed. "Not quite. But you'd have to ask Ayden the behind-the-scene specifics."

My stomach knotted, but I couldn't pelt all the questions I had at Sammie because she kept going.

"Anyway, the first night I showed up to some secret location and was given a skimpy bikini to wear. It was so awful with its hot pink glittery sequins sewn all over it. Completely classy. The guy that found me explained that all I had to do was walk through the makeshift ring between rounds, holding up the poster. The money was amazing, and I just gave up a couple hours once a week. They were really paying me for my silence, but I didn't figure that out right away."

"So that's where we met," Ayden interrupted, pouring some wine into his glass.

"I don't buy it," Aaron replied. "There's definitely more to the story."

"Oh, there is," Sammie assured us, grinning.

Ayden looked completely uncomfortable, and I almost felt sorry for him, but I was far too nosey to let my sympathy get in the way. I didn't want to stop this train!

"It was my second week on the job, and when the fighters were announced, I glanced over and saw Ayden. He didn't look like any of the other fighters I'd seen, and his smile was so endearing."

"Wait what?" Brandy and I both shot back.

I glanced at Ayden, and his lips were pressed together, his arms folded in front of him as if he was bracing himself.

"You were a fighter?" Brandy asked, her voice a click higher than normal.

Ayden's eyes bounced to mine, and then met his sister's as he nodded.

"Did you know about this?" Brandy demanded, staring at Mason who also gave her a slight nod.

Somehow this admission stirred something completely carnal inside of me. As if I wasn't having a hard enough time keeping Ayden in the friend zone, this latest revelation made it almost impossible. I wanted to find out more about this side of Ayden.

"How come you don't have any scars?" I asked.

"I'm good," he replied flatly, his jaw tense.

"Anyway, I didn't think much of it. I'd seen how girls completely threw themselves at the fighters, and I thought it was kind of gross, but Ayden didn't seem to be into any of that. He just showed up, did his job, and left," Sammie continued. "It was like the fourth or fifth time I worked the event, and some guy was hassling me. I had just changed into my outfit, and this really creepy guy followed me down the long, empty hall to the restroom. When I came back out of the bathroom, my heart raced once I saw that the guy was still there. The guy pushed me up against the concrete wall and wouldn't let me go. Before I knew it, Ayden came out of nowhere and stepped in to end it. And boy did he end it."

"What did Ayden do to the guy?" I asked Sammie, completely avoiding Ayden's gaze on me. I was completely enthralled.

"Let's just say the guy was in need of extensive dental work. That was my last night working the fights. I didn't want to be a part of the scene any longer, but it got me thinking about modeling."

"God. That's horrible," Gabby replied, shaking her head.

"It actually turned into a good thing. I decided to try out the modeling thing in a legit way and I got lucky. I was able to finish college without loans and put enough away for, well, this little bundle. Things always happen for a reason," Sammie said, patting her non-existent belly. "Needless to say, Ayden and I started to see one another, but we both realized we were better friends than anything else."

"Really?" Gabby asked.

"Turns out I'm into dark haired men and as you can see, Ayden's a complete blonde. Just doesn't work for me," she teased.

"There's nothing wrong with blondes," Mason spoke up, laughing.

"No, there's not," I laughed, turning my attention to Ayden. "So how long did you fight?"

He shrugged. "Too long."

"Do mom and dad know?" Brandy asked, still obviously pissed about being in the dark.

Ayden bit his lip and glanced over at her. "No, and I'd appreciate you not saying anything."

Brandy nodded and her gaze shifted to Sammie. "Well, that was quite enlightening."

"I know. I want to hear more about these fights," I said, taking a sip of wine. "You know, having hot dogs and ziti isn't so bad."

"I don't know about that," Sammie chuckled. "I'd say one or the other, but that's just me."

"Oh, this girl can eat," Ayden said, laughing. "Anyone who finally can make her settle down will be in for a really big grocery bill."

"Hey, I'm not that bad," I argued.

"YES, you are," Brandy and Gabby echoed in unison.

"You're just jealous," I teased, rubbing my hands along my side in a pinup pose.

"Actually, we are," Gabby agreed.

I felt Ayden's gaze on me, and I glanced over, feeling a pool of warmth take over my body. I looked around the table, wondering if anyone noticed, but everyone was too busy chatting about our mystery man at the table.

I glanced back at Ayden, and his scarless face as he flashed me a lopsided grin, his words settling over me, *I'm good.* His proclamation wasn't *I was good.*

Was he still fighting?

I narrowed my eyes on Ayden. His lips parted as if he was going to answer my silent question, but instead he turned to Sammie and whispered something before taking off from the table.

I followed him out of the dining room and grabbed for his hand as he glided down the hall toward the entry.

"Where are you going?" I asked.

"Just out," he replied, his gaze dipping to the floor.

My hand latched onto Ayden's, trying to stop him from leaving. My stomach fluttered with his touch, but I felt his hand shake mine away.

"I thought you brought her as a date..." my voice trailed off.

He shrugged and walked out the door, leaving me to wonder what just happened.

Seventeen

'd gotten a message from Austin about dinner tonight, which I was looking forward to, but I was also excited about hanging out with everyone today. I started to hear the group slowly wake up with doors softly opening and closing, and the sound of voices following every so often.

I quickly knotted my hair in a bun and dabbed some lipstick on. I was already wearing my snow pants and t-shirt. I'd just put my jacket over everything before we left, and I'd be good to go. As I walked slowly down the hall, my nose alerted me to the wonderful smell of coffee, and I knew today was going to be a nice day. There was a plate of pastries on the breakfast bar and a row of empty mugs. I glanced over to the great room where the television was on, but no one was around.

I poured a cup of coffee and grabbed a croissant just as Ayden came into the kitchen. My eyes skated down his pecs, and my heart nearly jumped out of my chest.

"Do you ever wear a shirt?" I snapped, as my eyes fell along his abdomen before stopping at his jeans.

He chuckled as he poured himself a cup of coffee.

"Didn't hear you get in last night," I mused, leaning against the counter.

I wanted to act like it didn't bother me, but it did. Listening for any sign of him to come home last night, I'd stayed up in bed until my eyes wouldn't stay open any longer. I was actually relieved to see him here this morning.

"Late night," he agreed, but offered no more information as he sipped his coffee.

"It'll be fun today," I said, putting my pastry on a napkin.

"Should be," he said, reaching for a bagel. "Will Austin be joining us?"

I hadn't even thought about inviting him! I apparently wasn't the best at this whole getting to know a long-lost-love type of thing—inclusion would probably be a good start.

"Uh, no. I didn't ask him. I kind of forgot."

"You forgot to ask Austin?" Ayden asked, completely bemused.

"Well, maybe I didn't forget, but we're having dinner tonight so that's probably enough of me for him to handle."

Ayden frowned and took a step forward, bringing us much closer than I'd planned on for the morning. "Why do you always talk about yourself as if you're a disease or a pest or something?"

"I didn't really know I was doing that," I said, looking into Ayden's eyes. "I didn't mean for it to come out that way. But anyway, I thought it would be nice to just hang out with my friends today." I took in a slow breath as Ayden moved even closer to me, and my pulse began pounding. His blue eyes darkened as his gaze fell to my lips, which I instinctively moistened.

"So you were a fighter?" I whispered.

He traced his finger along my jaw and nodded slowly, not taking his eyes off of my mouth. "There's a lot about me that you might find interesting, if you'd let me show you."

It felt like a band of butterflies took flight in my stomach as he continued watching me, and all of the emotions that I'd been bottling up came crashing into my world. His touch was soft, gentle, sending chills up my spine, but the look in his eyes was so much more. I wanted to experience whatever was going on in his mind, in his world. I took a step toward Ayden, closing our gap and reached up to touch his neck to bring his lips toward mine.

Ayden dipped his chin, his mouth hovering next to my ear. "I don't think this is something you want to do right now." The breath from his words tickled my skin, but the meaning completely shattered me. I looked up at him quickly as he took a step back.

"What was that for?" I asked, a mix of anger and relief wafting through me.

Thank God I didn't kiss him!

"I've told you before," Ayden replied, his voice low. "I don't want you to do anything you'll regret. I don't want to do anything that makes you doubt why you're here. I shouldn't have…"

Brandy and Aaron's voices interrupted Ayden's words, and I spun around, grabbing my croissant off the napkin.

"Good morning," I said, giving Brandy a big hug.

"Are those okay?" she asked.

"Delicious. Are you the one we can thank for getting these this morning?" I asked.

"Aaron and I went out for espresso and thought we'd bring something back to give you energy for the big day on the mountain," she said, grinning.

"I don't think hot dogs are a good idea any longer," Sammie groaned, as she came into the kitchen. "I'm not going to make it today."

"Oh, no. That bad, huh?" Brandy asked.

"Not so hot," Sammie laughed. "Do you mind if I hang with you today?"

"Sounds a lot less lonely. I'd love it." Brandy took a sip of coffee and smiled.

"Should we get going soon?" Jason called from down the hall.

"Totally, but we have to wait for Brad Pitt to go put on a shirt," I laughed. "The whole talk about his past glory days made him take his role a little too seriously."

Brandy started laughing and pointed at her brother. "Why are you going shirtless so much when we're all freezing to death in the mountains?"

Sammie almost spit out her orange juice in laughter and I just grinned. "Yeah. Why is that?" I arched my brow at him.

"So who said those days were behind him?" Mason said, appearing from the hall and slapping Ayden's back.

"Seriously?" Brandy asked, crossing her arms.

"He's kidding," Ayden laughed, as he walked away, but I wondered if he really was.

"Hurry up," Mason shouted at his brother. "You're holding us all up."

Everyone started pulling on their jackets and hats in the entry as Brandy and Sammie gave us the puppy dog faces.

"Have fun in the snow for us," Brandy said.

"Don't worry. We will," I replied.

I was sitting down on the bench, lacing up my snowboard boots when Sammie walked over to me and leaned down. "Ayden's a really great guy."

I looked up at her and smiled nervously. "He's a very confusing person is what he is."

"I think the situation is confusing, not his..."

"What are you up to?" Ayden asked Sammie, coming up behind her in stealth mode.

"Absolutely nothing." Sammie grinned and tapped my knee.

"Good. Nothing is exactly what you should be up to." He glanced over at me, and I looked away, still annoyed with him.

"At least, you don't take long to get ready," Mason said, glancing at his brother. "Everyone ready to get this started?"

We all nodded and walked out the door with our equipment as Sammie and Brandy were left waving goodbye to us all. Snow was gently falling, but it wasn't as cold as the day before, which was nice. Jason and Gabby broke off as a pair, while Aaron and Mason walked quickly ahead of Ayden and me.

"What's the rush?" I asked, watching Aaron and Mason leave us in the dust.

"Beats me."

We walked in silence over to the lift where Aaron and Mason had already uploaded. I glanced behind me and saw Jason and Gabby hugging. They were in no rush.

"You wanna just pair up?" I asked.

Ayden nodded as we snapped into our equipment, but he didn't say anything else. We pushed over to the lift and loaded up. Still nothing.

"Okay, so I've just gotta say this," I said, turning to look at Ayden. "I really have no idea where you stand, or where I want you to stand. But I'm just one of your little sister's best friends, and things were usually pretty cut and dried between us. I knew where I stood in your eyes, which was not anywhere in particular. Now, I have no idea what's going on. One minute it feels like you want to devour me and the next you push me away, literally."

"Boy, you have never been one to beat around the bush," he said, staring straight ahead.

"Not usually my style. No."

"You're wrong, though," Ayden said, shifting so that his eyes met mine.

"About what?"

"You've never been my little sister's friend. You've been Lily...Lily who calls bullshit when she sees it, who knows how to take care of her friends, who is more brilliant than any person I've ever worked with, and who is sexy as hell." His blue eyes darkened a shade. "But some of those qualities seem to have evaporated when it comes to Austin. And because of that, I'm staying out of it."

"You think I'm sexy?"

"Out of everything I just said, that's what you latched on to?" His lips tugged up slightly and I laughed.

"A girl's gotta have her priorities."

"I almost canceled on this trip, Lily. But Sammie convinced me that I needed to come and have fun. But I keep running into a roadblock."

The lift slowed and stopped, leaving us to dangle in the middle of the mountain. The sway of our chair lift freaked me out so I slid over to Ayden and held onto his arm.

"What's the roadblock?"

"I'm the roadblock."

The chill as we stayed stationary made me tremble. I looked up the line and didn't see anything that would've caused the lift to stop, but we definitely weren't going anywhere.

Ayden wrapped his arm around my shoulders, and my body relaxed into his.

"You're your own roadblock to having fun?" I asked, looking up through my lashes at him. "Doesn't sound like the Ayden I know."

He smiled and squeezed me into him. "It's not, and as of this morning, I'm done with being a roadblock." He grinned and pressed his lips against my cap. "I love spending time with you. You're a lot of fun, and I don't want to spoil my trip or yours; so after last night, I decided to let go."

My stomach felt like it was twisting too tight as I wondered what happened last night? Was he talking about after he left?

"I wouldn't want you to do that either." I felt the tightening continue as my imagination went wild with what gave him this sudden freedom. "I'm glad you can start enjoying the trip."

The lift sputtered to life and began carrying us farther up the mountain.

"I might have been the cause of one of the stoppages yesterday," I revealed.

Ayden's deep laugh melted my insides as I glanced over at him. I knew that Austin was the roadblock, not Ayden. But he still didn't want to stop me from doing what I needed to do, and that was beyond kind of him.

"How the hell?" he asked, breaking me out of my thoughts.

"I got stuck on the lift as we were unloading so it whipped me back around as it started to go back down the hill. I was dangling from the lift until I dropped into a snow bank."

Ayden was laughing so hard his eyes watered. "It wasn't that funny." I scowled.

"I wish there was video of that. I really, really do," he said, his laughter finally subsiding just as we were about to disembark. "Sure you got this?"

I rolled my eyes and stood up gracefully as the board hit the hill. I glided down the small hill without a hitch and waited for Ayden to catch up.

"I find it hard to believe you had an incident yesterday," he said, coming up behind me.

"I got really good instruction," I assured him.

Ayden's expression fell slightly, and I felt bad for referring to Austin, even though I had no idea why I should feel bad.

"Hey, check that out," I said, pointing in the opposite direction, while I scooped up a ball of snow.

"What? I don't see anything," Ayden replied, glancing back at me just as I pelted him with a snowball right on his forehead.

"Oh, it's so on," Ayden laughed.

I shrieked and took off down the hill, but not before a snowball smacked me on my ass.

War had been officially declared.

I spotted a little outcrop of trees with plenty of non-compacted snow and turned off in that direction. I landed on my knees and began quickly assembling an arsenal of snowballs as I kept glancing up the mountain, waiting for Ayden. A few too many seconds passed and my heart started beating quickly. Did he fall down or something? What happened to him?

I unstrapped my boots and removed my snowboard, sticking it upright into the ground before standing back up. I walked several feet back up the mountain and stared at all of the people snowboarding by. None of them were Ayden.

"You've done it now," Ayden's deep voice came from behind me.

How did he do that?

"Damn you," I said, my gaze lingering on my stockpile.

"You shouldn't have." His gaze followed mine to the stash, and he reached toward the balls.

I dove toward the ammo, but not before he snagged as many as he could and backed away. Snow shoved its way down my neck, and I didn't even care. Instead, I grabbed two perfectly shaped ice-bullets and pelted them right at his chest. He was still attached to his board, which got caught in the powder and he fell over.

"Score!" I yelled, dusting myself off.

"Not even," he shouted, unstrapping himself from the board and standing back up in a flash. His eyes meant business as he glanced at the ten or so snowballs I still had, only inches from my grasp. I grabbed the first one and felt more of the snow melting down my back. Apparently, more snow snuck in than I realized.

Without hesitation I aimed squarely at Ayden's chest and let the snowball fly toward him at record speed, but he dodged it. His eyes glinted determination as he lunged toward me, tackling me into the powder. The cushion of snow underneath me compacted slightly as Ayden climbed on top of me. My pulse raced as I felt him slowly move up my body. He pinned my arms down, away from the snowballs, and my breathing hitched.

As he inched his way up, my heart felt like it was going to explode as the rush of feelings pounded through me. I'd been close to Ayden before, but this was almost unbearable as his gaze finally met mine. I couldn't stop laughing as I squirmed underneath him, but all it did was push me deeper into the snow. His lips were only inches from mine and his gaze anchored me in place as my laughter diminished. Unpinning one of my hands, he sprinkled some snow over my cheeks.

"Payback for taking me down," he murmured.

"Indeed," I replied. His blue eyes narrowed as I slowly licked the snow from my lips.

"You're driving me insane," he whispered, as I let my free hand wander down his back.

I never knew being covered head-to-toe in snow gear could be this hot, but with every movement I felt from Ayden, my world was crumbling. His eyes fell to my lips as he released my arms and took off his gloves.

"Are you cold?" he asked, his fingers tracing down my cheeks.

Hypothermia wasn't going to stop this moment, hell no!

"Not at all." I looked up at him from under my lashes. His eyes were heated and the expression behind them, raw and intense.

"You're so beautiful."

Holy Hell!

"Kiss me," I whispered. I probably sounded like I was begging, but I honestly didn't care any longer. He pressed his forehead to mine, keeping his mouth just out of my reach.

"I can't, Lily. I won't do that," he murmured. "There are too many factors."

My body trembled, which was apparently Ayden's breaking point. He cupped my chin in his hands, and hovered his lips deathly close to mine. My body was aching with desire as he pressed his mouth to mine, and the sensation immediately heated me all the way through. The warmth of his lips contrasted with the chill of the snow, and with each deepening kiss, an intense craving so spectacular drilled into me. His tongue brushed along the seam of my lips, and I shuddered as I parted my lips. My pulse was running wild as the intensity of our kisses deepened with every passing second. His hand ran along my face as we barely even took a breath.

"Sir, that's against resort rules," a man's voice echoed through the peaceful mountain air.

Ayden let out a groan and pressed his forehead against mine, my lips still tingling from the amazing kiss.

"Sir, did you hear me?" the man asked again.

"Yeah. Loud and clear. Our snowball fight got a little carried away," Ayden apologized, trying not to laugh as he rolled off me. "Sorry about that."

I stayed completely motionless until I heard the snow patrol ski away and then wriggled my way out of the snow.

"Did we just get busted by snow patrol?" I giggled.

"Guess so," he laughed. "I'd do it again in a heartbeat."

Ayden scooped me up out of the snow and brushed the snow off my back.

"You've got to be freezing," he said.

"It was worth it. Beside I'm completely layered," I teased.

"I'm so sorry," Ayden said, strapping on his board.

What? I just had the best kiss of my entire life and the guy was apologizing.

"Why are you sorry?" I asked, trying not to let my hurt show.

"Did you listen to anything I said earlier?" he asked, his brow arched.

"Yeah, but I guess I figured you got over it," I offered, spiraling into the endless pit of my stomach. Why was he doing this again?

"It won't happen again," he replied, and I watched the wall rebuild itself right in front of me, which was fine. I was done with these false starts, back to business, back to friend zone.

"I can't believe the snow patrol caught us. That ought to at least go down in the scrapbook," I said, securing my board.

"Not just the snow patrol," Gabby's voice startled me, and I looked up to see Jason and her standing about ten feet away, grinning.

"It's not what it looked like," I stuttered, glancing at Ayden.

"It was pretty much what it looked like," Ayden said, laughing. "But we've both come to our senses. I think there was something in this morning's coffee."

And just like that, he stole my heart and took off down the mountain without looking back.

Eighteen

"I can't do this anymore," I muttered to myself as I plopped onto my bed. Things today had started so great, and then turned to shit in an instant, which seemed to be a theme for me. The only thing I had been able to figure out so far was that I was the common denominator in that equation. With that revelation, I vowed that I was no longer going to fall for Ayden's looks, or his touches, or his shirtless ways. He was just as confused as I was, and there was no way I planned on making it any worse. I had about an hour before meeting Austin for dinner, and I had planned on spending it with a good mystery. I pushed my feet under the comforter and organized my pillows perfectly just as a thump rattled the walls out in the hall.

I slipped deeper into bed and then heard a faint knock on my bedroom door—so faint I wasn't sure I'd actually heard it until it happened again. I slid off the bed and grabbed my fleece robe. I'd washed off all my makeup and had left my hair in the ponytail before I had to put myself back together again. I had to take a hot shower to warm up after leaving the slopes. I was sure if the kiss had ended differently, I wouldn't have needed it, but such was life.

I trundled over to the door and wondered who it was, or why they didn't just come in. Jason and Gabby were getting couples' massages and Brandy and Aaron were having a romantic dinner out somewhere. Mason was bar hopping and Ayden was god knows where since he'd taken to vanishing in the night, so I had no idea who would be on the other side of the door.

I wrenched on the handle to see only Ayden standing in the hallway, leaning against the doorframe. His eyes were glassy, and he was wearing the adorable grin that I'd come to miss in the last few hours. He had a knit cap on and was dressed in jeans and a wool sweater. He looked incredible, but I was disappointed in myself for noticing. He wasn't who I needed to be focusing on. He had made that clear up on that mountain, several times.

"Aren't you supposed to be bothering someone else?" I asked, taking a step back.

He shrugged but didn't move from the doorway.

"Are you drunk?" I asked, raising a brow.

"You're so damn sexy," he murmured, not answering my question.

He had to be drunk. I was in a pale pink fleece robe, sporting polka dot knee-high socks, and my nose was all red from too much sun on the slopes.

"What's up, Ayden?"

"Won't you invite me in?"

"It's not like it's my apartment. It's a bedroom. I didn't think it'd need a formal invite." I gestured to the pair of chairs that were by the fireplace, but he didn't budge. "Okay. So either you want in or you don't."

I wasn't really sure what his intentions were. This trip had been full of awkward moments and remorseful comments. Or at least that was how I took it, took him, at this point.

He walked a few steps forward and the slight breeze as he walked by had more than a hint of a few drinks. I kept the door open and followed as he swayed toward the closest chair. All of my snowboard clothes were hanging in front of the fireplace, drying from the day's runs.

"I've missed you," he muttered, as he slammed into the chair.

I sat down in the other chair, tucking one leg underneath me as confusion settled around me.

"You've missed me?" I questioned. "We just spent half the day together before you bolted. So that's a little hard to imagine. I didn't go anywhere. I was pretty easy to find. So I find that hard to believe."

"It's true, more than you can imagine..." his voice trailed off.

His eyes connected with mine, and I felt the familiar charge run between us, but there was no way I would act on it. Not with what he did to me on the mountain. Not with his inability to make up his mind. Not with what was coming up tonight. And definitely not with what led him here.

But then my heart was completely disloyal to my mind.

"I've missed you too."

His eyes narrowed on mine.

"I think you've just had a little too much to drink tonight. Tomorrow morning, you'll wake up and realize that. But right now, I want to stop you from making any embarrassing whiskey admissions," I teased, trying to distract him. "We've already had more than our fair share of false starts, and I don't intend to have any more."

My heart was pounding as I waited for his reaction. I didn't know if I wanted him to call my bluff or take my words at face value.

He reached up and swiped his knit cap off, ruffling his hair up. My mind went to thoughts of running my fingers through his hair, and a wave of heat rolled through me as his eyes connected with mine.

"So are you gonna meet up with that guy tonight?" he growled.

"You mean Austin? Uh, yeah. That's kind of why I was brought here, apparently. You made that very clear last night and today. And my suspicions are that poor Sammie was brought as a prop and you intended to make me think—"

"About that," he muttered.

I crossed my arms and pinched my lips together. "Yeah. About that."

"I didn't mean anything," he began. "I just wanted an easy out. I wanted to be here and give the illusion that I wasn't here for you, but I am. I am here for you."

"I find that hard to believe," I replied, feeling the knot in my stomach tighten.

"Of course you do." Anger lingered on his last word.

"Don't turn this around on me. I haven't been the one waffling. I haven't kissed you, only to run away. I didn't lead you on and then tell you to stop. That's all you."

The warmth of the fire was beginning to make me overheat or maybe it was Ayden's reaction to something I didn't even understand. I wanted to peel off my robe, but I was certain that would give him the wrong idea so I sat simmering in front of the fire, watching him.

"You made yourself clear, Ayden. And tonight you've just had a few too many. By tomorrow, you'll wish you never stopped by to say hi. I guarantee it. This fits your pattern perfectly."

"That's bullshit and you know it," he replied, standing up.

"Is it?" I questioned, standing up to face him.

Big mistake!

Our bodies were only inches from each other, and I felt the heat rolling off of his. Ayden's eyes were boring right through me as I looked up at him. I could smell his cologne and the faint caramel hint of whisky that must have been his drink of choice tonight. The combination was intoxicating, but I refused to do anything he or I'd regret in the morning.

"Lily, it's been so hard playing along with everything. Damn it. I've tried, but I can't take it any longer," he whispered, as the warmth from his breath skated across my cheeks.

Chills ran across my skin as the look in his eyes intensified. His eyes fell to my lips and his hands ran up my arms. My breath caught, and I couldn't move as I felt him take a step closer to me as the energy between us strengthened.

"I can't let you go to someone who doesn't understand how amazing you are. So what? You made a mistake when you were a teenager. You're carrying all of this guilt from something that happened a long time ago, like eons ago, and I feel like I'm running out of ways to get you to understand that you don't need to spend your entire life apologizing. The first time you reached out to him, he should have responded. If your love was as strong as you think, he would've."

His words stung, but they were all things I'd thought about over and over again, and here Ayden was calling it like it was, once again.

"Don't go to him tonight," he whispered. "Stay here with me."

I began to shake my head, but Ayden's hands ran up my spine, sending a powerful surge through me as his arms cradled my body against his. I pressed my cheek on his chest, feeling the heavy beat of his heart as he waited for my response. I attempted to steady my breathing and tell him no, but being held in Ayden's arms was like some fairytale, wiping away all my worries and concerns. Every time. But I had to remind myself of all the moments when he found some sort of clarity and managed to push me away. Feeling like I was just some mistake wasn't what I'd consider a fairytale ending. I needed to be a sure thing. I needed to be *his* sure thing.

I took a step back and looked into Ayden's eyes. "I'm sorry. I need to make my dinner appointment. But it's not even about Austin. I just don't want to keep being your second-thought. I've already made plans and I intend to keep them."

His stare turned icy as he dropped his arms from me. "Do you want to know where I was last night?"

I wasn't sure I did.

"I went over to the lodge and sat in the bar, trying to figure out how to make you see that I was the guy you needed, not Austin," Ayden's voice was gravelly as he looked into my eyes. He started laughing. "You know, I saw Austin last night when I was at the bar. And unless he makes out with all of his clients, I don't think he was being completely honest with you."

I felt like I was slapped in the face when I heard Ayden's words.

"Was it Stephanie?" I asked, not that it really mattered. We weren't a couple. He could date whomever he wanted. I just didn't want to be lied to.

Or at least that's what I told myself.

"No. It wasn't Stephanie."

"Well, it's really no concern of mine, or yours, for that matter. He's single. I'm single," I replied, loosening my ponytail, hoping to rid myself of the sudden headache that appeared. "It doesn't matter who he makes out with or doesn't make out with."

I was lying through my teeth, and Ayden saw right through it. I could tell as he crossed his arms.

"So you're okay with being lied to?" he questioned.

"There's nothing serious between us so it's no skin off my nose." I pressed my lips together, and I tried to hold in the mix of embarrassment and anger that was rising. I wasn't even sure who to direct it at any more.

"Don't you think better of yourself?" Ayden asked. His touch startled me as he placed his hand on my waist, but it gave me something I so desperately craved with him, closeness

"I do, which is why I don't want you to do anything you'll regret when you sober up. I don't want to put myself through that. So yeah, I do respect myself enough not to continue to be toyed with. I didn't kiss you because I was bored. It actually meant something to me, and I'm tired of getting mixed messages from you."

"You don't think you've been sending me mixed messages?" Ayden's jaw tensed.

"How?" I asked.

Ayden looked around the bedroom like that alone would alert me to something.

"What?"

"We're in Utah. You're going out with him tonight," he replied.

"All of us flew down here so that I could hash stuff out with him. That's what I've been doing," I replied.

"That's not the only reason you came, Lily. And we both know it. So that alone, I'd say was a big red flag for me to step away from you, to stay away from you. But I just can't keep away from you any longer. I swear to God the only thing that made my brand successful was all the ideas I thought up to launch just so we could work together on campaigns. I'm not going to keep playing games, pretending that you don't matter to me. You matter and you're not a regret or a mistake. You are what I need, Lily. What I crave. And this trip has shown me that."

Ayden pulled me into him, his lips crashing down to mine before I even tried to resist. There was no holding back as his mouth parted with mine, his tongue sweeping through my mouth as I kissed him deeper than on the mountain, deeper than with anyone ever before. Our mouths stayed on one another's searching for an easy resolution to make this moment last. But we both knew it wouldn't. It couldn't. I pulled my fingers though his hair as his lips slowly worked up my cheek toward my ear, sending a shivery sensation clear to my toes.

"Your lips are addicting," he murmured. "But so is the rest of you."

I pulled back slowly and looked into his eyes, the intensity in them overwhelming. This entire situation was teetering on devastation as I continued to fall deeper for Ayden Rhodes because I knew by tomorrow he'd be second-guessing every single second of what just happened; like he had done every single time there was an almost or not quite between us. Every time I heard an apology come from his lips, it killed me because I wasn't *ever* sorry. I didn't want to hear it again.

I looked up at him and glanced at the clock on the wall.

"I should get ready," I said softly.

"Don't. Please, don't." Ayden's blue eyes were so dark, they were almost black as he watched me move away from him. I forced a smile and fought the urge to fall into his arms. I couldn't afford to go there.

"Alright, whatever," he said, walking out of the room, not even giving another glance in my direction.

And that was why I couldn't fall under his spell.

Nineteen

I shut the door behind him and pushed down all of
the memories of Ayden and I spending so much time
together over the years, and me never once recog-
nizing the signs. We'd spent countless hours working
on building his business, and it never occurred to me
that he might have been interested. Or maybe he wasn't.
Maybe it was only a recent thing. I'd always been attracted
to him, but only recently did the feelings come crashing
down anytime he was near me.

I had absolutely no desire to go out tonight, but
after chasing Ayden out of the room, I certainly
couldn't call it off now. I quickly put on some founda-
tion and powder. My cheeks would probably stay rosy

all night from Ayden, which was just wrong on so many levels. Then again, it sounded like Austin certainly wasn't missing out between us seeing one another so no biggie there.

I pulled on some black tights and boots and slipped a black sweater dress over my head. Running a brush through my hair, I decided to put my hair back into a ponytail and be done with everything. I turned off the light by my bed and bid adieu to the book I never got to finish as I walked out of my bedroom. Ayden's door was closed as I walked down the hall. I didn't see any sign of Sammie. I wondered if she was in there with him.

I put on a jacket and walked outside. The snow was still coming down, and it was hard not to think back to the afternoon on the mountain, and how much fun I'd had with Ayden. How wrong was it of me to be walking to see one guy, and daydreaming about another. But tonight was just a friendly dinner. I was sure of it. Following the lighted path, I found my way inside the warm lodge and looked for Austin in the restaurant. He waved me over and was already seated with a bottle of wine at our table and a starter ready to dig into.

"Hey," I said, walking over to the table.

He stood up and gave me a big hug. Austin was dressed in a pair of jeans and a blue flannel shirt. He looked really good, relaxed. I guess a good make-out session would do that to a person.

"Those look delicious," I said, eyeing the beef skewers.

"They are. I thought it'd be nice if you didn't have to wait."

"That's very nice of you. You obviously know me well," I teased.

"I actually think I do," he laughed. "You haven't changed as much as I thought you would've after you left."

"Really?"

"Yeah. I guess I thought you left to reinvent yourself or something, but you're the same old Lily." His smile was genuine and the compliment was actually really sweet.

"Thanks. So how'd the business meeting go last night?" I asked, unable to resist.

"It went great," he replied, pouring me a glass of wine.

"That's good. Was it for the resort or a different venture?" I inquired.

"The resort. I met with a rep for one of our local breweries. They like to go over the seasonal offerings before they're launched."

"Makes sense. How'd she get that job? I think working for a brewery would be so awesome."

"It wasn't a she. It was a he. His name was Zach."

"Oh, huh. I just figured. Not sure why I figured, actually." I glanced at the menu and wondered if Austin was really good at lying, or if Ayden had been mistaken. But like I told Ayden, it didn't really matter. None of us were in a serious relationship. "I think I'm going to have the roasted chicken."

"That makes two of us," he said, placing his menu on mine. "So did you have fun on the mountain today?"

"I did. I had so much fun, especially thanks to your lessons. Ayden was quite impressed."

Austin's brow furrowed.

"My best friend's brother," I said, wondering why I was assuring him of anything. "Brandy couldn't go on up on the mountain because she was in a bad motorcycle accident."

"That's horrible."

"It was. It was so scary. There were moments we weren't sure—" I stopped myself.

Austin nodded. "How's she doing now?"

"Amazing. You wouldn't even know she was in a wheelchair, only months ago. But the doctors want her to heal another year before she tries skiing or snowboarding again."

"Is she as talented as you on the slopes?" he laughed.

"Exactly. She's just as talented as me so she knew she'd be going down and that wouldn't be good right now. So anyway, Ayden is Brandy's brother."

The server came to take our order and the rest of the dinner flew by. We caught up on old friends, which made us old for doing it, and talked about what he enjoyed about his job and what I loved about mine. Before I knew it, we were outside walking toward my condo, and I got an urge to do another snowball. I had no idea what came over me, but before I knew it, I grabbed a pile of snow and threw it on him, laughing.

"Jesus, what the hell did you do that for?" Austin asked, his eyes flashing with annoyance.

"Seriously?" I asked.

"Yeah, seriously," he said, brushing the ice-crystals off his jacket. "That shit's cold."

"I didn't even get you hard or on flesh," I teased.

"Is that supposed to make me grateful?" he asked.

Whoa. Which Austin was this, and can I please have the old one back?

My mind flashed to Ayden and I shrugged. "I guess some people would be grateful. Yeah."

"It's just really immature," Austin said, shaking his head.

"Really? It was that bad?" I asked, now standing still, looking at Austin, trying not to laugh.

"I'm not broken, though. I'll mend," he laughed, sensing my agitation.

"I would hope so," I said, biting my lip. "It was a fun night. Hopefully, we can catch up again before I leave."

"We're done for the night?" Austin asked.

"Yup. I'm beat. Isn't it like close to midnight?"

Austin nodded. "Is this because of the snow thing? It wasn't that big of a deal. I'm just not into surprises."

I started laughing. "No. It's not the snow, but I'm exhausted and should probably get back before my friends worry."

He was clearly not pleased. I wondered what he was expecting for the night? He leaned in and gave me a quick kiss on the cheek, which did nothing for me.

Of course it didn't.

"I'll text you tomorrow," I offered.

"Sounds good," Austin said and walked back to the lodge slowly.

I stood on the path and looked up at the night's sky. I hoped with everything in my heart that Ayden would wake up tomorrow and feel the same way he did tonight, but until then I could treasure the memories of the world's best snowball fight and remember that everything happened for a reason. My hair was beginning to get wet as the snow began to melt so I made my way back to the condo. It was completely dark; the bedroom doors closed.

Our big day on the mountain must have killed us all. I fought back the urge to laugh at the partiers we all turned out to be and threw my jacket on the entry bench. I quietly made my way to the bedroom and flipped on the light, almost screaming at the same time. There was someone in my bed. I slowly walked over and saw Sammie's head sticking out of the covers and chuckled. She certainly was determined. I grabbed my yogi bear pajamas, turned off the light and slipped out of my bedroom. I changed into my pajamas in the spare bathroom and felt my entire body tense up as I thought about what I was about to do.

I took a deep breath in and walked to Ayden's door. Opening it slowly, the light from the hall cast enough light to see that he was sleeping. I closed the door quietly and locked it, before walking slowly to where Ayden was lying. He looked so peaceful I didn't want to wake him. Gently pulling back on the comforter, I noticed he was shirtless and the teddy bear was under his head.

Dear God help me!

I climbed in next to him and curled around his body, feeling the warmth of his skin through my pajama top. He moved only slightly as he wrapped his arm around me and brought me in close. His steady breathing was like being hypnotized as I fell asleep in his arms.

Twenty

I was teetering on the edge of the twin bed, awakened by the sunshine that was filtering into the bedroom. Where'd the snow go? Ayden's arm was still wrapped tightly around my waist, and his steady breathing signaled that he was still deep in sleep. I loved how our bodies fit together, but the thought of him finding out that I'd snuck into his bed scared me. Feeling unsure of what I'd actually done, I slowly slid and rolled out from under his arm, softly falling onto the wood floor. I didn't want to embarrass myself with rejection once more. I stood up and looked at Ayden one last time before sneaking out of the room and into my bathroom that was attached to the bedroom where Sammie was still sleeping. I brushed my teeth quickly and quietly and then made my way back through the bedroom without waking her up.

Score!

All the bedroom doors were closed, including Ayden's. I was definitely the first one up and wasn't even sure what time it was until I saw the stove clock glaring six o'clock.

Yuk!

I'd go back to bed, but I had nowhere to sleep. Rinsing out the old coffee in the pot allowed my mind to wander to Austin and his ridiculous reaction to some snow in the face. Actually, it wasn't even in the face. He'd be a real treat when something actually went wrong. I wasn't sure what happened to the caring and protective boyfriend I remembered from high school, but he didn't appear to be around much.

In fact, I wondered what the gift of time actually erased about Austin from back then. The incident last night seemed to trigger some things I'd done a good job of burying over the years, like the one night he came unglued at me for not meeting up with him after his baseball practice. I'd come down with the flu, but that excuse didn't fly with him even after he visited me in bed with a bucket next to me. I had definitely shoved that memory far back in the old brain.

It was funny how we tended to put someone on a pedestal the more time away from them we got. My mind flashed back to Jake and my stomach knotted. The crushing feeling of losing him spread through me, yet again. With Jake, there were no bad memories though. None. He was an amazing guy, my first love. I just wished he had allowed himself to find that out before...

"Hey, you're in charge of coffee duties this fine morning?" Ayden's voice interrupted my twisted trip down memory lane.

Staying focused on the task at hand, I refused to turn and face him. I was sure he was shirtless, and I honestly didn't think I'd be able to handle myself properly in a kitchen. It was hard enough being snaked against his firm, warm body all night.

"Yup. Couldn't sleep for some reason," I said, filling up the coffee filter with grounds. "Bet you need some caffeine after last night."

"What do you mean?" he asked, coming up behind me. I felt the warmth from his body without even having to turn and look.

"You know...I think you hit the sauce pretty hard."

"The sauce?" he laughed. "Did we just get whisked back to the fifties?" he laughed.

I couldn't help but laugh as I pushed the button on the coffee pot and turned to face him.

Mistake!

"So how did it go last night with Austin?" Ayden asked, with a possible smirk hiding under his expression, which made him absolutely adorable. At least, he was *trying* to hide it.

"Pretty good," I said. "I got a lot of answers and feel really good about coming out here. I'm glad your sister set it up. Everything happens for a reason, and I think last night I found mine."

"Really?" he asked, perplexed. A dash of disappointment darted through his gaze as I toyed with him momentarily.

"Yup," I replied, not offering an explanation.

"You know, the guys and I were planning on snow-shoeing today."

I shivered. "That sounds like a lot of work."

"It does, doesn't it?" He took a step forward narrowing the gap between us even more.

"Uh-huh."

"I think I'd enjoy another snowball fight more," he whispered.

Me too!

"Is that so?"

He nodded and took in a slow, deep breath as his fingers slid through my hair. Pulling me into him, my body pressed against his, and my hands slid along his bare chest, savoring the dips and peaks.

"Are you okay with my change of plans?" he whispered, as his breath scattered along my scalp, sending a prickle of delight through me.

"Completely," my voice breathless, as I felt his firmness press into me.

It didn't take long to be completely mesmerized under his spell. My only hope was that he wasn't going to do take-backs on me.

He kissed my tangled hair and I shuddered.

"Are we just going to go straight for the snowball fight, or did we want to put other plans in there too?" I asked, thankful that I was being propped up by the counter behind me and his body in front of me.

"I guess we should probably lead into the snowball fight with something first. How about breakfast, and I'll surprise you with the rest of the day." He took a step back, smiling wickedly.

"It's too early to make plans," I said, reaching for his hands and pulling him back into me. "No place would be open."

"But sometimes anticipation is everything," he said, grinning. His eyes landed on the coffee pot behind me. "And I think one of the things that became clear last night was that you wanted to ensure that..." his voice broke off as my arms slinked around his bare waist. I pressed my lips to his chest and slowly opened my mouth, gliding my lips along his skin. Ayden's breathing quickened, and I knew my job had been done. I released my arms from his waist and giggled.

"You're right. Anticipation is *everything*," I said, pushing him playfully away from me.

"That isn't anticipation. That is male cruelty," he laughed.

"You started it." I looked into his eyes, and his gaze intensified as his hand stroked my cheek.

"And I just might finish it," he said, dropping his hand as my breathing hitched. A smile spread along his lips in pure satisfaction as he watched my reaction, but I was still going to win this one.

"Want some coffee?" I asked, turning away from him.

"Sounds good to me. So, how'd you sleep last night, beautiful?" his voice low and teasing.

My heartbeat quickened at the realization that he knew. I wasn't as sneaky as I thought.

"Never better," I confessed, pouring the coffee into a mug for him.

"I think I could make it a lot better," he said, and I spilled the coffee all over the counter.

"Whoa," he laughed, grabbing a towel.

"I don't know what it is about you," I laughed, mopping things up with another towel.

"That's a good thing, right?" he asked, his voice turning gentle.

"Absolutely intriguing. I've never experienced it before..."

"So it's not the whisky and wine?" he asked, wringing the coffee out of the towel. My eyes cascaded down his beautiful torso, and I laughed at myself, and my reaction to him.

"Definitely not the whisky and wine," I said, as he caught my gaze.

He reached for the cup of coffee that was almost overflowing and took a sip, as I wiped the rest of the liquid from the counter.

"I'm going to go take a shower," he replied, winking and it took every ounce of self-control not to follow that man right into the shower.

"Okay." I leaned against the counter and watched him trundle down the hall as my body felt completely on fire. I needed to shower as well, but Sammie was sleeping in my bed, and I didn't want to wake up a pregnant woman who's done everything in her power to guide me in the right direction. It would just have to wait. I walked into the family room and sank into the couch and flipped on the television.

"You're up so early," Gabby stated, walking into the great room and sitting next to me.

"Yeah. I think with everything that's been going on, I'm on high alert or something."

"Well, welcome to my life. With the bakery, this is sleeping in for me."

I started laughing. "You know you love it."

"I do." She smiled, but there was something in her expression that concerned me.

"How's everything going with Jason?" I asked.

She twisted her lips into a pout as she contemplated what to say. "Not sure."

"I know this might sound weird but hear me out."

"Okay," she agreed.

"If Brandy can find my old high school boyfriend without even a name to go on, maybe she can help Jason find out whatever's bothering him. I mean you think that's what this is about, right?"

Gabby nodded. "Do you think Brandy would do that?"

"Please, you know she would love it."

"I wonder how to do it without him finding out."

I shook my head. "Oh, no. I think he definitely needs to be in on it. Otherwise it could turn into a complete fiasco. You both should talk to Jason, see if it's something he'd be into and go from there. Maybe he needs more information about his sister or something."

"What if he doesn't want me involved?" Gabby asked, shifting on the couch.

"Well, that's something you guys would need to work through, but as a couple, those are the types of things that you need to hit head on. Whatever he finds out about his family, might be your family someday, and if he can't deal with it now before he's met any of them..."

Gabby nodded. "No. You're right. I agree. I think that's what's bothering me. Like he's seen me at my worst. Why won't he let me in? I want to be there for him."

"Exactly."

"But there's a part of me that worries that it's not his family..."

"What would make you think that?" I asked.

"Nothing. That's the kicker. I think it's just because I've had so many horrible experiences in the past."

"My advice on that one is not to let your imagination get carried away. If there's nothing that's led you to think that, then deal with the obvious. I'd be willing to bet there's nothing like that going on."

"Enough about me," Gabby said, pulling a blanket on her lap. "Tell me how it went with Austin. I was actually wondering since you're up so early if maybe you never went to bed." She wriggled her brows, and I busted into laughter.

"Not quite like that, my friend," I said, grinning. "I need to fill you in."

"Uh, yeah. Please do," she laughed.

"So this trip has been absolutely amazing. And if I believed in any of that self-help stuff, I'd even venture to say that it qualifies as a turning point in my life."

"Seriously?" Gabby couldn't contain her excitement. I only hoped the excitement would remain as I continued talking.

"Yeah. Totally. I've learned a lot. One of the most important things is that people can change, and not necessarily for the better. Actually, it's not even that. It might just be that lives can go in different directions and different interests arise."

Gabby's expression fell slightly. "So the Austin thing wasn't a good idea?"

"Meeting up with him was the best gift ever. I kept fooling myself about him. I actually buried the real Austin and held onto the one I wanted him to be. When my first boyfriend passed away, Austin was there for me, completely. But that's all that we had actually shared, a shattered past. What I didn't realize was that it wasn't Austin who I hadn't gotten over. It was Jake. I'd never properly grieved for him. I was stuck in denial and still so angry with him. I felt like I could have saved him or helped him, but instead of asking me for help he broke up with me and shut me out. And that's where I stayed stuck. I isolated myself, even from you two. I mean, we've been best friends for how long, and you didn't even know what happened."

Gabby nodded and placed her hand on mine. "Grief is a tough thing and everyone goes through different stages. When my mom died, I blamed my father and I think that's why I relied so much on Aaron. And then when he took off, I was just completely devastated, but it's hard to deal with the emotions as they come up."

"It is. I've been going after something that wasn't even real just so I wouldn't have to deal with things that were. I felt safe when there was no emotional pull to any of the guys I'd met in the past. I actually think I liked feeling numb, like it was my safety net. But there was a part of me that wanted Austin to be the one to pull me out of it, not realizing someone else already had." I bit my lip and glanced at the floor.

"What?" Gabby asked. "What do you mean someone else?"

"There's definitely someone else who has seen me at my worst and my best..."

"It's Ayden, isn't it?" Gabby's brows shot up, and she couldn't keep the smile off her face.

"How'd you know?" I asked.

"Seriously? I think he's been in love with you for years."

"No way," I whispered.

"Yes, way."

"How do you think Brandy's going to take it?" I asked.

"Please. She'll be fine with it. She better be fine with it. She's dating my brother and I didn't care. I just want my best friends to be happy."

"I think I might tell her tonight if things continue the way they have been."

"Oh, my God. I'm so excited about this," Gabby gushed, completely in her own world. "So the Austin thing is completely okay, and you're not going to kill us?"

I laughed. "Definitely not going to kill you, but I do think you owe me a lifetime of free baked goods."

"I think that's fair."

"Good morning," Sammie said, fussing in the kitchen. "How'd everything go last night?"

I stood up from the couch and turned around to Sammie beaming.

"Apparently things went according to your plan," I said, rolling my eyes.

"What plan?" Gabby asked.

"Since I can't have caffeine or alcohol, Lily's just helping a poor pregnant girl stay amused." She grinned and took a sip of orange juice.

"So what's our plan for the day? I heard the guys were going to go snowshoeing," Gabby said.

"I think most of the guys are going to go snowshoeing, but one has other plans," I confessed.

"So no girl time?" Gabby teased.

"If Lily stayed behind with us, I'd lock her outside in the freezing cold," Sammie vowed.

"She knows?" Gabby whispered.

I nodded.

"You're probably right. So are you planning on seeing Austin any more, or is that kind of behind you?" Gabby asked.

"Oh, no. Did something go wrong last night?" Brandy asked, coming into the kitchen.

I glanced at Sammie whose eyes were as wide as saucers, and I couldn't help but laugh.

"Well, yes and no," I laughed nervously, walking into the kitchen.

"I think that's our cue to exit," Gabby announced and Sammie followed.

"Why did the kitchen suddenly turn into a ghost town around here?" Brandy asked.

Not wanting to wait any longer to tell her, I offered Brandy a cup of coffee and decided to repeat everything this vacation had taught me as her expression remained unchanged.

Twenty-One

I took a sip of my coffee and waited for Brandy to say something, anything. But she just sat there and sipped her coffee slowly. This wasn't exactly the reaction I was hoping for, and I wanted to get everything out in the open before Ayden reappeared.

Unable to handle the silence any longer, I hopped off the stool and began making toast. What was it with food and me? After popping the bread in the toaster, I glanced up at Brandy who was beaming from ear to ear.

"What?" I asked, placing my hands on my hips.

"I've known," she laughed. "I just wanted to mess with you a little since you obviously didn't feel any of the same pressures I did about dating Gabby's brother." She scowled at me teasingly.

"Are you serious? How'd you know?" I asked.

She started laughing and shook her head. "I'll always protect my sources."

"That's totally my line," I shot back. "So he told you?"

She nodded. "He asked me if I was okay with it. And, of course, I was okay with it. Like I'm in a position to not be okay with it?"

"True." I teased, narrowing my eyes at her.

"Anyway, I've never seen Ayden so serious about anything in my life, and I've been a nervous wreck this entire time, worrying you'd break his heart and actually find your happily-ever-after with what's his face."

I started laughing. "You mean anti-snowball man, Austin? Definitely not happening. But to think I'd break Ayden's heart? I'm kind of feeling like I might be the one who should worry about that. He's been hot and cold for so long..."

"Well, you're the one in Utah visiting your old boyfriend," she scoffed, her face expressionless.

"Oh, my god! You pulled me down here," I laughed.

"Still." She smiled. "I'm sorry. I know I should be taking this more seriously, but I just don't understand how I could've been torn up inside when I first started seeing Aaron, and you've got nothin' going on about it upstairs. No remorse. Nothing," she laughed. "I've gotta be able to mess with you a little."

"Because I came to you right away. That's why I didn't feel bad about it. Plus, your track record already told me it would be fine," I laughed. "Besides, you created your own inner turmoil with Aaron."

My toast popped up and without buttering it, I began to munch on it.

"So, seriously? You're okay with everything?" I asked again.

Brandy's expression turned serious as she nodded. "I couldn't be happier. You are my best friend and Ayden is well, amazing. He's an awesome brother and—"

"Whoa. Why's Ayden getting all these props all of a sudden?" Mason asked, coming into the kitchen with complete bedhead, but unlike his twin brother, he was fully clothed in flannel pajamas. "I thought I was the favorite brother, knucklehead."

Mason stole my toast and finished it off. "So what's the big idea making me second fiddle?"

"Don't kid yourself. You've always been second fid-dle," Ayden laughed, walking into the kitchen. His eyes landed on Brandy, who gave him a quick nod and smile as he slid his arm around my shoulders for a hug. "So I'm going to bag out on you guys today."

"What? We've even got turkey sandwiches chilling in the fridge for our snow picnic today," Mason whined, slapping the counter. "And who's going to be the one who saves the day when one of us rolls down a hill? Ayden, please, you're so needed for today's expedition or we won't all sur-vive." Mason's brow arched as he held in his laughter.

"I've got my priorities," Ayden laughed, kissing the top of my head, sending a flutter of pure exhilaration through me. This was what things were supposed to feel like. "And laugh all you want, but who had to haul your ass out of the Cascade mountains after you slipped down an embankment?"

"Whatever, dude," Mason joked. "That's totally cold. I was like fifteen."

Ayden laughed as Gabby, Jason, and Sammie appeared in the kitchen.

"Boy, did I luck out with the right brother," I teased.

"I resent that. I'm completely the catch between the two of us," Mason replied.

"So everything's out in the open?" Gabby asked, sliding next to Brandy on a stool. "Did you have any idea Lily was swooning over your brother?"

"I hid it well. Thank you very much," I said, rolling my eyes at Brandy. "Don't tell me you knew."

"No, definitely not, but I don't know how I didn't see it coming. I mean you were always telling me how cute they were."

"*They*?" Mason and Ayden yelled at the same time and I cringed.

"No. Not *they*," I corrected. "Ayden. Only Ayden."

Gabby and Brandy started laughing while Mason turned to face me with a huge grin.

"Not even," I said, rolling my eyes.

"I don't know about that," Gabby said. "I kind of remember the whole trip to their cabin and you—"

"I did not. I've only had eyes for Ayden. He's way hotter."

"So you talked about me?" Ayden whispered, grabbing me into a hug.

"Maybe."

"Hmmm," his whisper sent chills through me.

"Only in passing."

"You two definitely need to spend the day together and get this out of your system," Gabby said, waving at us.

"It's not like that. We're only going to play in the snow," I protested.

"I saw how that worked out for you yesterday," Gabby laughed.

"What do you mean?" Brandy looked over at us, amused.

"You don't want to know," Jason said. "But it certainly made a snowball fight look hotter than normal."

"That's it. Enough with the unjust persecution," I said, as Ayden released me. "I did nothing wrong or out of the ordinary. I'm off to shower."

I walked down the hall, leaving the excited voices back in the kitchen when I felt Ayden come up behind me and scoop me into his arms.

"I just wanted to tell you how hot the Yogi Bear pajamas are," he teased.

"I'm glad you like them. They're my favorite."

"And holding you in my arms last night was—"

"Incredible," I finished as I got to my door. "Now, if you'll excuse me, I've got to get ready for a date with a really hot guy."

I pushed him playfully out of my door and closed it behind him. Everything felt completely perfect, too perfect. But I didn't want to get wrapped up in my usual paranoia. Instead, I picked out a pair of jeans and a grey sweater and headed for the shower.

Turning on the water, I let it warm up and stripped out of my pajamas. The fact that I crawled into bed with Ayden wearing them was oddly wonderful. Normally, I spent so much time on perfecting the right look with lingerie that I was never actually comfortable or myself. I stepped into the warm shower and let the water droplets cascade down my back, allowing me to fully relax for the first time since we arrived in Utah. I was absolutely amazed at how things had turned for the better because I stopped trying to force something that wasn't natural.

I lathered the shampoo in my hair and was rinsing it out when I heard a rustle in my bedroom.

"Hello?" I called out but got no response.

I heard a few snickers and then more rustling so I hurried and rinsed my body and hair before turning off the water and drying off. I walked into the bedroom and there was no one around and no sign that anyone had been here, but I knew someone had definitely been snooping. Actually, it was probably two somebodies, but I couldn't tell what they were up to as I looked around.

I went back into the bathroom and began blow-drying my hair and daydreaming about Ayden. I wondered what it would be like when we got back to reality, after our vacation in the winter wonderland. First of all, there was the distance. I lived in Portland. He lived near Seattle. Second, I was jobless, but when I did find one, I knew I'd throw myself into it, and that never left much time for a relationship. And third, his job kept him completely tied up and traveling. By the time I put down the blow dryer,

I was depressed and annoyed until I heard his voice from the doorway.

"You look magnificent," he murmured, his eyes cascading down my towel-wrapped body.

I blushed and decided to put all my worries behind me, at least for the next few days, while we enjoyed each other's company.

"So was it my imagination or were there two accomplices in my bedroom while I was in the shower?" I asked.

"I have no idea what you're talking about," he said, grinning. "So I've got the whole day planned out."

"Are jeans and a sweater okay or do I need more?"

"That'll be perfect." His blue eyes sparkled as his eyes fell along my body once more. "I'm sorry, but I just can't..."

He took two large steps and had me in his arms in under a second. My entire body melted into his as he gently slid his lips against the crook of my neck, sending shivers down my spine. I slid my hands around his hips as he pressed into me.

"Ayden," I whispered, as my breath caught, feeling his firmness press against my body.

"I love how my name rolls off your tongue," he whispered, right before his mouth came to mine. The sweetness of his lips was completely intoxicating. It took everything I had not to slip out of his arms. With each new kiss, my world spun into a whirlwind of emotions. Tasting his lips only created a deeper desire within my body, signaling how badly I needed more from him.

My fingers grasped along the hem of his sweater, finally finding an entrance. Feeling his bare skin against my fingertips as my hands glided along his abdomen, created a rush of nervous excitement through me. I wanted so much more with Ayden, and with each deepened kiss, it felt like he did as well. His breathing became jagged as his hands slid down my back, against the terrycloth of the towel, when he picked me up and gently placed me on the counter, our mouths never parting from one another.

He stood between my legs, placing his hands on my knees, which sent a prickle across my skin. Ayden took it slow as he slid his hands up my legs, stopping just short. His gaze darkened as I pleaded with him for more, but his hands returned to my back as he slid me forward into his arms, placing more kisses along my chest as my body trembled.

"Please," I begged.

"Anticipation," he said, placing one long kiss along my mouth. "Now, maybe this'll give you something to look forward to after our day's activities."

"Are you sure today's activities can't include more of this?" I asked, my voice almost hoarse.

"We shall see," he said, slipping his mouth over mine as his hand cupped my chin.

"Are you guys still here?" Brandy asked.

Ayden broke his mouth from mine, and I threw my head back in laughter.

"Maybe, I should move to Portland," he whispered.

"Your sister will always find you," I teased.

Twenty-Two

"Who wears earmuffs?" Mason asked, laughing.

"Someone who has cold ears." I scowled at him, as I rubbed the furry contraptions attached to my head.

"Hey, don't diss this girl's methods for staying warm," Ayden laughed. "It's cute."

"Not sexy?" I teased.

"That might be stretching it," Ayden replied. "Actually. No, you make it sexy."

"Right answer." I smiled as he laced his fingers through mine.

Even though we were all planning separate activities today, we left with the guys and planned to meet up tonight for dinner. The girls were planning on a movie marathon of romantic comedies, and I was grateful for an excuse to not indulge since it wasn't my thing anyway.

"So are you going to tell me what you've got planned?" I asked Ayden.

"Breakfast first," he said, pointing toward a small café.

"You know me well."

"Have fun," Mason said, giving his brother a quick fist pump while Aaron and Jason waved.

"Thanks. Be safe," I said, as Ayden opened the door to the café.

The strong aroma of cinnamon hit me and I knew I'd be in heaven.

"They're supposed to have the best cinnamon French toast in the area," he said, grinning.

The server sat us near the windows overlooking the slopes, and now that the clouds were pushing their way back into the sky, there was a good chance we'd get some more snow, which made me completely happy.

I scooted the chair in and didn't even bother opening the menu.

"Already know?" Ayden asked.

"Cinnamon French toast, of course."

His gaze focused on mine as my mind wandered back to this morning. I felt the flush in my cheeks and Ayden started laughing. "Thinking about something?"

"Possibly."

Ayden ordered two mimosas and French toast as I attempted to remind myself that we were in a public place.

"I have a question for you..." my voice trailed off.

"Go for it." The heat in his eyes almost distracted me from wanting to know the truth behind his fights so I dipped my eyes toward the red-and-white-checked paper placemat.

"I feel like the fighting isn't past tense. Do you still do it?" I toyed with the paper napkin in my lap and waited for his response.

Ayden let out a deep sigh, and I felt his gaze fall from me as he contemplated what exactly to say. I hoped, unlike Austin, that he'd stick with honesty.

The server set down our drinks and I quickly took a sip, returning my eyes to Ayden. He looked back up at me, and the rawness behind his eyes was no longer hidden.

"I started fighting when I was in college because I knew I didn't want to work in construction with my dad. I love him to death, but we were never on the same page. I wanted to own my own business, but everything I came up with needed a lot of financial backing to get it off the ground. Initially, I got into the fighting to save enough to start the drink company."

"But you obviously don't need the money now," I said.

He shifted uncomfortably in his chair and laced his fingers together. He took another deep breath in and pressed his lips into a thin line before speaking again.

"I don't want to sound like a monster..."

"You never would."

He ran his fingers along the stubble on his jaw. "You're absolutely right. I don't need the money any longer, but I love the rush I get when I step into the ring. It's an incredible surge of adrenaline and it's a good outlet."

"A good outlet for what?" I asked, searching for something deeper. I knew it was there, I just hoped he'd share it with me.

"I enjoy what I do, Lily," he paused as his gaze darkened. "But it's not my passion. I don't know what is. I'd hate to think it's fighting, but I really do enjoy it. There's something about treating your body as a machine and stretching it to its limits that's incredible."

The look in his eyes was almost primal as he explained his love for getting in the ring, and the heat from earlier began spreading through me as I hid my smile and my thoughts.

"I hope you don't think less of me."

"Think less of you?" I questioned. "You have no idea the thoughts that are running through my head at the moment."

"How so?" he asked, perplexed.

"Let's just say the idea of dribbling syrup on something other than the French toast sounds like a great idea."

His gaze fastened on mine at my admission before breaking into a grin. "Seriously?"

I nodded. "I'd love to see you at one of these events, if that's okay?"

"I have one coming up when I get back in Seattle. I actually had a fight that Monday when I was in Portland breaking the news to you."

"I don't understand how you don't look all beat up..." A lump surfaced in the back of my throat as I spoke. The reaction completely took me off guard.

"I told you. I'm good. Although, I'm getting a bit long-in-the-tooth, I suppose. But it hasn't slowed me down yet."

"Does Mason know?" I asked.

"It's hard to keep things from Mason. It's the twin thing. But he doesn't know how often I fight."

"How often do you fight?" I asked.

The server placed a giant serving of cinnamon French toast in front of both of us, and the strong aroma of cinnamon and nutmeg wafted through the air.

"About every six weeks. Any longer and I lose my edge, but between this fight and the last it'll only be about three weeks."

"Why the rush between fights this time?" I asked, feeling uneasy.

"The winnings are pretty incredible. It's the first fight of the year and it was too hard to resist."

"But you're not doing it for the winnings..."

He shook his head. "No, but that doesn't hurt." A smirk appeared and my worries slipped away.

"You're sure you'd be okay if I came?"

"I'd love it. No one has ever come to one of my fights."

"What about Mason?"

"I mean no female. Other than Sammie when she was a model."

A sinking feeling appeared as my mind drifted to the conversation from the other night. "So who's the organizer of these things?"

Ayden's expression fell and his gaze locked on mine and I knew.

It was Mason.

"Your brother?"

He nodded. "It also helps him out."

"What do you mean, helps him out?"

"This can't go anywhere, Lily. You promise me that, right?"

I nodded, his gaze not leaving mine.

"He got into some gambling trouble. Sorry, that's not being completely honest. He's in some financial trouble still. He stopped gambling, but on his salary working with my father, he still owes a lot to some very unfriendly people. I tried to offer to pay it off, but he won't take my money."

"Wait, he won't take your money, but he'll take your blood in exchange."

"It's not like that. I don't lose and he always wins. This is the last fight he'll need to be free and clear."

"And then after?" I questioned. "Will you still fight?"

"I don't know yet."

"Wow. I don't know what to say."

"Don't think less of him. I know it looks like our family's got it all together, but my dad was pretty hard on both of us. I guess 'cause we're guys. Brandy always got off pretty easy. But Mason and I have both used the fighting circuit to our advantage. He just kind of got into trouble recently and…"

I shook my head. "You don't have to make excuses for him. We've all done things we wished we hadn't. It's just the thought of you getting hurt makes things…"

"I won't get hurt. I promise."

I hated hearing promises that weren't a sure thing, and I knew this was one of those, but I also knew Ayden confided something that he hadn't shared with anyone, and it made me feel even closer to him.

"I'll support you however you need."

Ayden shook his head in disbelief. "You're an incredible woman, Lily. I feel so lucky to have you in my life."

"I feel the same way about you," I whispered, feeling my heart rate increase as he continued looking at me in such an intense way. "Our toast is probably getting cold."

"Do you think they'd let us take any syrup to go?" he teased.

"I don't know what you're talking about," I quipped, slicing into the delicious breakfast. "So are you going to tell me where you're whisking me off to after this?"

"Tubing."

"No way! I haven't done that since I was a kid."

"I'm sure it's like riding a bike. Once you know how..."

"That will be so much fun." My phone buzzed and I glanced down, surprised to see a text from Austin, asking if I was free tonight.

Shit! I wasn't expecting to hear from him today.

"What's up?" Ayden asked.

"Awkward, but uh..."

"Austin?" he asked bemused.

"Yup. He wanted to know about dinner tonight. Think I should invite him out?" I teased.

"Probably not. Unless he doesn't mind being a third-wheel."

"Wouldn't he be like a ninth wheel or something since we're all doing dinner together?"

"Actually, I fibbed. I thought it would be nice just you and me."

My stomach fluttered with a parade of butterflies as his request settled over me.

"Unless you..."

"I'd love it," I interrupted, already texting Austin that tonight wouldn't work but maybe lunch on another day might be nice. I got no immediate reply so I tucked the phone away and enjoyed the rest of my breakfast with Ayden.

AFTER AYDEN COLLIDED into me on the latest run, I was determined to show him some payback.

"You certainly don't take it easy just because I'm a girl, do you?" I laughed, dusting myself off.

"Would you want me to?" His brow arched.

"No, but I don't think it's called bumper tubes," I replied, eyeing my surroundings.

"Fair enough." He grabbed his tube and mine, as we walked over to the rope tow.

"Let's do doubles. That looks like fun," I offered, watching a mother-daughter duo slide down the hill.

"Let's do it," he said, tossing our tubes on the ground.

I sat my butt in the hole and held onto the rope as I sailed up the mountain. I let go of the rope but didn't get out of the way until the last second so Ayden crashed into my empty tube and it went flying. It didn't quite have the effect I was hoping so I grabbed my tube and trudged to the top of the hill, pushing the black rubber tube to the side.

Ayden walked over and threw the tube toward me, and I jumped out of the way as it slid by and hit my tube.

"Whose tube are we using?" Ayden asked.

"Yours." I crinkled my nose to make sure it still moved as the numbness from the cold began to spread to my cheeks.

"What was that for?"

"I think my nose might fall off."

"That wouldn't be the best look. Wanna call it quits after this run?"

I nodded as he took a seat in the big donut and motioned for me to come over. My stomach flip-flopped when I realized exactly how I would be positioned on top of him.

"What's that big grin for?" he teased, adjusting his knit cap.

"Nothin'," I laughed as I looked down at him. "Maybe we'll do more than one run."

He started laughing, and I sat on the edge of the tube in between his legs as I adjusted my earmuffs and hat.

"Ready?" he asked.

I nodded as he snaked his arms around my waist and pulled me onto him. My legs stuck out in front of me, but my body coiled into his perfectly. I felt his body tense underneath mine as I wriggled into place. Sensing a smile on his lips, my body relaxed into his, and I knew it didn't matter how cold my nose got, I never wanted to leave his arms.

"Ready?" he murmured next to my earmuffs.

"Go for it," I squeaked, as his legs began to work us over to the peak of the hill. Every movement of his body made it impossible for me to sit still as I imagined his muscles working and flexing to get us to the top of the hill.

"On three...One. Two. Three," he yelled, pushing us down the hill.

The added weight made us sail down the hill even faster. The freezing air pelted my cheeks as our tube began to spin down the hill. It felt like we were on the teacup ride at top speed. Ayden's arms wrapped around me even tighter as we hit the midway point, and I couldn't contain my screams as we headed down the last bit of hill.

"I gotcha, babe" he yelled, half-laughing, as I shut my eyes and gripped his arms so hard I thought he was going to bleed out.

My breathing was so erratic, I didn't even notice that our tube had started to slow down until Ayden congratu-lated me, and our tube hit a soft snow bank. Instead of jumping out of the tube, I just leaned the back of my head against his chest.

"Damn. Apparently you weigh too much to make that safe," I laughed. "But I'd totally do it again."

"Anything that puts you in my lap is worth the risk," he said, giving me a long squeeze.

An announcement about the park's closure over the loudspeaker interrupted our rest, and all I could do was groan.

"I had no idea we were here for so long," Ayden said.

"Me neither. I guess I should get up."

"Unless you want snow patrol to yell at us again," Ayden laughed.

"That was kind of fun. I felt like such a rebel." I slowly made my way off his lap and stood up. I decided my payback could wait until he really wasn't expecting it. Instead, I offered him my hand, and he jumped out of the tube.

"You can ride up and turn in the tubes. I'll walk up."

"Nah. I bet this thing can haul us back up. We'll just both hold on tight."

We walked over to the rope tow, and he sat in the tube once more, motioning for me to get comfortable. I collapsed onto him, hearing a tiny groan as my weight hit his body with a thud.

"Maybe I should lay off the French toast."

"No way."

We both grabbed the rope and the tube bumped and slid back up the hill, hitting the bank with a thud. I jumped off, allowing Ayden to hurry out of the way from the incoming tube traffic, and watched as he nervously glanced behind him to dodge the mother-daughter unit flying in behind us.

"Ready for dinner?" he asked, grabbing my hand and placing the tube in the large bin.

"Do I need to change?"

His smile deepened, and he shook his head as we walked down the hill. "I've got a nice private dinner planned for just the two of us."

"Really? Where at?"

"It's a surprise."

We walked down the rest of the hill in silence, hearing laughter from kids and adults as they relived the day's snow experiences, and things just felt right—more than right. I couldn't wait to see what the rest of the night held. Not realizing how hot the tubing had made me, I unzipped my jacket as we made it to the base of the hill, and Ayden did the same. Slowly taking in the scenery, we stopped on a small bridge and looked over the village.

"Beautiful," I replied.

Ayden slid his hands around my waist, and my body immediately reacted to his touch. It felt as if I were on fire wherever his hands went. I slid off my jacket and let it fall to the ground as he brought me into him.

I ran my hands through his hair as he held me close. Looking into his eyes, I felt his fingers press through my sweater as he gripped me securely.

"I'm the luckiest man in the world," Ayden murmured, his lips touching softly down to mine. My world began to rock as his tongue softly graced mine, and my body begged for more than I could have standing on a bridge. I felt his heartbeat quicken as our kisses deepened and the surrounding world fell away.

Until I heard *his* voice.

"Wow, Lily. This definitely wasn't something I ever imagined stumbling across," Austin's voice jolted through me as Ayden's embrace broke from mine. "You must just love to mind fu—"

"I wouldn't finish that statement," Ayden warned, taking a step back from me, his eyes darting to Austin's.

"What? You think I'm worried about you?" Austin laughed, glaring at Ayden.

"Please don't pay attention to him," I whispered to Ayden.

"Yeah. Don't worry about me. Take her advice. She certainly has," Austin's eyes shot to mine as my breath caught.

"That's not...not...what I meant," I began, stumbling over my words.

"I don't know why I expected better of you with your track record..." Austin's voice trailed off as his words cut through me, and he shook his head. His eyes looked like he'd been drinking and his balance didn't look so great either.

"Let's get going," Ayden said, grabbing my hand.

"Yeah, run away like you always do," Austin sneered.

"It's not like that," I said, taking a step toward Austin.

"Really..." Austin replied. "I would've thought you'd show some sort of decency, flying down here and all, but I guess your reputation..."

Ayden's gaze darkened as his eyes darted from mine to Austin's. "Don't," Ayden's voice cautioned, cutting off Austin's statement.

"Whatever," Austin mumbled, throwing his hands at us. "She's not worth my time."

A muscle throbbed in Ayden's jaw, and I knew something bad was about to go down. Ayden took a step away from Austin and a faint whisper of "whore" floated through the air. I let out a gasp as Ayden released my hand and lunged toward Austin.

"Stop," I hollered, but it was too late.

Ayden landed an uppercut, sending Austin against the bridge railing, his body completely sinking as he slid down the concrete. Ayden stood over a dazed Austin and leaned in closely, only inches from Austin's face.

"Don't ever call a woman that. Ever. Piece of shit."

Ayden took a step back and shook his head before turning to face me. My eyes fell to Austin who was already on his way to standing back up, rubbing where Ayden's fist made contact, but I wasn't worried he'd come for Ayden. There was no comparison. He'd be foolish to try.

I couldn't come up with anything to say. Instead, I dropped my gaze and felt tears begin to prick my lids, embarrassed about how my past had ruined a perfect day.

"Come on, babe," Ayden whispered, touching my chin softly. "Let's get out of here."

I nodded slowly, throwing Austin one more glance before we walked off the bridge, leaving my history behind.

Twenty-Three

"That's not quite how I thought tonight was gonna go," Ayden said, pulling me closer as we walked slowly. "Are you okay?"

"Yeah...I'm just so sorry for—"

"You have nothing to be sorry for," Ayden interrupted, stopping us in our tracks. "You didn't do anything wrong."

"I shouldn't have—"

"Shouldn't have what?" His brow arched. "Kissed me?"

"No." I shook my head. "You're right. I would never take that back."

A faint smile appeared on his lips as Ayden tugged on my arm slightly, and I worked myself into his arms. "Can you promise me something?"

"I'll try," I murmured.

"Quit trying to carry the weight of the world on your shoulders. You're not responsible for all the bad things that happen in this wonderful world we live in," he replied. "You think you can work on that?"

"I think I can." I nodded as he let go of me.

"I didn't freak you out back there, did I?" he asked.

"Not even. It was actually pretty..." I stopped myself and started laughing.

"Pretty what?" His eyes mischievous.

"Nothing."

"Pretty nothing, huh?" he teased, as he led us toward a large building that looked similar to the lodge near our condo. "That's too bad."

"Pretty hot," I mumbled.

"Hot, did you say?"

I rolled my eyes. "Yeah. I said it."

"Right this way," he said, opening the door into a grand lobby filled with oversized log furnishings, and a stone fireplace warming the place up. There was a restaurant to the left, which was where I thought we were going until he pulled me across the way to the check-in desk. My heart did a somersault with this sudden turn of events.

"Checking in under Rhodes," Ayden told the friendly woman behind the counter. She gave me a quick smile, and her gaze lingered on Ayden a beat too long.

"Everything has been taken care of. Your room is on the top floor. Just call down when you're ready."

Ready for what?

"Thanks," he replied, tapping the key cards on the desk. "All set?"

I looked up into his dazzling blue eyes and smiled, trying to keep the butterflies at bay.

I nodded as an overwhelming amount of curiosity began pulsing through me with each step closer to the elevator. He held my hand tightly as we waited for the elevator to arrive. There was no one else around, and I swear if he listened hard enough, he would've been able to hear my heartbeat.

The elevator chimed and opened right up. He led me into the elevator and pressed the top floor as the doors shut. I glanced at him through the corner of my eye, wondering if he was going to try anything.

He didn't.

I stood on my tiptoes and gave him a quick kiss on his cheek and turned back toward the closed doors. I caught a smirk trace along his lips as he stood still. Two could play this game. The doors opened wide, leading to a long hallway with only one door at the far end. I turned toward him, furrowing my brow and waiting for an explanation.

He gave none.

I followed him down the long hall and became increasingly impatient as he slowly slipped the key card into the door. Finally hearing the click of acceptance, my pulse quickened at what might be on the other side.

Before opening the door, he gently touched my chin and his eyes traveled down to my mouth. His lingering gaze returned to mine as he smiled, pushing the door open.

The penthouse was stunning. Outside the large windows, the ink blue of the night provided the perfect backdrop against the streetlamps, illuminating the white specks of snow as it fluttered magically through the air. The large great room was modern with a rustic flair. In the middle of the room, a table, set for two, was covered in rose petals and candles.

He walked me over to the table as I took in the beauty of everything.

"I thought lilies might be overdone," he said, pulling the chair out for me.

"You have no idea," I laughed, sitting down as a server came from behind.

Ayden took a seat across from me, his smile absolutely captivating.

"Sir," the server gave a slight nod and began pouring champagne into the flutes.

Ayden's eyes stayed on mine as the server left us alone.

"This is incredible," I whispered.

He took a sip of champagne while I glanced around the room. I saw one of my bags in the corner and now realized what the rustle was in my bedroom this morning.

"You didn't have to do all of this."

"I thought we might like some privacy for dinner."

"Just dinner?" I brought my attention back to his simmering gaze and smiled. His lips looked so inviting as I imagined my mouth running along them.

The server came up behind me, placing a spinach salad down for each of us, but my mind could no longer concentrate on the meal. I glanced down at my salad and back at Ayden as I bit my lip, wondering what I should do.

I reached for the flute as I felt Ayden's eyes burning into me. In less than a second, he was up from his chair walking behind me. I heard murmuring and then watched as the server left the room. I took a couple sips of champagne and felt Ayden's finger's slowly slide along the back of my neck. My breath shuddered as his touch lingered, and he gently pulled my hair to the side. The prickle of his stubble against my flesh sent a wave of desire through me.

"I've waited so long for you, Lily," he murmured, pulling out my chair.

I stood up, and he scooped me into his arms. His mouth crashed against mine as he carried me out of the dining room. My sensitivity to each kiss, each movement as he glided his mouth away from mine, sent a tidal wave of emotions through me.

He carried me down the hall and through another room until we hit a beautiful master bathroom. A large soaking tub overlooked the snowy, night sky. He placed me gently on the tiles edging the tub and turned on the water. I watched his careful movements as he poured soap into the water. He turned back toward me, and softly kissed my mouth once more before standing up.

"I'll let you relax—"

"Please don't leave," I said, reaching for his waist.

"Are you sure?"

"More than anything." I traced my fingers down his legs.

He smiled and let his gaze dip to my mouth. I parted my lips about to say something, beg for something, but he pulled me back into his arms, his hands gliding along the hem of my sweater. But he didn't pull it off. Instead, his hands slipped under the material and gently slid along my flesh. His fingertips softly circled my back, sending chills along my body, but he wouldn't kiss me. He only wanted to tease me. His hands explored one sensitive area after another, creating a hunger that was insatiable.

Ayden dropped his head slightly, bringing his mouth to my neck, slowly releasing kisses along my skin. My breath hitched as his tongue slid along my throat while his hands still ran along my spine.

I teased my fingers along the waistband of his jeans, but he gathered my hands and continued scattering kisses along my jaw. I never wanted to be kissed on the lips so desperately. I let out a whimper as his hands held mine. His breathing changed, but he didn't bring his lips to mine. Instead, he took a step away from me, and turned the steaming bathwater off. Ayden's eyes danced along my body, and I was still fully clothed. I couldn't imagine what it would be like to be naked in his arms, but with every passing second, it was getting harder not to rip my clothes off and find out. This pace was torturous. No one had ever held this power over me. Ever.

Ayden bent over to check the temperature of the water, but the drive inside of me couldn't handle it any longer. I grabbed his fingers and brought them to my mouth. Gently licking the tips, I looked up at him through my lashes and watched as his jaw tightened and his eyes closed. Placing two of his fingers in my mouth, I slowly twirled my tongue around before releasing his hand from mine.

"Two can play at that game," I teased. His eyes opened and a wicked grin covered his lips as he came toward me.

"Yes, two can..."

I grabbed the hem of his sweater and raised it slowly as I began to place kisses along his hard stomach. His breath caught as my mouth worked its way up, my tongue gliding along his chest. I felt his hands take the sweater from me, tugging it over his head as I continued to work my mouth along his chest. But he stopped as he cupped my head in his hands and brought my lips to his. Ayden smelled insanely good, a mix of cologne and pure male, but the way he tasted was out of this world. With each stroke of his tongue my world spun into another reality, and I couldn't imagine ever coming out.

"The water will get cold," he whispered, as his hands slowly lifted my sweater over my head.

I took a step back, only wearing my red lace bra and jeans, and smiled. His breath caught as his gaze explored my body. The way his eyes consumed me sent a rush through me.

"You've seen me in a bikini before," I said, suddenly feeling shy.

"Never when I thought I could have you as my own," his words sent as many shivers through me as his gaze.

To be possessed so fully by Ayden was something I craved. I needed him, all of him. He took a step toward me, and his fingers rested on the waist of my jeans. I nodded as he began unbuttoning them. The sensation as his fingers softly brushed my stomach while he unzipped my pants sent my sensitivity soaring. I slowly slid my jeans down as he watched me, his gaze darkening.

I stepped out of my jeans, now standing in only my matching bra and panties. I motioned for him to take a step toward me and he complied. He brought his mouth to mine and as his kisses deepened, I snaked my fingers along his waist and unfastened his pants. Quickly sliding them down, I pressed my body against his, feeling the different temperatures of our flesh come together as his breathing turned more ragged. His hardness pressed into my abdomen as I reached down to feel him in my hands. I felt his muscles jump as my hand rested on top of the thin fabric separating us.

His hands ran along the curves of my body, and my heart rate continued to ascend with each new area he explored. His hands rested on the small of my back as he attempted to steady his breathing, his gaze focused on mine. I flashed him a smile and slowly began to slip my panties down. A devilish grin appeared on his lips as he realized what I was doing. Before stepping into the tub, I flipped my panties off and smiled sheepishly.

Ayden shook his head and slid his tongue over his lips. I don't even think he realized what he was doing as he watched me.

"Absolutely beautiful," he murmured, his gaze coming to meet mine again.

"Take it off," I whispered.

He smiled and inched his knit boxers down. My heart almost stopped when I saw his beautiful body in front of me, so close. It was even more magnificent than I imagined. His shoulder muscles were taut, each cord defined as he began to step into the tub. His abdomen hard, his muscles etched like marble, led my eyes down to where only dreams were made of. He caught me watching him, and his laughter completely wrapped around me as he slid into the tub at the opposite end. Ayden read my mind and reached his arms out, pulling me toward him in the tub.

My body floated toward his in the water as he brought me into him. His lips crashed onto mine as I felt his hands slide up my back, releasing the clasp on my bra. I pushed my chest to his, as I shifted my body, and Ayden began pressing hot kisses along my jaw leading down my throat, to my chest. The flick of his tongue changed as he cupped my breasts in his hands, shooting a burst of awareness through me.

As his lips traced along my breasts, his warm breath clashed with the chill in the air, and the drying water droplets on my skin. Not able to contain myself any longer, I ran my fingers along the prickle of his jaw, leading his mouth back up to mine. His hands slid along my legs, teasing my emotions. His touch did such amazing things to me as I felt him flick his tongue along my mouth. The ache that was growing deep inside of me was almost unbearable as his kisses became more dominant. I savored every touch, every motion as his fingers worked along my thighs; my breathing shifting with each new movement. Ayden broke his lips from mine as my body heaved with desire.

"Lily, I want you to know that I love you. I've loved you for a very long time."

I looked into Ayden's scalding gaze and nodded. "I love *you*, Ayden Rhodes."

And I did with every ounce of my being. I loved this man who made me stop doubting myself and my choices and made me understand that everything happened for a reason.

I pressed my hips into his hard body, unable to get close enough to Ayden as I felt his bare, wet skin against my abdomen and breasts.

Ayden's expression turned brooding as I began to kiss him ever so softly along his jaw as my fingers combed through his hair. I skated one of my hands down his chest as his breath caught. Ayden slipped his fingers around my wrist and drew me into him. His expression darkening as I wriggled around in the water, begging for more. I needed more. The want in me was so strong, it almost hurt, and he wasn't making it any easier as he explored each new place, slowly.

"Kiss me," I begged.

"Is that all you want?" he asked, his tongue sweeping along my breast.

"No," I said, shuddering as he brought his lips back to mine. With each deepening kiss, I lost myself in Ayden completely.

Savoring every movement, every moment, as his hands traveled down my stomach, my breathing quickened. His hands slid along my thighs, slowly working their way inside of me. My body quivered as he looked at me with hooded eyes, his fingers teasing me endlessly.

"Please," I moaned, before his fingers slipped away, leaving me in complete devastation.

"Please what?" he asked, his lips sliding along my throat.

Before I could answer he moved my body ever so slightly as I felt the length of him finally break into me. The amount of pleasure that swelled inside, made my responsiveness to every touch, every breath, almost unbearable as it collided with the strength of his body. As his hands gripped my waist, our bodies moved into a slow rhythm of ecstasy that I'd never imagined possible. His mouth continued exploring parts of my body with a renewed sense of awareness as our bodies intertwined with one another.

My hands ran along his chest as my mouth followed the delicious taste of Ayden. His pelvis pushed into me harder as his mouth crashed onto mine with passionate kisses that only made me beg for more. When I thought I couldn't take any more, his thumbs began stroking my breasts in the same rhythm as our bodies, and I knew he was the only one who had this kind of power over me.

I felt his body tense as mine filled with ecstasy, peaking into sensory overload as my body shook with every pulse he provided. It wasn't until Ayden slowed his kisses, bringing me back to reality that I realized how absolutely mind-blowing love was meant to be. This was what I had been chasing.

Twenty-Four

I t was only six hours until midnight, when a new year and a new beginning was about to ring in. But I had to admit I loved how the old one was winding down. I glanced at my friends as we all sat around the fire pit on the patio. Jason was holding Gabby, and Brandy was sitting on Aaron's lap. Sammie had recovered from the hot dogs and was now working her way through cheese and crackers, while Mason was pleading his case for another round of *Call of Duty*. Snow was expected later this evening, but until then we were all bundled up enjoying the outdoors and roasting marshmallows on the patio. The only light was from the fire pit and one patio light.

I, of course, received an apologetic text from Austin, which made me laugh. There were certain characteristics about Austin that I really liked and many more that I couldn't handle or understand. But I never would've found that out if my best friends hadn't thought this trip up. Austin enjoyed his freedom, and while I might have been a temporary blip on his radar, he was more than happy with the steady stream of females the resort town brought in. I was absolutely positive of that.

"Do you have any New Year's Resolutions?" Ayden murmured, as he held my hand. We were sitting on a long bench pulled as close to the fire as we could get it.

I looked into his eyes and smiled. "I guess I should set a resolution to find a job," I laughed. "That's probably a smart one to put out there. But that's all I can think of. All of my other wishes have come true, and a few I didn't even know I had dropped in my lap."

Ayden brought me into him, and as I looked around, I couldn't imagine anywhere I'd rather be. Surrounded with such love and kindness was the best gift of all and a magical way to start the New Year.

A delightful pulse ran through me as I leaned my head on Ayden's shoulders. "Do you know what would make this moment perfect?" I asked.

"What's that?"

"A marshmallow."

Ayden started laughing and shifted so he could grab a marshmallow out of the bag to stick on the skewer.

"Your wish is my command." He stuck the marshmallow in the fire and slowly turned it.

"So are we staying in or going out for midnight?" I asked the group.

"Let's stay in," Mason said.

"Second that," Sammie said. "But I'd be game for anything."

"I'd like to stay in," Gabby said, nodding.

"Me too," Brandy agreed.

"Well, that makes it easy."

Ayden slid the marshmallow off the skewer and brought it to my lips. "Careful," he said. Ignoring him, I took a bite of the melty goodness, and it burned my lips before it tumbled to my lap.

I picked it up, blew on it, and popped it back in my mouth. "I should probably rinse this out." I glanced at the trail of sugar down my lap.

"Yeah, definitely should get on that," Ayden teased, standing up. "Don't want it to stain."

I tried not to giggle as I followed him off the patio and into the kitchen where he grabbed my coat and pulled me to him.

My tongue found some more sugar on my lips, and I started to lick it off, but not before Ayden brought his lips to mine. The chill from his fingers skated across my cheeks as he ran his fingers through my hair.

Laughter from the patio made my heart race, and I slowly withdrew my lips from his.

"Do you want to help me with the mess I've made?" I asked, lacing my hand through his.

"Absolutely." He grinned and pulled me out of the kitchen, down the hall, and into my bedroom.

I slipped off my jacket and tossed it on the chair as I heard the lock on the door click.

"Why would you need to do that?" I teased, his eyes fastening on mine as I slowly inched up my shirt.

"I want some of your last memories of the year to be some of your best." His eyes darkened as his gaze traveled along my stomach.

"I would like that," I agreed, as he finished pulling my shirt up for me, revealing my pale pink bra, but rather than continue to undress me, he picked me up and placed me on the bed.

My breath caught in my throat as his gaze darkened and his fingers began sliding along my stomach. I motioned for him to strip, and his smile deepened as he slid off his sweater.

"Now I don't feel so vulnerable," I teased, slipping my fingers along his waistband and pulling him onto me.

Gently, he brought my bottom lip in between his teeth, nipping and teasing as a tingling sensation shot through my veins. I sucked in an astonished breath as his mouth left mine, and his gaze intensified as he moved down my body.

He slowly worked my jeans off, and I shook my finger at him, commanding him to do the same. I wanted to feel his flesh against mine. I needed to feel his body next to me. As he removed his jeans, he began to place soft kisses along my leg. A bolt of electricity shot through my body as his lips worked along my thigh, his fingers teasing me through my panties.

A moan escaped my lips as I clutched onto his shoulders, leading him back up until his lips found mine. His hands drifted through my hair as he shifted his body to align with mine. As I fumbled with my panties, desire strummed through me at an unstoppable rate. Every part of my body hummed with a thirst that only he'd be able to quench. Ayden's hands slipped down my sides as his mouth left mine, and he skated kisses along my neck. This was definitely the best New Year's Eve ever. I guided him into me and felt the longing only grow. Ayden's eyes met mine as I sucked in a deep breath as our bodies melded into one. He held me tightly as our bodies lost control and worlds collided.

"Happy New Year, indeed," I breathed. My eyelids felt heavy with sleep so I tucked my body into his, and the warmth from his skin wrapped around me.

"This is probably one of those nights where they'd miss us," Ayden said, his lips by my ear.

"You don't think we could get away with staying in bed?" I flipped around to face him, and he brought his lips to mine, kissing me once more.

I let out a groan as his lips moved away from mine, and I sank deeper into the covers before I flipped them off both of us.

"I guess you're right," I said, slowly rolling out of bed.

I opened the closet and grabbed a dress with a cute cutout on the back. It had long sleeves, but skimmed my curves nicely. Slipping it over my head and adjusting the fabric I walked over to Ayden who was pulling on his jeans.

"You like?" I asked, wiggling in front of him. I had been in mostly jeans and sweaters all week so it was nice to get a little dressed up, even if it was just to play video games until midnight.

Ayden ran his fingers through his blonde hair and let out a whistle. "Amazing."

I twirled around one last time and laughed as he pulled me in for one more kiss before leaving the bedroom.

The kitchen was bustling with Sammie and Gabby preparing all kinds of food as I heard Brandy and the guys yelling upstairs as they competed. I grabbed a piece of celery as Ayden headed toward the loft.

"Get the marshmallow issue all figured out?" Gabby laughed.

"It was a tough one," I teased, sinking the veggie into some dip.

We carried the food upstairs and played endless matches, until the New Year almost slipped by us. We almost missed the countdown until fireworks outside started going off, and we all hurried down the stairs and outside as the loud explosions on the mountain began soaring through the sky.

"Ten, Nine, Eight, Seven..." Everyone shouted and Ayden didn't even wait. He pulled me into him, his mouth crashing onto mine to welcome the New Year. My mouth tingled as our kiss continued long after the stroke of midnight; it only ended when Mason kept blowing a horn in his brother's ear.

"Happy New Year, babe," Ayden murmured, his eyes locked on mine, and I pressed my lips to his once more, ignoring Mason and the rest of the world.

Twenty-Five

Waking up in Ayden's arms was a beautiful thing. It was our last morning in Utah. I looked around the bedroom as my mind raced with thoughts from the last couple of nights. The tenderness of Ayden's kisses and the loving way he looked at me, continued to take my breath away. Ayden's breathing changed slightly as he pulled me into him, and I couldn't help but giggle as his whiskers scraped along my cheek.

"Good morning, beautiful," he whispered.

"Good morning," I said, snuggling into him.

We were back at the condo, but he was no longer in the bunkroom. Sammie was glad to chase him out, and

I was glad to welcome him in. It was hard to believe so much had transpired on our trip to Utah, but I never would change a thing about it.

"Ready to go back to Seattle?" Ayden asked.

"What do you mean?" I asked. "My flight goes to Portland."

"Not anymore. I thought since you wanted to see my fight in a few days, it only made sense to have you fly in with me, hang out..."

I didn't say anything as his words settled over me. What would we do once this was all over, him in Seattle, me in Portland?

"They're open tickets, so I can change them back if you want. I can come to Portland..."

Not realizing what my silence implied, I flipped over and looked into his worried eyes. "I'm beyond excited to fly into Seattle with you. I just got sidetracked...thinking about where we both live and..."

"One step at a time, baby. Things always work out the way they're supposed to." He nipped at my ear, and I started laughing as my body immediately responded to his.

"So I thought you could make yourself at home while I prepared for the fight."

I nodded and traced my fingers along his mouth, imagining what it would be like to hang out with him on his turf.

A loud knock on our door interrupted my next idea, and I just started laughing.

"Maybe we should just have you come to Portland," I teased.

"If we want to get a decent meal before the flight, we've gotta get going," Brandy called through the door.

"Which is code for get your ass out of bed," I teased.

I heard Brandy's laughter through the door as she walked back down the hall. I shoved off the covers and groaned. Ayden's fingers traced along my arm and I smiled.

I was in a camisole and boxers, not exactly winter pajamas, but being wrapped in so much goose down and Ayden more than made up for it. I glanced at Ayden as he sat up, his blonde hair in complete disarray and blue eyes still a little sleepy.

"What?" he asked, pushing his hand through his hair.

Of course, he was shirtless, but he was wearing a pair of boxers and my gaze fell to his abdomen.

"Nothing," I laughed, as he pulled me into him. "Not fair. I don't want to get in trouble with Brandy."

Ayden pulled me on top of him and pulled my hand to his, kissing the knuckles softly.

"Did I ever mention how that drives me insane?" I teased.

"I don't think you did. No." He pulled my hand to his lips once more. "When did that start?"

"At the launch party," I confessed.

"I had no idea," he laughed, as I crawled off him.

"Yup. You've had me for a long time, Mr. Rhodes. You just didn't know it, and neither did I."

I walked into the bathroom and began brushing my teeth as I turned on the shower. Ayden followed and grabbed a razor.

"Just one more day?" I mumbled, in between tooth-paste spits.

"One more day what?" he asked.

"With the whiskers," I laughed.

"Whatever you say." He beamed, tossing the shaver on the counter and trading it for a toothbrush.

I walked into the bedroom and picked out a pair of navy yoga pants and a white hoodie and brought them back into the bathroom. I felt the suds about to escape into my mouth and hurried to the sink as Ayden grabbed two towels and placed them next to the shower.

He quickly stripped, and even though I'd spent more time with him naked than clothed in the last couple of days, I couldn't help but be impressed as he climbed in the shower. I watched through the glass as he let the water trickle over his hair and lathered up his face and body. But instead of pure enjoyment, fear crept in as I thought about what it was that gave him this exquisite body, the fighting. I wanted to see him fight. I really did, but every day that got us closer to the date made my nerves work overtime. He ran his fingers through his wet hair, and I reprimanded myself for getting worked up. He knew what he was doing and I couldn't doubt him or I'd be doubting his ability.

I wriggled out of my boxers and pulled the camisole over my head, dropping them on the floor.

"Room for one more?" I asked, pushing away the fear.

"Always," he laughed, rinsing the soap out of his hair.

I stepped into the steamy shower, and he quickly began sliding soap along my body as I let the water run over my hair. Ayden poured shampoo over my hair, and I began massaging it into my scalp when I felt his hands glide up my thighs. My breath caught as he pressed me against the tile, his fingers circling inside me. The water was pelting me as I watched his gaze steady on mine bringing me to the end, my body shuddering into his.

He gave me one last kiss before he stepped out of the shower, and I was left to rinse off by myself, still completely lost in the world Ayden had created for me.

WE ALL SAID our goodbyes at SeaTac Airport as we climbed into our separate vehicles. I gave Sammie an extra long hug and thanked her for everything. She looked even cuter than usual because she found out Mario was going to be arriving in less than an hour to surprise her. He had gotten everything handled ahead of schedule and would be able to stay in the states now.

Ayden linked his hand with mine as we each pulled our carry-ons toward his Audi. Brandy and Aaron offered to drop Mason off since he rode with Ayden to the airport, which allowed for Ayden and I to go straight to his house. I'd actually never been there before. I'd seen pictures from when he'd bought it, but I'd never had a reason to go over there. Now I was full of them.

We walked over to his car, and he popped the trunk, placing both of our bags inside. I quickly sat in the passenger seat and let out a deep breath as he was just ducking inside.

"Everything okay?" he asked.

"More than ever," I said. "I just can't believe this is how the trip ended."

"Pretty incredible." He smiled, glancing over at me.

"Insanely incredible."

"Beyond insanely incredible," he laughed.

"Pretty beyond insanely incredible." I grinned.

He started the car, and we circled out of the parking garage, finally hitting the highway. The airport garage was like a maze. One wrong turn and a person had to start all over again. The traffic was pretty nonexistent since it was a Sunday, but we also weren't going directly into the city. Ayden bought a house toward the Cascade Foothills, which was close to the city if needed, but it felt worlds away. I'd stayed at a Spa there during a girls' weekend and loved the area. It was very peaceful. I think it was close to one of the wineries that Gabby's parents had hosted functions.

Ayden placed his hand on my knee, and the intense sensations ran through me once again. I glanced at him and wondered if I had the same effect on him so I slid my hand along his thigh. A huge grin gave me my answer as I sank into the seat.

"I've got a gym at the house that I'll be doing my workouts in so I'll still be around."

"I wasn't worried. Do what you need to do to make sure you knock the guy out," I laughed.

"Yes, ma'am," he teased. "I had no idea you had this streak in you."

"Neither did I," I laughed.

We pulled off the highway and onto a road that wandered through thick Douglas firs and cedars as I admired the many sprawling homes that sat back from the road. I loved the amount of property that was attached to the homes out here. I wondered if Ayden's home had property too.

He turned onto a long, gravel drive and my heart began to beat quickly and I had no idea why. As we followed the road, trees spotted the grounds, along with huge rhododendrons and holly bushes.

"Is this all your property?"

"It is. It backs up to Wolf Creek," he said, pointing in front of us.

The drive bent and that was when I saw Ayden's home. It was a large timbered home with stone facing along the garage. It didn't resemble the pictures I had seen in any way.

"You've done a ton of work on the house," I said. "It's beautiful."

"I did a lot of it on my own, but of course, my brother and dad have helped," Ayden said. "So you like it?"

"I love it."

I caught a smile of satisfaction touch his lips as he opened the garage and we pulled in. There was an old Ford Truck sitting one stall over. It looked to be refurbished and extremely cute. Although, cute might not be what Ayden was going for.

I got out of the car and walked to the back where Ayden was pulling out our suitcases. I rolled mine along, following him to the door that led into the house. He pushed the button on the wall, and the garage door closed quietly behind us as we stepped into his house. He quickly punched in a code on the alarm system and grabbed my suitcase from me. We were standing in a mudroom that had built-ins along the wall and a place to hang jackets.

He motioned for me to follow him into the kitchen, which was enormous. He set the suitcases down on the tile floors and took my hands.

"I'll show you around so you can make yourself at home. And then I've gotta get training."

"Totally."

The kitchen opened into the family room, and then from there, we walked down a long hall, which was where the master bedroom was. It was beautifully decorated and had windows overlooking Wolf Creek. The king-size bed was in the center of the room, and there was a sitting area next to the windows. He led me into the bathroom and my jaw dropped open.

It was huge and the tub twice the size as the one at the lodge. He caught my gaze and started laughing.

"I know...Just imagine..." he murmured. "I'm gonna change real quick."

I took a seat and looked out the windows as the rain began to fall. It was so relaxing out here. I could see why he liked living in this area, away from the city. He went into his closet and within minutes came back out in a pair of sweats and a shirt.

He led me back out of the room, down the hall, and up the stairs to his gym. It was awesome and filled with tons of equipment. I saw why he had no need to have a gym membership. He walked me past the many guest bedrooms, all decorated wonderfully, until we hit the door at the end of the hall.

"This is one of my favorite places in the house," he said, opening the door.

He flipped on the lights to reveal a huge media room. I spotted the PS4 and started laughing.

"I'm totally going to kick your ass," I said.

"In your dreams." He bent down and gave me a quick kiss. "Mind if I get started on my workout?"

"Not at all. I've had a mystery I've been trying to read all week but kept getting interrupted," I teased.

"I'll be done in a few hours. If you need anything just come on in." His eyes focused on mine, and I swiped a quick kiss along his lips.

"Maybe I'll join you at the end?"

"I'd love it."

He walked into the gym and turned on the stereo and began lifting. The way his eyes locked on mine, as he caught me watching, told me there was no way I could go in there while he was working out. He needed to concentrate on training and I'd only be a distraction. I grinned, feeling completely satisfied as I walked down the hall and stairs, but as I heard each thump from his footsteps above, my worry began to take over. The thought of him getting hurt, or worse, was beginning to force its way back into my head. I needed an escape.

I grabbed my book out of the suitcase, and a pulse of excitement ran through my body as I thought about how my life was turning out. That was what I needed to focus on. I quickly walked into Ayden's bedroom and flipped on the flat screen television as I heard the rhythm of his music pounding through the walls. I smiled, knowing there was nowhere else I'd rather be.

Feeling like my vacation was far from over, I crawled into Ayden's bed and cracked open my mystery, feeling like the luckiest girl in the world.

Twenty-Six

W e pulled up to the large warehouse, the parking lot already full. I spotted Mason, and my nerves immediately went into high gear as he gave Ayden a quick wave before seeing me in the passenger's seat. And that was when his expression fell.

That was nice!

Mason jogged over to the car as Ayden turned off the engine and opened the door.

"Dude, what's she doing here," Mason's voice low.

"She's part of my life now, and this is part of my life. Plus, she's my good luck charm," Ayden said, getting out of the car. "Chill out."

Mason walked to the front of the car and ran his fingers through his hair. I glanced at him and waved, hoping he would loosen up some.

"What's the problem?" I asked, stepping out of the car.

"Nothing," Mason said, his gaze darting between his brother and the warehouse. "Better get inside. It's a full house tonight."

"Isn't it every night?" Ayden asked.

I was wearing a pair of jeans and a huge pink sweatshirt with an oversized neck. The chill in the air caused me to shiver, which Ayden picked up on.

Mason nodded and Ayden slid his arm around my waist, keeping my body shielded from the breeze. We walked down what seemed like an endless row of cars, and my heart began sputtering out of control with what I was about to witness. I thought I was okay with seeing him fight, but now I wasn't so sure. I didn't want anything to happen to him. Nothing in this world was ever a sure thing.

As if sensing my unease, Ayden leaned over and kissed the top of my head. "I'll be okay, babe," he murmured. "I've got this."

Not wanting him to think I doubted him in any way because I really didn't, I nodded. "I know you do. I can't wait to watch you lay the guy out on the ground."

"That's my girl," Ayden laughed, as Mason opened the rusty metal door.

The inside of the warehouse was freezing. I wasn't sure what I expected, but I guess I assumed the place would have heat. In hindsight, that was obviously not the case since everything was meant to be impromptu and untraceable. I shivered as I walked into the small entry that could pose as an office if needed. The window on the back wall of the office overlooked the larger warehouse space where the crowd was assembling.

Mason motioned for us to follow him up the stairs that were directly to the left. Ayden let me go and jogged up the stairs behind Mason, and I followed them both. The upstairs hallway smelled musty, like the warehouse had been vacant for a very long time, and that only added to my concern. The beige carpet was torn, and the paint peeling from the walls. I got a sinking feeling as I followed them both to an empty room overlooking the warehouse from above.

"You can stay up here if you want," Mason offered. "It'll give you a good vantage point."

I shook my head and glanced at Ayden. "I'd rather be down by the ring, if that's okay."

"Fine with me," Ayden said. "In fact, I'd prefer it. These things can get out of hand sometimes."

My stomach tightened, but I did nothing to expose the amount of fear that was threatening to swallow me whole. I also didn't ask what he meant.

"We've got forty minutes 'till fight time," Mason replied "I'm gonna go see how collections are going."

Mason dropped a duffel bag on the floor, and I glanced at Ayden who nodded at Mason. Ayden leaned against an old metal desk that was shoved in the corner and crossed his arms.

"What'll we do until then?" I asked after Mason left the room.

"I've got a few ideas," Ayden said, his gaze boring into me, igniting a longing that I forced back. Now was not the time.

"That's bad to do before a fight. All the great fighters know that," I teased, glancing at the gathering crowd down below.

"That's a myth."

"How can you be so sure?" I asked, scowling.

"I can't be sure, but I'd be willing to test out the theory." He pushed himself off the desk and walked slowly toward me, his gaze following down the length of my body, which created a thrilling sensation as I thought about all the people down below having no idea what we were doing up above.

"Didn't you say this one should officially pay off..."

I couldn't finish my sentence as his gaze devoured me. His fingers gently followed the curves of my body, and my breath caught as he pushed his hips into me. I felt his hardness against me and prayed I'd have the self-control to say no.

"We can't," I whispered.

"Oh, but we can," he moaned, bringing his lips to my exposed shoulders.

The feeling of power that pulsed through me, knowing that I created this inside of him, made it almost impossible for me to think straight.

His mouth slowly worked its way down my shoulder, and I silently cursed myself for wearing something so revealing. It never dawned on me that he'd find it sexy.

"Ayden, I'd never forgive myself if you didn't win, and I'm about to lose control."

"That didn't help your cause," he said, giving me a hard kiss before letting me go.

My heart was racing and the heat at the base of my stomach was spreading as I tried to catch my breath.

"Thanks for caring about me," he said, giving me a wicked grin. "But don't think I won't find you after the fight."

"I'm counting on it."

A loudspeaker clicked on below, followed by several high-pitched squeals and then a boom of bass.

"Guess it's getting close to showtime," Ayden said quietly, as the music began playing.

I nodded and looked below at the crowd. There were people of all ages and sexes mixed together. I could almost smell the excitement in the air as bets were made.

"Where's the other guy?" I asked.

"We're the sponsors of this one so we get to prepare on premises. He's probably just down the street or something."

"Does that give you an advantage?" I asked.

"I think it does." He nodded. "Although I win them when we're the visitors so I guess it just depends."

I nodded and watched Ayden unzip the duffle. He pulled out a pair of shorts and my pulse quickened again, realizing just how close we were to the event.

He pulled off his shirt, revealing his beautiful lean torso, and it became painfully obvious how he created such a beautiful body, fighting. I watched him unzip his jeans, and my gaze followed his hands as he slid them off. Letting out a sigh, I was met with Ayden's laughter.

"At least I know you're suffering too," Ayden's tone serious, his eyes dancing with satisfaction.

"You have no idea," I muttered.

He pulled on his shorts as Mason returned.

"Ready?" he asked.

Ayden nodded and my heart literally stopped for a split second. It was really happening. I was about to watch the man I loved step into a ring and willingly put himself in harm's way.

Mason grabbed towels, a mouth guard, and balm out of the bag and motioned for us to follow him.

"Okay. You need to stay by me the entire time," Mason instructed.

"Don't wander off," Ayden agreed. "I need to know you'll be by him the entire time."

"I promise," I vowed, as we walked down the hallway. "Are there no gloves?"

"Not that kind of fighting," Mason replied.

When we reached the bottom of the stairs, the music lowered and the crowd hushed themselves immediately. The fighters were spotted.

"First time in this weight class, let's hear it for Maverick Stone," a man's voice boomed.

The crowd started booing, and I almost felt sorry for the guy as I watched him march down the cleared path toward the ring.

I said *almost*.

I glanced at Ayden one last time, his beautiful blue eyes connected with mine.

"Love you," he mouthed.

"Love you." I smiled, looking away quickly, not wanting him to see the fear about to boil over. My nerves were so raw it was hard to concentrate as I saw the sea of gawking eyes on us, waiting for Ayden to be announced.

"And now making his way back to the ring, the Defending Champion, Ayden Rhodes."

I watched Ayden begin to walk the path as the crowd erupted into cheers. His back muscles worked with each movement he made. Mason nodded at me and gestured for me to follow as we made our way through the crowded aisle.

All of the hands reaching for Ayden like he was a piece of meat stirred my guts up something fierce, and I wanted them to all back off, but he was obviously used to it as he made his way into the ring.

Mason grabbed my wrist and quickly pulled me with him before the crowd threatened to swallow me up. I saw a man step into the center of the ring and things slowly began to blur together. I heard him rattling off rules or something, but all I could do was concentrate on Ayden.

Dear God, let him be safe. Let him win.

It felt so weird using up my prayers on my boyfriend, asking that he beat someone up, but I didn't want to think of the alternative.

I watched Ayden's gaze darken as he watched his opponent, analyzed him. There was something going on inside Ayden's mind as the time ticked down. I didn't see the same thing going on behind Maverick's expression. I wondered what it was that Ayden was thinking about.

The announcer exited the ring, and then before I was ready, a bell dinged from somewhere above. I leaned against Mason for support as he shouted commands at Ayden. I seriously doubted Ayden actually listened, but I could be surprised. Once the fight began, I watched Ayden begin a dance like nothing I'd seen before. His feet barely touched the mat as he bounced from one foot to the other. Maverick came at Ayden with a quick punch, but Ayden rolled away from it long before it even had a chance to connect. Ayden took a few steps back and I watched as Maverick tried again.

Ayden bobbed away from the punch and threw one himself, landing a connection right into Maverick's ribcage with a crunch. The crowd went wild, and I stared in horror, praying that nothing like that was reciprocated. Maverick took a stumble back, but quickly jumped onto the balls of his feet, ready for another go. Ayden's movements soared through the ring, his hand connecting with Maverick's cheek before landing another punch on Maverick's chin.

Maverick stumbled back, falling onto the mat. I looked around at Mason for a sign to see if it was over, but Maverick stood back up. This time his expression filled with disdain as his shoulders bulged with ammunition. Maverick lunged for Ayden, and I gasped as I watched Ayden stand his ground.

He didn't roll away.

He didn't move.

He watched.

He waited.

And when Maverick was within arm's reach, Ayden's knuckles connected so hard against Mavericks jaw, I heard a snap. And watched as Maverick's eyes went blank and he fell backward against the mat. Not knowing if it was like the other time when he'd pop back up or not, I didn't let myself get excited until Ayden spun around.

His eyes connected with mine as a huge grin spread across his lips when the fight was called and Ayden was announced the victor. His body was slick and his muscles defined as the blood continued to pump through them. He was beautiful. He was a fighter.

I looked quickly around the crowd and watched more money trade hands than I could even fathom as the crowd erupted into craziness.

"We need to get her out of here," Mason called over the commotion.

Ayden's brilliant blue eyes stayed locked on mine as he nodded and walked over to me.

Ayden quickly bent down and cradled my jaw in his hand, giving me a long passionate kiss. As I tasted his mouth the desire to make love to him only grew. It was as if all of the fear and worry turned into something far more powerful that needed to be satisfied. He broke his lips from mine and smiled at Mason and then at the crowd.

"Told you she was my good luck charm," Ayden laughed as Mason shook his head. But Mason was smiling too. Something more was going on than I understood.

"I thought you won all the time?" I asked.

"Not in the first round. Not a TKO in the first round. Not like this," he said. "You just made us a lot of money."

"How did I make you a lot of money?" I asked. "That was all you."

He grabbed my hand and pulled me through the crowd toward the stairs not bothering to answer until we got away from the noise.

"Because what I'm about to do to you is all I thought about once I stepped into the ring," he said, pulling me up the stairs. "I need to lick each and every part of you."

My body quivered as his words lingered, and he hauled me with him into the room where we'd only just left. He grabbed the bag and flashed me a smile.

"I thought—"

He laughed, "Not here."

"Wait," I said, pulling him toward me.

I kissed him softly, my hands gliding over his abdomen as my lips dared to find the saltiness that my mouth craved.

"I'm not going to be able to stop," his voice wary.

"Then don't," I moaned, dropping to my knees. The saltiness under my lips never tasted so delicious as my mouth trailed down his abdomen. His hands ran through my hair as I placed kisses along his v-muscles.

"That should hold you..." I whispered, standing back up.

"You're so cold." His eyes steadied on mine as his breathing evened out.

"And you're trouble," I teased.

He grinned and slipped a shirt on.

"You're going to be so sorry," he growled.

"I hope so."

Twenty-Seven

"You were amazing out there," I said, as we pulled into Ayden's garage.

"You okay with me continuing?" he asked, as he pulled the key out of the ignition.

My heart leapt into my throat at his question. I would never ask someone to quit doing something they loved, but I'd be lying to myself if I didn't admit it scared me. The idea of losing him terrified me. And if it hadn't been Maverick who hit the mat, it would have been Ayden. There's only one winner in the ring.

"I'm here to support you," I said, glancing at him.

He turned in the seat and gently touched my chin, bringing me into him. I closed my eyes as I felt his mouth touch mine. There was no teasing this time. His mouth pressed against mine, determined to continue the connection from before. I grabbed onto his t-shirt and twisted it in between my fingers right before he leaned back.

"Let me go shower," he said, catching his breath.

"I was kind of looking forward to something dirty," I laughed.

"Oh, it'll be dirty," he replied, smiling.

I rolled my eyes as he got out of the car. I took a deep breath in and watched as he made his way into the house. I wanted to tell him the good news, that I'd gotten a job interview here in Seattle. I didn't want to tell him before the fight, but I was hoping that his reaction wouldn't disappoint me. It was like I still kept waiting for the sky to fall.

My phone buzzed, and I pulled it out of my pocket. It was a message from Gabby.

Jason's going to go on a trip and he won't let me come.

I quickly typed my question.

You asked?

She wrote back that she had asked and he said not this time. I let out a sigh as all of the amazing emotions from only moments before were quickly displaced by impending dread. This didn't seem like Jason. Gabby and Jason needed to get this settled, whatever it was. She needed to confront him, demand answers, which was what I texted back to her. My phone was silent for

a few moments as I got out of the car and walked into
the house.

*I know you're right. I just kept hoping he'd open up. I'm going to go talk to
him and I'll let you know what I find out. Are you still in Washington?*

My heart sank. I knew how much Gabby hated con-
frontation, but it was for the best. Whatever was going on
needed to be solved together, not solely by Jason. I heard
the shower turn on down the hall, and I felt the familiar
butterflies return as I thought about Ayden.

*I'm still at Ayden's and plan to interview for a job up here. I'll keep you
posted. Everything's going to be fine. Things will work out. XX*

I hit send and hoped that everything would work out
for Jason and Gabby. Not knowing exactly what was going
on only made me worry more. My imagination was probably making whatever it was ten times worse, and I was
sure Gabby's imagination was even worse.

I tossed my phone on the counter and slowly made my
way down the hall, relishing every part of where things
were right now. I didn't know what the future held, but I
was determined to enjoy the present. Learning to let go
was one of the biggest gifts I'd been given. Some people
learn that in life sooner than others, but it took Ayden to
show me how freeing it was to just trust.

The sound of the shower turning off made my heart
speed up as Ayden walked into the bedroom with a towel
wrapped around his waist. Water was still rolling down

his chest as he motioned for me to walk over, and it was impossible not to obey his wishes.

"I hope you forgive me for not coming after you sooner," Ayden murmured, his arms wrapping around my waist as the wetness from his skin soaked into my sweatshirt.

"Everything happens when it's meant to," I replied, looking up into his vivid blue eyes. "Opening up to you about everything turned out to be the beginning. I don't know if that would've happened if the timing had been any different. Those were things I kept close to my heart. That was how you got into my heart."

"I'm one lucky man," Ayden whispered.

"You've made me the luckiest woman." I kissed his mouth softly and slid my fingers along the towel's edge.

"Do you ever wonder what it is that you really want in life?" he asked, his eyes searching mine.

"I think I'm pretty close to finding it," I laughed.

He smiled and brought me into him even closer.

"But in all seriousness, I just set up an interview at a firm up here..."

"You'd be willing to move up here?" he asked.

"I've been thinking about it for awhile. Brandy and Gabby are my family, and I've missed them tremendously."

His grin looked absolutely delicious. "That's the best news I've ever heard."

My fingers loosened the towel, and it fell to the floor as a wicked smile spread across my lips. Ayden's gaze filled with desire as I played innocent and took a step back, smiling.

As I stood there waiting for his next move, my heart hammered in my chest like this was our first time once again. My heart was beating so quickly that when he touched me, I realized I hadn't taken a breath in far too long.

I was amazed at my reaction to this man. It was like every time was a first; every touch as passionate, every kiss more intense, and I never wanted these sensations to end. His fingers slid against my skin as he slowly pulled my sweatshirt over my head and tossed it onto the floor. He slid his hands around my waist and picked me up, carrying me to the bed. He set me down gently on top of the fluffy goose down, and I squirmed into position, grasping for him. But he stayed just out of reach as he leaned over me, until his elbows propped on each side of my waist.

I felt the warmth of his lips as they began working along my belly, sending shivers down my spine. Squirming, I ran my fingers along his back, hoping to be fully undressed by him. His mouth continued working up my stomach until he hit my cotton bra, which his tongue trailed around, causing my breath to break. Twisting his hair between my fingers, I gently pulled him up to me, to my mouth. I felt the hotness of his mouth against mine as his kisses deepened, his hands sliding under my back to unhook my bra. As his touch made my longing for him burn wildly, my hips ground against the fire he created inside of me.

His hands quickly removed my bra and began working on my jeans, as my mouth trailed along his neck, down to his chest. Feeling him work my jeans off created something frantic inside of me. I wanted to feel him against me, in me. He pulled my jeans the rest of the way as I began pushing my panties down, waiting for his body to press against mine. As he dropped the jeans to the floor, he began pressing soft kisses along one of my legs, while his fingers traced a long path up the other one.

Ayden began to slide his body against mine as my breath quivered. Feeling him taunt me with unevenly dispersed kisses, made my soul completely beg for him, to be connected with him.

"Ayden," I whispered, gripping his shoulders. He looked up at me with hooded eyes, and my world began to spin as his fingers slid between my legs, along my seam as I opened wider.

"You feel so amazing," Ayden murmured, as he guided his body along mine.

I let out a moan as his fingers continued to circle in me, and his mouth teased each of the peaks of my breasts. Sliding my hands along his shoulders as his kisses deepened created a swell of emotion inside of me as he moved his hands to cradle me as my body quivered in his arms.

"You're so beautiful when you let go," Ayden murmured, as I closed my eyes and felt him glide into me, my world shattering with each new connection. As our worlds merged into one, I felt our hearts begin to beat to their own rhythm, and I knew Ayden had made me his.

"Everything you hoped?" I whispered, as I felt the heaviness of his breathing begin to calm.

"And more," he whispered, tenderly kissing my lobe. "Your taste is intoxicating. I wish we had found each other sooner..."

"If I could go back in time, I wouldn't change a single thing," I whispered, as he peppered kisses down my belly, my fingers lacing through his hair before he sank into me once more.

There was one thing I now firmly believed, and life had shown it to me time and again. Everything happened for a reason, and I was willing to give my heart to Ayden Rhodes.

I wanted my Happily Ever After.

BEYOND INTENT
COMING SOON!
(Jason and Gabby)

Hope you enjoyed the third book in the Beyond Love Series. I absolutely love these characters and am so grateful to you all for allowing me to share their stories with you.

To follow Gabby, Brandy, and Lily, be on the lookout for BEYOND INTENT!

There are currently six books planned in the Beyond Love Series. To learn about New Releases, sign up for Karice's mailing list at her website.

Acknowledgements

I want to say a simple thank you to Amazon, iBooks, Barnes & Noble, and all of the other avenues available for the indie publishing world. It allows the art of storytelling to continue to flourish in unexpected ways!

Thank you also to:

Cover artist: Phatpuppy
Typography: BB Designs
Female model: Anya Kod
Male model: Steve Alario
Makeup/Hair artist: Nadya Rutman
Photography: Teresa Yeh

Contact the Author

To contact the author, please visit her online at http://www.karicebolton.com or via Twitter/Facebook/Pinterest @KariceBolton.

If you'd like to be included on her mailing list to find out about new releases, go to Karice Bolton's website at www.karicebolton.com

LONELY SOULS
WITCH AVENUE SERIES

One

"**M**om!" I hollered more for my benefit than hers.

I wasn't in earshot yet, but I loved the way my voice carried into the wind off the sea. The constant sloshing of the waves guided me to the rocky beach where my mom was collecting her thoughts and anything else that might catch her fancy. It was a pleasant night with only the moon's warm glow lighting my way on the very uneven path that weaved through the overgrown black-berries and tall beach grass. Doing my best to dodge the prick of the thorns, I carefully managed to stay on the trail. I didn't need to be all scarred up for my upcoming celebrations.

This little stretch of beach was hard to get to and rarely frequented by anyone, which was why we loved it. The beach wasn't what most people pictured when they thought of a beach. The beaches along Washington's coast, more often than not, had tiny rocks and pebbles in place of sand and many boulders and downed logs that made for awfully fine seating, not places to spread out on a beach towel and soak up the rays.

The makeshift trail finally ended, allowing me to spot my mom's pile of things. I hoped she was ready to leave. It was getting a little chilly, and I hadn't prepared to be here long. We had a crockpot full of chili waiting for us both, but she wanted me to meet her here at our special spot, so she could tell me something. I had no idea what it was that she wanted to tell me, but since so much was going on in my life right now it could be about anything. I just graduated from high school. My eighteenth birthday was almost here. Our huge summer solstice celebration, Litha was fast approaching, along with the big event, my acceptance into the Witch Avenue Coven on the same day.

"Mom?" I yelled, as I trudged my way over to her bag, looking around the empty beach.

Only the crashing of waves answered.

I didn't see her anywhere.

"Mom?" I tried again, batting down the worry that wanted to make its way into my consciousness.

Realizing my voice was no match for the roar of the waves, I started walking toward one of the larger boulders, in case she was sitting where I just couldn't see her. The pebbles were loose, creating an extra treacherous journey since I was only in flip-flops. Poor planning on my part, but I didn't think that I'd have to hunt her down. She could be sidetracked so easily.

Finally making it to the mammoth piece of black rock, I became annoyed when I saw she wasn't there. I wasn't in any way prepared to be marching up and down the beach looking for her. I grabbed my cellphone out of my pocket and dialed her number as I went back toward her pile of things to sit. Maybe I should stay put, and she'd return soon enough. As the phone rang on my end, I got closer to my mom's pile and heard her bag ringing. Darn! She didn't take it with her—odd. That was always a rule of hers when hiking or at the beach. We carried our phones with us at all times.

I squatted down to see what she brought with her, hoping an item might lead me in the right direction to find her. If she were gathering plants, then I'd know better where to go. I opened up her bag and panic set in immediately. The shirt she was wearing when she left our house was stuffed in her bag, wrapped around the shoes she was wearing. This made no sense. Her wallet and jewelry were in this bag. She wouldn't just leave all this stuff for a stranger to steal. Something was wrong. Jumping up, the insides of the bag dispersed onto the beach, but I didn't care.

"Mom!" I screamed, kicking off my flip-flops so that I could run up the hill closest to me.

Reaching the top of the hill, I scanned the grassy area quickly seeing nothing. Spinning around, I looked back toward the rocky beach. From this vantage point, I was able to see everything and nothing. My heart started pounding as I began dialing 9-1-1.

"911, what is your emergency?" The operator answered.

"My mom. She's missing," I cried into the phone, dread spreading everywhere.

"Calm down, ma'am. Where are you located?"

Calm down? I'm not hyper, just scared!

"I'm at the beach just off of Snoqualmie Avenue, down the trail," I replied

"Is your mother in the water? How long has she been missing?"

"I don't know!" I screamed into the phone. "Please just send help."

Okay, now I'm panicking! I can't calm down. My mom isn't where she's supposed to be.

"Ma'am, help is on the way. What is your name?"

"Triss," I replied, as I ran back down the hill to search the beach or the water, or anywhere but where I was.

Could my mom be in the water? I didn't even think of that. She wouldn't be in the water, would she?

"And what is your mother's name?" the operator asked blandly.

"Veronica Spires," my voice panted with the exertion.

"Where are they? When will they get here? She needs help!"

I reached the edge of the water. The waves were lapping against my bare feet. Looking out toward the sea, I saw nothing but water and rocks illuminated by the moon's light. There was no way she would be out there.

She never went into the water without someone with her. Oh, my God, where could she be?

The police sirens, off in the distance, were becoming louder by the second. Help was on the way but not nearly soon enough.

"Veronica! Mom! Veronica!" I kept hollering. "Where are you?"

"Ma'am, help has arrived. They're making their way down the trail. I'm going to stay on the phone until they reach you."

My body crumpled. Falling on my knees, the tears began pouring down my face. This couldn't be happening. I turned off my phone. The police were almost to the beach, and I didn't need the operator to hear my cries. The police chatter of CB radios began rolling through the air mixed with the barks of the K-9 units.

This was a nightmare. There was no way this could be happening. My eyes darted back to the hilltop that I had just left. A man was standing on the hill, watching me, with the darkness working in his favor.

"Hey," I yelled, looking at him, trying to see any sort of distinguishing features. He froze in place.

I jumped back to my feet, with my jeans soaked from where I had been sitting. I started running up to the hill, and the stranger took off.

"Miss!" a policeman yelled.

"Someone was watching me!" I cried, not stopping my run. "They might have my mom!"

I reached the top of the hill in a flash, and there was no one to be seen.

A policeman came up right behind me.

"Are you, Triss?" His voice was gentle, probably used to dealing with lunatics, not sure which way they were headed in any given situation. "I'm Officer White."

"Yes, my mom. She's not here." The tears started again. "I was supposed to meet her and all that's here are her things. I can't find her. Clothes, wallet, jewelry are all that's here." I took a deep breath. "Then there was a guy, I think staring at me."

"Where at?" he asked immediately.

"Right here," I replied. "He was standing right here. I think it was a guy. That's why I came this way. It's so dark it's hard to tell. I was sitting on the beach right before you got here and noticed the person."

"Where are your mother's things, Triss?" he asked, scanning the area and coming up with the same thing as me, nothing. There was no one here.

I pointed over to the beach, completely defeated.

He nodded and looked briefly at the ground for any sign of tracks besides mine; he then turned to the officers at the base of the hill and signaled for them to wait.

We walked back down the hill, and Officer White explained to the others the situation. I had no idea how he got so much from my few sentences. He pointed at the two officers who were in control of the German shepherds, and he motioned for me to come with them to where my mom's belongings had been dumped by my carelessness.

"Triss, we are going to allow our K-9 members, Sunny and Brandy, to smell some of your mother's items, okay?" Officer White asked, looking intensely into my eyes. He had to be well over six feet tall and commanded the attention of anyone who looked in his direction.

All I could do was nod. It felt like if I even opened my mouth to breathe, I would break down again.

One of the female officers, who had her hair pulled back in a severe ponytail, came over to me and touched my shoulder softly. She quieted her chattering CB on her belt.

"Is there someone we can call for you?" she asked.

"My aunt," I muttered, staring off over the darkened sound again, my eyes filling with tears.

One of the other female officers gave commands to Sunny and Brandy and off they went in the direction of the hill. The very same hill I had just come from with Officer White. They were racing off into the distance with the humans following right behind. My mom had been in that area. The dogs caught her scent.

It seemed like hours, but Aunt Vieta finally arrived. Her eyes wide with horror from the scene she witnessed in the parking lot. I couldn't even begin to count how many police and search and rescue arrived. There were divers already out in the ocean, and everywhere I turned, there was activity.

I had shutdown. I was merely operating on autopilot. Aunt Vieta started running toward me and scooped me into her arms.

"We'll find her, Triss. We'll find her," she kept mumbling into my ear, but it did little to comfort me.

"I know we will," I nodded in agreement.

She released me and stood back looking at me.

"Here, I thought you might be freezing." She shoved a coat into my arms that she had tied around her waist.

"Officer White's over there," I said, pointing toward his direction. He was busy getting updates from the teams that had spread in various directions. "He'd be the best person to fill you in. I don't think I could."

I appreciated my aunt's presence, but I would rather just sit on the beach listening to everyone's updates, hoping I would find something out that would bring my mom back immediately. Instead, I was bombarded with statistics about the longer the victim was missing how exponentially the odds of finding them decreased. I doubt that was for me to hear, but I did. And those words would forever haunt me.

"The waters are getting a little rough. We'll start again in the morning," were the first of many sentences that etched a place in my mind, creating a level of despair I didn't think possible.

AWAKENING
THE WATCHERS TRILOGY

One

The screams shattered my sleep. My heart was pounding seventy miles an hour. I felt for my fleece blanket to throw off, since I seemed to be stuck to my sheets with gallons of sweat. I looked around my blackened room, with only the red glow of the alarm clock displaying 2:00 am to comfort me. My heart sank as I lost the battle for another night's sleep. I heard the gentle snore of my bulldog, Matilda, rattling through the air. She was used to my screams by now. I promised myself with a little whisper that I was safe. It was only a nightmare—another nightmare. That was all it was. It couldn't possibly be real, that kind of terror. The dreams were coming closer together now, and worse yet they seemed to lead to nowhere but sleep deprivation.

I commanded myself to take deep, steady breaths to stay calm. Still shaky from the last images that had blasted into my brain, I tried to rid myself of the awful scene replaying over and over in my mind—my death. The mere thought of the attacks made me want to hide from the world in my closet. The black, swirling creatures were coming at me and through me from every direction. Their mouths open, displaying several sets of teeth with blood dripping from their lips, waiting for me to make a mistake. This was not a world I recognized. How could my mind even create such deadly monsters? The elements of realism spooked me beyond belief. I grabbed a tissue from my nightstand and wiped the dampness from my forehead, unsure of how much longer I could keep this up. Every night and every dream seemed different. They all had similar storylines, to a degree. Sometimes the unfamiliar characters reappeared to haunt me over and over again. It just depended on the night. Part of me felt as if I should know these people or at least the events that kept taking place. Why else would they keep reappearing? However, the events were so fantastical, the thought that I should recognize them made me feel even crazier for thinking it.

Fully awake now and completely disappointed in the prospect of another long and drawn out day without sleep, I trudged to the window and opened my heavy, red velvet curtains to expose the serenity of a dark out-side world. The snow was slowly floating down leaving a beautiful pattern on the sidewalk, illuminated only by the streetlight. The sight brought a shiver to my bones. Even though a minute ago I'd had to wipe the wet heat of fear from my body. I couldn't keep chasing and being chased like this. I couldn't go on thinking my life was in danger every time I closed my eyes. I needed rest. I needed sleep. Lack of sleep was making things worse. I was sure of it.

"What is all of this telling me? I don't even know the people in my dreams!" I whined to Matilda.

She responded with her usual snorts and snores, sprawling out even more on my mattress now that I had left a larger area for her enjoyment. I flipped on my night-stand light, which cast its familiar glow, as I attempted to move back into bed without displacing Matilda. A sigh escaped as I grabbed my latest book, which was ready and waiting for another night like all the others.

I opened the book to the third chapter as my mind attempted to identify the people in my dream. Seeing crumpled remnants of humans discarded all over was never something that I could get used to regardless of whether it was a nightmare or not. I was getting used to seeing the swirls appear to attack me, but I was also intrigued by the thought of trying to figure out the iden-tity of the random strangers who appeared time and time again. Sometimes they were the same people. Other times, a completely new set would make an entrance. I always avoided looking into their eyes because, during one of my very first nightmares, all I saw was the dull glow of death staring right back at me. I couldn't stomach it twice, and somehow my subconscious self knew to never look them in the eyes, whoever they were.

Thankfully, the latest batch of characters had seemed kind—as if I knew them from somewhere although that wasn't possible. I'm sure they must have made an appearance in other dreams. I just don't remember them. One stood out in particular. He was trying to save me, but it was too late. The black, soulless swirls got me. My nightmares had never gotten to that point before. Never did I know the conclusion to these nightmarish adventures before tonight.

This time, I saw how it ended. I didn't make it. It wasn't a painful process. I didn't feel tortured. It seemed like I should have felt the attack. I didn't. What I was left with were horrible feelings of despair and loneliness wrapping their way through every aspect of my life. My soul felt like an empty cavern as I saw myself being blown away into the wind. I remembered looking back at the strangers on the ground. They were looking up towards the sky at me as I left to wherever bodiless souls go. The one guy who was so memorable was staring back at me, tears streaming down his face. He was the one who tried to save me. He'd risked his own life against the monsters for me. He was only a minute too late. My heart now longed for him, this figment of my imagination. I didn't know why.

I couldn't shake the images this time. They were too haunting, too real. And now I was going crazy believing that these things had some sort of significance. Lack of sleep was finally catching up with my fragile state of mind.

Made in the USA
Middletown, DE
07 July 2021

43756908R00194